A VISION OF BEAUTY

Molly wrung water out of her long hair as she walked, enjoying the feel of the grass beneath her bare feet. She smiled sweetly as she approached Hawk, then sat down on a quilt he had spread out for her.

"I have never had anything feel so good!" Molly sighed as she pulled a brush through her hair.

You have never felt me touching you, Hawk thought to himself, fighting the urge to speak out loud.

"That water felt like satin."

My touch would be a feather stroking your skin.

"If it hadn't been a little chilly I'd still be in there."

There would be nothing but heat when I touched you.

"And that water tasted nearly as good as it felt."

Nothing could compare with the taste of you, Hawk thought feverishly, his desire running rampant throughout his body. *I would taste and touch and sample until neither of us knew where you began and I ended.*

Molly stopped brushing and stared at him. "You're awfully quiet. Is something wrong?"

"No, Molly. Come over here . . ."

PAMELA K. FORREST

WILD SAVAGE HEART

ZEBRA BOOKS
KENSINGTON PUBLISHING CORP.

for Helen J. Price

I love you, Mom.
Me II

ZEBRA BOOKS

are published by

Kensington Publishing Corp.
475 Park Avenue South
New York, NY 10016

Copyright © 1993 by Pamela K. Forrest

First Printing: January 1993

Printed in the United States of America

Prologue

Ohio River Valley
Late Winter 1785

The morning sun painted a radiance of golden light as it slowly rose over the eerily quiet Shawnee Indian village.

Days earlier the voices of happy, excited children had rung through the clearing as they played games in the deep snow, cheered on by parents and grandparents. Sometimes, in the very excitement generated by the childish contests, those same spectators would forget that they were no longer children and would briefly join into the game in progress.

White puffs of breath had risen past reddened, chubby cheeks and sparkling black eyes to be lost in the air somewhere above glistening blue-black heads. The children had no reason to fear the men who joined their games. A warrior, whose terrifying countenance struck fear in the hearts of the white

5

people at the nearest settlement, could be an uncle; that one an older brother; another a cousin. The stern faces of the warriors would break into smiles as they were willingly brought to their knees by the combined forces of the children.

Now the only sign of the deep snows that had fallen were pristine white patches hidden in the shadows beneath the trees. Even that final proof of winter would be melted by the end of the day. Only deep in the woods, well hidden from the sun and the warm spring breezes, would the snows last for another day or two.

Garden plots, whose boundaries were carefully laid out and fenced, waited for spring thaw. Winter had been harsh but the people of the village had been prepared, sharing both the labor and the fruits of that labor from their gardens.

In the fall, game had been plentiful and had been carefully dried and preserved for the days when winter winds made hunting impossible. The snug, warm lodges had been a gathering place of happy people as the snow flew and the winds howled.

When the cold drove even the strongest inside, stories were begged for by the youngest and happily told by the oldest. Mothers hid their smiles as grandfathers told tales so tall that childish ebony eyes grew wide with wonder.

It had been a peaceful time to sew the hides that had been carefully tanned earlier, to repair or replace weapons, to prepare for spring.

But as the sun began to warm the new day no sound of laughter was heard; nor were childish screams of excitement or voices raised in greeting.

6

There was no visiting from lodge to lodge, no measuring of the thawing earth to see if planting could be begun. In the village of several hundred people the silence was oppressive.

Linsey McAdams walked outside of the lodge of Wolf and Morning Moon to allow them some privacy. With her arms wrapped around her waist in a disheartened manner, her troubled green eyes searched for sight of Luc LeClerc. She desperately needed his strong arms to hold her, to reassure her that this nightmare would end. He was somewhere in the village but she could not find the strength or willpower to go in search of him.

Seeking solitude the evening before, Linsey had walked through the village. She knew that the sounds that had drifted from the lodges would forever haunt her dreams: agonized coughing as pain-racked bodies searched for one more breath—groans from the dying and from those still alive as loved ones left on their journey to Manitou—whimpering of the babies too sick to cry—the sounds of anguish as the people died from a disease that was a legacy of the white man.

A few short weeks earlier, Linsey, too, had been terrified of the Indians. She firmly believed every horror story she had ever heard. But Luc, known to the Shawnee as Bear Who Walks Alone, had taken her hand in his and shown her the truth of the people so different from her own. With his patient understanding and the friendship of Wolf and his gentle wife, Morning Moon, Linsey had come to know and love the Indians.

Now a different type of horror stalked Linsey.

With every passing hour the death toll mounted. Young or old, infant or warrior, few of the people were surviving more than a few hours of the disease. Their fever-racked bodies could not fight an illness that had been unknown to them before the white man invaded their lands.

Spring Flower, only daughter of Wolf and Morning Moon, had died quietly the evening before. Linsey had sent their son Chattering Squirrel away with the old trapper, Kaleb Smith, but she worried that it might be too late and the precious toddler would succumb to the disease.

Inside the lodge, Morning Moon, heavily pregnant with another child, fought for her life—a fight that Linsey feared the gentle Indian woman would lose. The baby, as if knowing that time was an enemy, had chosen now to be born. Morning Moon's labor had begun days too early and at a time when she was far too weak to survive the strain.

Later, Linsey would remember this day as the longest of her life.

Morning Moon moaned, the pain of labor or the disease viciously attacking her body, reaching through her delirium. Linsey continuously sponged her overheated flesh, hoping to bring her temperature down. Wolf and Bear had come and gone frequently during the day, giving Linsey news of any development in the village. When the death toll had climbed to over two hundred by midafternoon, she quit asking.

The grandmother, a woman so old that even the

8

oldest members of the tribe couldn't remember her as a young woman, had also stopped in several times. Somehow the old woman had not caught the disease and she worked unceasingly to ease the suffering of the sick and dying.

"Lin Zee?"

"Morning Moon?" Linsey's attention was quickly caught by the Indian woman.

"Spring Flower?"

"She's resting." The lie came easily to Linsey's lips as she pushed damp hair off her friend's fevered brow. There would be enough time later for Morning Moon to learn that her oldest child was dead.

"Squirrel?"

Linsey smiled into the glazed eyes. "Kaleb took him to our cabin so that he wouldn't get sick. They were going to see how much trouble they could get into."

"My baby?" Her hand tried to move to the mound of her child but fell short of its goal.

"Your baby moves frequently." Linsey placed her own hand lightly against the firm flesh. A smile crossed her lips, the first in days, when she felt the baby kick against her. "He is strong and wants to be born."

"Lin Zee," Morning Moon stopped to cough, a sound that was far too feeble. "You will care for my children."

It was neither a question or request. It was a statement of fact and Linsey busied herself with wringing out a rag and placing it on Morning Moon's brow. "Until you are better," she replied firmly. Her

9

troubled emerald eyes met a knowing ebony gaze.

"Until I am better," Morning Moon whispered raggedly. She closed her eyes as she drifted back into a delirium that offered protection from the debilitating truth.

Sometime in the late afternoon, Morning Moon's labor stopped. The old grandmother examined her patient and shook her head sadly. At Linsey's insistence, and in spite of the old woman's doubt of its success, she showed Linsey and Wolf how to massage Morning Moon's extended belly in hopes that labor would once more begin.

The afternoon turned slowly to evening. Linsey and Wolf worked well as a team, Linsey massaging while Wolf sponged his wife's fevered body. When Linsey tired they traded places.

When Linsey thought she'd drop from fatigue, Bear returned from an errand and understood the situation at a glance.

"Show me what to do."

Bear was startled by the heat beneath his fingers when they first touched Morning Moon's body. He almost withdrew his hands in shock as the baby kicked.

"It moved!" he said in amazement.

Tired beyond exhaustion, worried beyond hope, Linsey and Wolf looked at each other and suddenly grinned.

"What did you expect?" Linsey asked. "That poor baby is all scrunched up in there and wants out."

The light moment was over as quickly as it had come. Linsey rested while the two men worked, returning shortly to relieve Wolf, who rested, then returned to relieve Bear. Through the darkness of the long night, they shared the loving chore of saving Morning Moon and her child.

The inky darkness of the night slowly turned to shadows with the rising of the sun. The grandmother returned, her knowing eyes seeing the fatigue on the three faces as they stood back and watched her examine Morning Moon.

The words were Shawnee, but the tone might as well have been English. All of their work, their nightlong labor of love had done nothing. The child would not be born.

Lost in their dejection, they were not prepared for the sudden movement from the bed. Three pairs of eyes clouded with horror as Morning Moon suddenly stiffened then thrashed wildly; her eyes opened wide before rolling up into her head. The grandmother nodded grimly, her shoulders slumping with defeat. The convulsion lasted for a fraction of a minute but seemed to go on for hours as they stood back helplessly.

It ceased as suddenly as it had begun. Morning Moon relaxed, her body going limp. She opened her eyes, her gaze locking with Wolf's. Only because of the total quiet in the lodge were they able to hear her whispered words. As her eyes closed, Morning Moon released a deep sigh and was still.

"My husband," Linsey whispered, repeating one of the few Shawnee words she recognized.

Wolf moved to Morning Moon's side and laid his hand on her chest. His eyes closed, devastation aging his face beyond his years.

"She is dead."

"No," Linsey cried as Bear wrapped his arms around her. "Please God, no . . ."

Their gaze was drawn to the mound of her stomach. Three pairs of eyes gazed with horror and anguish as they watched it move and roll. The new life extinguished before it could begin as the infant fought its final battle.

"The baby . . . dear God, the baby!"

Horror never felt before gripped each of the observers as they watched the helpless child move. With no words to anyone, the grandmother moved to the side of the bed. Her knowing hands rested on the swollen abdomen, feeling the position of the baby. She snarled a command to Wolf, who responded in a daze by handing her the knife he carried strapped to his thigh.

Once more confirming the location of the baby, the grandmother placed the knife at the top of Morning Moon's abdomen. With a swift movement, she slit open the stretched skin.

Linsey's eyes widened in panic at the action, but the old woman ignored her startled scream; time was more important than a white woman's squeamishness. She cut through the uterus, exposing the membrane containing the child. Piercing through the sack, the grandmother lifted the baby from Morning Moon's body. Laying it on the edge of the sleeping-shelf, she quickly tied off the cord and cut it.

The child was still, its dark, wet skin tinted blue. Supporting the baby's head, the old woman cleared its mouth and firmly slapped its bottom.

In a world filled with dying and dead, one little

12

body filled new lungs with air. A voice, feeble at first, quickly gathered strength. Tiny eyes opened to squint in the light of a new day, small arms and legs waving as cool air rushed over damp skin.

"You have a son." The grandmother turned, handed the child to his father.

Wolf gently held his son, rubbing his cheek against the soft, wet one. Taking the child outside, he held him up to the morning sun. Repeating words older than memory, he thanked Manitou for blessing him with a son, promising to teach him of life, helping him to grow into a brave warrior.

Returning to the lodge, Wolf handed his new son to Linsey. "Many years ago Bear Who Walks Alone became my brother. Now I ask a difficult task of the woman of my brother. Name my son. Take him with you to your cabin and watch over him and his brother. When the time is right a name will come to you and you will know it is the right one.

"Protect my sons for me, Summer Eyes, so that they may live to know tomorrow."

In less than three weeks, the death toll at the Shawnee village climbed to over six hundred men, women and children.

And one birth—an event so miraculous that Linsey knew she'd never forget the moment. Much to her surprise, the baby's name came easily.

"My sister," Hawk said quietly when he finally came to claim his sons, "you have given my son a name?"

She nodded. "Morning Moon once told me that

13

Shawnee names have meaning but I knew few Shawnee names. One of the English ones I did know was Nathan, which means gift of God. I also chose Morning so that he can remember the mother who died before his birth. For several days when I was trying to make my decision a hawk seemed to be everywhere I turned. He was so strong and free."

Wolf nodded quietly. "It is a good name, my sister, a name worthy of a warrior. Nathan Morning Hawk."

Chapter One

North Carolina—Spring 1811

"Mary Helen Gallagher Royse," Molly whispered to herself as she twisted the shiny gold band on her left hand, watching it catch the sunlight. "Molly Royse . . . Adam and Molly Royse . . ."

"Did you say something, sweetheart?"

Molly felt heat warm her face as she turned to look at the man beside her on the wagon seat. Her husband of one day. Not quite a full day, she amended, since they had been married late yesterday afternoon and it was just past noon today.

"I was just practicing my new name," she admitted, with a shy smile. "I'd be terribly embarrassed if someone addressed me as Mrs. Royse and I didn't answer."

Adam smiled at her and released one hand from the reins to give her a quick hug. "You've got the rest of your life, Molly Royse, to remember your name."

"Molly Royse," she said. "I like the sound of it. Don't you?"

"Very much." Adam felt his voice catch as love filled him. "More than I can ever say."

Molly leaned against him and briefly closed her eyes. This much happiness almost scared her. Until Adam had come into her life she had been destined to care for her aging father. As the youngest of four daughters, Molly had had her fate decided for her. Her older sisters had all made desirable marriages with men carefully chosen by Charles Gallagher, while she had been raised with the knowledge that she would always remain at home, unmarried, childless.

Until Adam. Courageous, bold Adam, who dared to defy Charles Gallagher by sweeping her away from beneath his very nose. Clever, resourceful Adam, who further defied the influential banker by taking his daughter to the frontier of North Carolina and therefore out of his reach.

Gentle, loving Adam who had already given her more happiness than she had ever expected, or hoped, would be hers.

Sighing contentedly, Molly opened her eyes and they collided with the dark, intense gaze of their guide, and Adam's friend, Nathan Hawk. Intimidated, Molly sat up abruptly and folded her hands in her lap, wishing once again that she had told Adam of her dislike of his friend before it had become too late.

When Adam had first introduced her to him, Nathan had been dressed in a conventional dark suit and white shirt, his blue-black hair neatly curbed at

16

his nape with a dark silk ribbon. His prominent cheekbones, sculptured nose and well-defined jaw hinted at his Indian heritage. He was coldly polite as he looked down at her from the advantage of several inches and she knew he had found her inadequate for the trip. Or perhaps he doubted her ability to be the kind of wife Adam needed.

Whatever his reason, Nathan made no attempt to hide his contempt.

If the civilized Nathan had alarmed her, this Nathan terrified her. He had traded his dark suit for fringed buckskins and knee-high moccasins. His hair was still bound at his nape, now with a rawhide thong, but she wouldn't have been surprised if one morning she saw it hanging freely around his shoulders.

His massive chest and wide shoulders pulled at the seams of his shirt while his pants hugged his heavily muscled thighs. He rode his horse as if he had been born upon its back. And perhaps he had, she thought, acknowledging that this man was every bit as dangerous as he looked. His appearance no longer hinted at his Indian heritage, it now demanded that his heritage be recognized.

And he still looked at her with contempt.

Molly felt Nathan's stoic gaze linger on her and she forced herself not to fidget on the seat. She felt that he could read her every thought with those searching black eyes, reach right into her soul and find it wanting. She was still horrified at the thought of riding into the unknown wilderness with him.

"Are you sure you're all right?" Adam asked softly.

17

Startled, Molly forced her eyes away from Nathan and turned to her husband. She felt a vivid blush creep up her neck and she knew that Nathan would observe it and probably know the reason.

"Yes, Adam," she replied in the same way she had answered the same question several times earlier. "I'm really all right."

"I know a woman's first time can be painful, sweetheart, and I was a little rougher than I should have been." Adam lowered his voice as the memory of their wedding night brought a heavy sensation to his loins. "I wanted you so badly. I know that's no excuse but it is the reason."

"Adam, please . . ." she stammered.

"I'm sure Nathan will understand if you need to stop a little earlier tonight."

"Adam, don't you dare . . ." Molly broke off, completely mortified at the thought of Adam explaining such a situation to his friend.

"He's a man, honey, he'll understand."

"If you mention a word of it to him I swear I'll . . . I'll climb off this wagon and walk back to Charleston!"

Adam chuckled at the intensity of her reply. His sweet, shy Molly had hidden depths, a few of which he had discovered last night. Her delight in the pleasures to be found in their marriage bed had overwhelmed him. He felt himself begin to harden as he remembered her eagerness to please him.

Clearing his throat, Adam forced his thoughts away from last night. There were many long miles, and even longer hours, before he could once more make love to his wife. And he knew time would pass

18

even more slowly if he were to dwell on the memories. Ah, but those memories were glorious!

Nathan watched the newlyweds whisper to each other and he saw the blush cover Molly's face. Spurring his mount away from the wagon, he wondered, not for the first time, exactly what Adam saw in his wife. To Nathan, Molly was plain rather than pretty. She was too tall, far too thin for his tastes and she was shy to the point of being insipid.

She was like so many of the women he'd known since he'd left his home in wilderness of Kentucky for the civilized wastelands of Pennsylvania. He had come to know many beautiful women, women who had become fascinated with the tall, unbelievably attractive man.

Hawk shook his head at the memories. The more mercilessly he had treated some of them the more they seemed to have wanted him. He didn't understand that they were drawn to the ruthless savage that lurked just beneath his civilized veneer. They were as enticed by his intensity and the promise of violence as they were by his muscular body. The few women who thought they had experienced his savagery had become slavelike in their devotion to him. In fact, he acknowledged, they had become annoyances, until he had been forced to either move on to another city or to show them the truth of his cold-blooded cruelty.

Nathan almost smiled at the mental vision of the horror and terror that would have covered the faces of his former lovers if they had ever witnessed the real savage, the Shawnee warrior capable of every cruelty and atrocity credited to the Indian.

He was Nathan, raised by loving white parents, surrounded by gentleness and peace. He was Morning Hawk, full-blooded Shawnee warrior, born in death, witness of brutality and rage.

He was both and neither. He walked a line between two worlds, comfortable in neither. Feeling that the ingredient missing in his life was just around the next turn, Nathan Morning Hawk kept searching. For nearly six years he had lived as a white man, surrounded by the city and the trappings of civilization. Now he was going home. Maybe he would find that nebulous something in the wilderness rather than the city.

He refused to consider the possibility that he would never find the sanctuary he sought. He knew that somewhere, someplace, he would find whatever it was that had forced him to take this endless journey. He would find the missing part of his soul.

Molly was just another white woman who looked at him as others had. He read the curiosity in her gaze as her honey-colored eyes met his. But he also saw more than curiosity; he saw fear and contempt; he saw fascination and self-disgust caused by that fascination.

He had agreed to help Adam move to the unsettled wilderness of North Carolina. He'd help Adam set up a new home, would teach the other man the things necessary for survival then he'd be on his way. By winter he'd be home with the family that accepted him as he was and loved him without question.

He rode several miles ahead of the wagon, looking for potential problems, finding none. At this point in their trip the trail was clearly visible and well traveled. The gentle spring rains hadn't worked on the trail yet, as they would in only a few more weeks, filling it with potholes and ruts. Now they crossed gently flowing streams, but soon those same streams would be raging rivers, swollen from floods further upriver.

Reluctantly, Nathan returned to the wagon. He noticed that the well-sprung wagon rode smoothly enough for Molly to rest her head against Adam's shoulder. Adam, wearing the look of a man well pleased with life, nodded as Hawk rode up, being careful not to dislodge Molly. Adam thought she might be asleep; Hawk knew she was awake and listening to every word.

"Follow the trail. It forks about a mile down, take the right fork." Hawk looked the way they had come. "You expect the old man to send someone after her?"

"I don't know what he'll do," Adam replied quietly. "I wouldn't put anything past him, though."

Hawk nodded in agreement. He'd met Charles Gallagher and knew the man would make a formidable foe but he didn't really expect to be followed this soon.

"He'll search Charleston first, but I'm going to backtrack a ways, just in case I'm wrong." He watched the sliver of color showing beneath Molly's nearly closed eyes. "If I don't catch up to you by dark, find a place off the trail to set up camp. Start searching for a campsite before dark, keep your fire small. You can't get lost, but if you do I'll find you before morning."

"And what shall we do if *you* get lost, Mr. Hawk?" Molly opened her eyes, stung by the assurance in his voice that he would find them.

"Why, Mrs. Royse, do you fear for my safety?"

"No," Molly replied bluntly.

Hawk's eyes narrowed at the aversion evident in her reply. "Pray that I do return, Mrs. Royse; for your husband is the first to admit that he knows nothing of the wilderness. Should some harm befall me then you would have the choice of returning to face your father's wrath or becoming lost and probably starving to death.

"Starvation is a slow, lingering death," Hawk added quietly, his intense gaze riveted to her face as he watched for her slightest reaction. He was surprised when her eyebrows rose haughtily but no sign of fear marred her features.

"Surely, this close to town, even we poor travelers could find our way home. Should we become disoriented, however, I have every confidence that Adam is capable of shooting something edible. And while it may not resemble something anyone would recognize when I am finished with it, once it is dead I am more than capable of cleaning and cooking it.

"So, you are wrong, Mr. Hawk. We may become lost, but we won't starve!"

"Easy, love," Adam chuckled at her spirited reply. "He didn't mean to scare you."

"Good, since he did not succeed." Molly adjusted her bonnet so that it protected more of her face.

"Actually, I kind of like the idea of being lost in the wilderness with you." Adam's eyes drifted to the fullness of her mouth. He thought of the wine-sweet taste of her when she had opened her lips for his invading tongue. Swallowing back a groan he forced his gaze back to Hawk. "If we're lost don't be in too much of a rush to find us, friend."

"Stay on the trail. I'll be back by dark." Hawk turned his horse and headed back the way they had come.

"I am so glad he's gone for a while," Molly mumbled softly.

"Me, too." Adam reached for her chin and turned her face to his. "I can't wait until tonight to taste you, Molly mine." He lowered his mouth to hers and licked her lips with the tip of his tongue. "Open your lips for me, love, let me in."

Molly went willingly into Adam's arms. She felt her bonnet fall from her head as he stroked her hair. Opening her mouth, she grew dizzy as his tongue imitated the rhythmical strokes of mating she had learned so recently.

Adam tied the reins around the brake, freeing his hands to hold and fondle his wife. He pulled her onto his lap and adjusted her until her hip rested against his throbbing hardness. He found the buttons of her shirt and opened it to her waist, slipping his hand inside and covering the fullness of her breast.

The kiss went on and on until Molly thought she'd faint from lack of air. She felt Adam's hardness against her and she rotated her hips invitingly. She moaned when his warm hand covered her breast.

Forgetting time and place, Adam caressed his wife until they were both hungry for more. He fought with the yards of material in her skirt until he discovered her cotton-covered thighs. With practiced ease, he searched for the opening in the seam of her drawers and then found her, warm and wet and ready for him.

"Is there a problem?" a familiar voice called from the back of the wagon.

Molly nearly fell, trying to free herself from Adam's hold. She pushed his hand from beneath her skirt as she slid from his lap and onto the seat. Adjusting her clothing with hands that shook, Molly was forced to hold her shirt closed when her fumbling fingers couldn't work the buttons.

"When I didn't hear the wagon move on I thought I'd better come back and investigate." Hawk had seen enough to know exactly what he had interrupted. "There are better times and places for that kind of thing."

Adam grinned at the mild rebuke. "I'd have to disagree with you there, Nathan. I can't think of anything I'd rather be doing right now."

Molly turned scarlet with humiliation and couldn't decide which man she'd rather shoot first. Adam stared at her with hungry anticipation while Nathan looked at her with skepticism bordering on rudeness.

"By all means, continue," Hawk replied quietly. "I made enough noise to awaken the dead but you were so engrossed with each other that you didn't hear me coming. This is a heavily travelled trail. Don't get so involved that you forget to listen for land pirates or local Indians."

"Land pirates?" Molly asked incredulously.

"Outlaws, bandits, highwaymen, robbers, choose

whichever name, it means the same. They'll kill Adam, rape you before killing you, then take everything of value in the wagon."

Molly wrapped her arms around her waist, unable to stop herself from looking around the sunlit clearing.

"There's no need to frighten her, Nathan," Adam said softly.

"The realities of life are frightening. She needs to know exactly what to expect." Without further word, he turned his horse and rode away.

Molly quickly buttoned her shirt while Adam grabbed the reins and flipped the whip to get the oxen into motion.

"I realize the necessity of having a guide, Adam, but I do wish you had found someone other than Mr. Hawk."

"We needed someone we can trust, Molly. I've known Nathan since we attended the University of Pennsylvania together. I trust him with my life, and yours."

"But he just seems so . . . so . . ." she shivered at the memory of his penetrating stare.

"Does he frighten you, Molly mine?" Adam asked softly.

"Yes." She leaned against him, using his warmth as a security against her unfounded fears.

Adam was quiet for long minutes, gathering his thoughts. "He is a full Shawnee Indian, raised by a white family." He clucked his tongue at the oxen and rested both elbows against his knees. "I don't know much about his past, but I do know that he is both intelligent and honorable."

"Well I just hope you won't be offended that I'm not as impressed by your friend as you are."

"I'm delighted," Adam replied with a grin. "At the university all the women flocked around him and completely forgot about the rest of us. There seems to be something about him that attracts the ladies."

"Not this lady!"

He leaned over and kissed her nose. "That's good to know. I'd hate to have to fight my best friend over my wife!"

Molly smiled at his nonsense. A few months ago it had seemed an empty waste of time to yearn for a husband and children. Now she was sitting on a wagon, heading west, with her new husband who was talking about fighting to save her honor.

Her thoughts drifted to her father and she wondered if he really would send someone to find them. He was an inflexible tyrant who had ruled her life with an ironfisted control. She knew him well enough to know that he would be violently angry that she had defied him. It had been his decision that she would remain at home and provide for him. He had spoiled her, giving her every luxury available, allowing her everything her heart desired . . . except a husband and child.

It still amazed her that her escape had been so easy. But then, there really had been no reason for her father to expect anything. He had met Adam only once and had made it clear to Molly that she was to have no further encounters with the young solicitor. He had patted her hand, having no doubt that she would obey him.

26

Knowing that the only way she could ever be with Adam was to escape from her father's domain, Molly made the decision to travel into the frontier of North Carolina with him. Yesterday morning she had left home with a basket on her arm as if she had been heading for the market, as she usually did every morning. Adam met her a few blocks from her house and escorted her to the livery stable, where Nathan waited with the wagon and team. They left Charleston without anyone the wiser.

Late that same afternoon, when the excitement was beginning to wane, Adam stopped before an insignificant-looking structure. The humble building witnessed the greatest event of her life. Within its unpretentious walls she became Adam's wife.

A bittersweet sadness teased her as she wondered if she'd ever again see her sisters or their children. Perhaps a day would come when her father would forgive her and she'd be able to return to Charleston for a visit. A dreamy smile crossed her face at the thought of returning with her own children in tow— a son and a daughter, both of whom greatly resembled their father.

"How many children do you want?" she asked abruptly.

Startled by the question, Adam turned and looked down at her upraised face. "Oh, I guess a dozen or so."

"A dozen?" Molly asked, appalled at the very thought.

"One at a time, of course."

"Of course . . ."

"We could begin tonight . . ."

"Maybe we began last night," she suggested shyly.

"Ah, Molly mine, there is nothing in the world that would make me happier than to know my child rested beneath your heart."

Molly blinked back the sudden tears that brimmed in her eyes. "I love you so much, Adam Royse. You have made me so happy."

"It's going to be hard, Molly." He thought of the next few months and wondered again if he should have left her safely in Charleston until he could have established a home for her. She would have been safe with her father until he returned for her.

"I should have left you in Charleston," he mumbled his thoughts aloud.

"I'm glad you didn't. I'm not afraid of hard work, Adam, and I'd rather be with you in the wilderness than without you in the grandest palace."

"If anything happens to you, I'll never forgive myself."

"What could happen to me with you around for protection?" She smiled gently at him. "I'm sure your friend thinks I'm not worth much but I'm sure even he would provide protection if it becomes necessary."

They rode in silence, surrounded by the beauty of nature and the contentment of being together. Adam's thoughts twisted and turned as he wondered if he'd regret his decision.

"Molly, should anything ever happen to me . . ."

"Don't say such a thing!"

"We have to be practical, sweet. It is possible that something could happen and you'd be left alone." He silenced her protest with a quick kiss. "Should it happen, I've asked Nathan to see you back to Charleston."

"That won't be necessary because nothing is going to happen to you!" Molly felt a shadow drift over her heart. Nothing could happen to Adam, she loved him too much!

"Molly mine, we have to face the possibility . . ."

"Enough, Adam! I don't want to talk about this."

"I have no intention of leaving you, sweet, until I'm an old, old man and you are heartily sick of the sight of me."

"Never."

Seeing how agitated she was becoming, Adam let the issue drop. Life was too uncertain, accidents happened. He was reassured by the knowledge that Nathan would protect Molly. He couldn't bear the thought of leaving his sweet wife alone and helpless in the middle of nowhere.

The afternoon slowly slipped past. The trail was easy to follow and was wide enough to allow the wagon to pass without trouble. They stopped once when Molly spied a bush thickly laden with early berries.

After tasting a few to confirm their ripeness, Molly removed her bonnet and Adam helped her fill it.

"I'm rather fond of your bonnets," Adam said with a smile.

Molly agreed wholeheartedly. It had been because of her bonnet that they had first met. She had walked to market as usual that fateful morning, not knowing that her life was about to change forever.

Molly had walked slowly, savoring the sights and

smells of the shops. She was in no rush to return home, so that by the time she had finished her shopping a summer storm was brewing, turning the sky to black, as a fierce wind blew threateningly.

As Molly rounded a corner the wind caught her bonnet, pulling it from her head. She tried to catch it, losing her grip on her full basket. Watching her bonnet blow away, Molly contended with her scattered items and fought to maintain her dignity as the gale played with her skirts.

Her savior came in the form of a young man with laughing blue eyes who returned her hat to her and helped to gather up her things. He carefully kept his eyes averted when the wind raised her skirt nearly to her knees.

Hailing a hackney, Adam Royse escorted Molly to her home. Nearly every morning after that fateful meeting, Adam would be in the vicinity when Molly went shopping. It was only later that he confessed that their continued meetings were by design rather than accident.

And those meetings led to this, Molly thought contentedly as she swayed with the movements of the wagon. They spent the remainder of the afternoon nibbling on the sweet berries and talking about the past and the future, in the way of all new lovers.

Since it was not quite spring, darkness still came early and a chill filled the air. When Nathan did not return, Adam began looking for a place to spend the night. They had been following a river most of the day, so searching for water was not a problem.

He finally found a place slightly off the trail where

the trees thinned, allowing adequate room for the wagon. While Molly stretched, and gathered firewood, Adam unhitched the team. It was a chore that he was still unfamiliar with and therefore did rather slowly. By the time he was finished, Molly had cleared a spot for the fire, as she had seen Nathan do the night before.

Building and lighting the fire wasn't quite as simple as Nathan had made it look, but Molly persevered, smiling with delight when a feeble flame began to lick at the kindling.

"What's for dinner, wife?" Adam asked as he approached the frail fire. His blue eyes sparkled with delight that they had managed to set up camp by themselves. He knew he had a lot to learn before he could comfortably provide for Molly in their new home. But this was the beginning and already he knew more than he had known only a week ago.

Flopping down on the ground beside her, he watched as Molly slowly fed small sticks to the greedily growing flame. "You kill it, I'll cook it," she replied with a grin.

She jumped in startled surprise as two rabbit carcasses were dropped on the ground beside her.

"I killed them. You cook them."

She turned her eyes from the repulsive remains and met the challenge in the night-dark gaze that taunted her and seemed to find her lacking in every way.

Chapter Two

"You have to clean them before you can cook them." Hawk nodded toward the rabbits.

"At home I often helped our cook prepare our meals," Molly said defensively, "I admit to lacking the ability to clean a carcass, however, I am willing to learn."

Glancing quickly at the dead animals, Molly raised her chin and met his detached gaze. She wouldn't let this civilized savage see her revulsion. As she climbed to her feet she wondered if Nathan was as civilized as Adam liked to believe. It seemed to her that the further they traveled from town the more his veneer of culture slipped from his shoulders.

She nearly bit through the side of her cheek as she bent over and picked up the rabbits by their fuzzy hind legs. She kept telling herself they were just like the plucked chickens she would sometimes carry home from market when their cook had been too busy to clean one of their own that they kept for that purpose. But the chickens had claws and skin on their legs, not this soft fur. And the chickens didn't have long, soft ears that flopped gently against her skirt.

"I'll clean them, Molly," Adam volunteered. "You get the fire going and you can cook them when I get back."

It was so tempting to hand them over to Adam but one look at Nathan's face was all it took to reject that idea. She wouldn't give him proof, so early in their journey, that she was useless.

"No, Adam, cooking is my job. You and Mr. Hawk have enough to do without adding that chore to your list." She smiled bravely at her husband, then she turned and headed toward the river, the rabbits held at arm's length from her body. "Keep the fire going, please. I'll be back."

Finding a conveniently large rock beside the water Molly laid the rabbits on it and then realized she had come away without a knife. One appeared almost magically just as she turned to go back to camp.

"Thank you," she said graciously, reaching for the knife. Molly studied the animals and wondered where to begin. "Thank you, little rabbit, for sacrificing your life for us," she mumbled to the body. "I know you were innocently enjoying your life and I am sorry it is you who must provide nourishment for our hunger."

Hawk was startled by her words to the animal. It was common for the Indians to pray for forgiveness to animal spirits but he had never heard of a white person, particularly a white woman, doing so. He wondered if it was a calculated move on her part to win his sympathy so that he would take over the chore she so obviously abhorred.

Perhaps it was that short prayer that changed his mind. Maybe it was the bewildered way Molly studied the rabbit. Whatever the reason, Hawk took his knife from its sheath on his thigh and moved up beside her. He had intended to let her clean the animal without guidance, now he would show her.

Without a word to her, Hawk began to clean one of the rabbits. He worked slowly, waiting for her to follow each step as he did it. He bit back a grin as her face took on a green hue at the grisly job. His admiration for her moved up several notches when she completed the chore without a word of complaint.

Molly looked at her carcass and compared it to Hawk's. He had removed the fur in one neat piece while she had clumps of matted fur scattered all around the rock where they worked. Her rabbit had nicks and gouges, his was clean and smooth.

"Guess it takes practice," she mumbled as she knelt and washed the rabbit.

"You did good."

Never had such limited praise meant more. Molly grinned and washed the blood from her hands. While she finished cleaning up both herself and the rabbit, Hawk buried the remains. He rolled his skin, intending to start the cleaning process later that night. He couldn't help wondering what her reaction would be when she saw him beginning the tanning process.

They walked companionably back to camp, Molly carrying her cleaned rabbit with a grip much firmer than the one she had used earlier.

"I did good!" Molly exclaimed to Adam, holding up her pitiful-looking rabbit.

"I'm real proud of you, honey." Adam kissed her quickly. "However it wasn't necessary for you to do such a chore." He looked at Hawk, his eyes conveying his message. "From here on out I'll clean the game."

"She has to learn," Hawk said quietly.

"Not something like that, she doesn't."

"Too much protection could kill her. Do you want her to starve if the day should come when she finds need to provide for herself?"

Adam's eyes narrowed. "She's been gently raised. She'll learn, but you don't need to force everything on her at once."

"You both have a lot to learn and a short time to do it in." Hawk's voice didn't portray the irritation he felt at Adam's overprotective attitude. "It's not going to be easy for either of you. And at times some of the chores are going to be downright unpleasant. She either learns now when I'm here to teach her or she learns the hard way later. The decision is yours."

Molly stood between the two determined men and would have stamped her foot if it would have done any good. The leaf-covered ground would have absorbed any sound, however, probably doing nothing but hurting her foot. But she'd had enough of them discussing her as if she wasn't there.

"If you two are finished planning my future instruction, I'd like to get these rabbits cooking. I'm hungry." Actually, after cleaning the animals, eating was the last thing Molly wanted to do. She wondered if she'd ever want to eat again!

Molly watched closely as Hawk made a quick spit out of a couple of hardy sticks. He spread the fire out so that it was wide enough to cook both of the rabbits.

"Fill the coffeepot with water," he instructed.

Adam stood to the side, the only signs of his agitation were his white-knuckled fists hanging at his side. When Molly returned from the river with the water she knew words had been spoken between the two men. Adam was working with controlled intensity, preparing their sleeping place. Nathan appeared calm and relaxed but Molly observed the pulsating muscle in his sculptured jaw.

Hawk poured some of the water into two other pots, then added coffee to the remaining water and set it on some hot coals to boil.

She watched as Hawk poured some corn meal into the dutch oven then added wild onion and enough water to make a smooth batter. He placed the heavy pan in a bed of coals and covered the lid with hot ashes.

Earlier in the day Hawk had found and picked some mushrooms and wild mustard. He combined them with more onions and put them on the fire to cook. He instructed Molly on how to watch the food so that it didn't burn, then he left her to finish their meal.

From the corner of her vision Molly watched as Hawk unrolled the rabbit fur. He made a frame from four pieces of wood then stretched the fur on the frame. Rather than being repelled, as he had thought she'd be, she was watching with fascination as he sat

37

in the light of the fire and began the long cleaning process. His movements were surprisingly graceful as he freed the remaining flesh from the hide.

When Hawk realized she was truly interested he explained the process of tanning a hide to her. Her nose wrinkled femininely at the mention of some of the steps, particularly when he talked about making a mixture of brains and urine.

Hawk watched for her reaction and for the first time he smiled at Molly. His black eyes twinkled, his white teeth sparkled and dimples appeared as deep creases beside his mouth.

Molly caught her breath at the male beauty in his face. She instantly saw the reason why so many women were fascinated by him. The smile changed his face from controlled ruthlessness to savage magnetism. He was the epitome of male beauty and perfection.

Molly forced her eyes away from him, feeling swamped by her attraction to him. She looked at Adam, and her guilt escalated. She was newly married to a man she loved and adored and yet she was attracted to her husband's friend.

Molly was too young and inexperienced to know that marriage did not create blindness to the physical attractiveness of other men. She had yet to learn that there was nothing immoral in appreciating that beauty and so she suffered an unnecessary guilt.

"I'll show you how to make beaver-tail soup one night," Hawk commented casually. "The meat of the beaver isn't to my liking, but the tail is sweet and tender."

"Uck!" was her only comment. Checking the cooking food, Molly decided it was ready and she called both men to eat. Still not sure that she was hungry, Molly placed small helpings of each item on her tin plate. She closed her eyes and forced herself not to remember the soft, furry body as she bit into the rabbit.

"It's good!" she exclaimed in surprise. She took another bite. She met Adam's gaze and smiled with pride. "Someday, I'll do this all by myself. But as much as I hate to admit it, I think we do need the instruction Mr. Hawk is willing to give us."

Her eyes twinkled as she thought of the lessons her husband had taught her last night. Later she would tell Adam that there was definitely one place where he needed no instruction.

The journey west became a series of everyday lessons for both Molly and Adam. Hawk was ever-vigilant in his determination to teach both of them as much as possible as quickly as possible. He deliberately avoided passing through towns or stopping at way stations. Not only was he trying to outwit Charles Gallagher, but he knew Molly and Adam both needed as much time as he could give them to learn the hardships of frontier life. Nearly everything they did was a lesson, and his opinion of Molly slowly changed.

In the weeks of travel he had never heard her express one word of complaint. She handled her share of the chores and even laughed at herself and at her lack of expertise. But he noticed that once she was shown how to do something, Molly worked diligently until that particular chore became natural.

He brought in different game each night—deer, quail, even the promised beaver tail—and showed her the different methods to clean and cook them. Her nose still wrinkled as she gutted the animals, bringing a smile to his stern expression.

And she never failed to thank the animal spirit for its sacrifice.

Adam also learned everything Hawk could teach him. And he no longer argued against Molly's learning some of the more unpleasant aspects of frontier living. He acknowledged that their very existence might someday depend on her knowledge.

For Molly it was one long, glorious adventure. She maintained a distance from Hawk, still infatuated by his beauty and repelled by the savage intensity that increased the further they moved away from civilization.

As she had anticipated, the morning came when Hawk no longer curbed his hair with a thong. It hung to his shoulders, a glossy blue-black proclamation of his heritage, held back from his face by a band of red cotton fabric around his forehead.

If the days were a glorious adventure, the nights were unsurpassed in sensual bliss. Adam spent hours teaching her the pleasures of making love. Molly would have been mortified to the tips of her toes if she had known that Hawk slept far away from them each night, not because of a desire to give them privacy, but rather because he couldn't tolerate hearing Adam's sounds of satisfaction.

The flat land of the coast quickly turned into

rolling hills. Thick pine trees gave way to huge oak, birch and chestnut trees that blocked the sky from view. In the far distance the smoky blue mountains reigned supreme on the horizon. Their destination was within sight, still separated from them by weeks of hard travel.

Soon after lunch Hawk called a halt. The farther they travelled the rougher the trail became. As he had known would happen, the spring rains made holes, then hid them in harmless-looking puddles. After falling into a particularly deep hole, one of the wheels on the wagon needed some work. They made camp in a spot surrounded by giant trees more beautiful than any Molly had ever seen before.

Deciding to take advantage of the stop and the warm sunshine overhead, Molly gathered up some of their dirty clothes. They'd had nearly constant rain for the last week, which had made it impossible for her to wash anything and get it dry. She hoped there might be enough daylight left to dry most of the things, and the few that remained damp could be spread out in the morning to dry inside the wagon.

As usual they camped within walking distance of a stream. It was crystal clear, deeper in the middle than on the banks. Humming cheerfully, Molly washed the shirts, skirts and pants she had carried to the river with her.

After she finished with the last piece of clothing and draped it over a bush to dry, Molly sighed with tired satisfaction. Pushing her hair from her damp forehead, she looked at the water that enticingly invited her to cool off in its silver depths.

She looked back toward camp and knew that she

was out of sight of the two men working on the wagon. No longer resisting the siren call of the rippling current, Molly stripped to her drawers and chemise. She would have liked to remove all of her clothes but without the protection of walls she couldn't overcome her innate modesty. She pulled the pins from her hair, shaking her head and letting the honey-colored mass fall to her waist.

Molly slipped into the stream until she was waist-deep. The water enfolded her in its promised coolness. She ducked beneath the surface and wished she had soap to wash her hair. It hadn't felt or looked clean since they had left Charleston.

Surfacing, she wiped the moisture from her eyes. And froze. A water snake glided on the smooth surface not more than a foot from her. Its body was nearly as big around as her forearm and its mouth was open, showing her the cottony interior that gave it its name. Beady eyes looked unblinkingly into hers as it turned its head back and forth, its tongue tasting her scent on the wind. Inch-long fangs dangled threateningly.

Too terrified to move or to even scream for help, Molly stood and watched as it swayed hypnotically in the gently moving water. She tried desperately to call for help but she could only manage a soft squeak. But in her mind, Molly screamed repeatedly for Adam, or even Hawk, to come to her rescue.

Hawk strained to lift the wagon the fraction of an inch necessary for Adam to slip the wheel back into place. He had removed his shirt because of the heat, and his sleek skin shone shiny with sweat over his muscular chest and shoulders.

Adam slid the wheel into place as a scream of terror thundered through Hawk's head, nearly driving him to his knees. Instinctively he reached for the rifle propped against a tree and took off at a dead run for the river.

Adam watched in bewildered amazement as his friend ran from the campsite. More out of curiosity than out of real concern, Adam followed him, wondering why Hawk had suddenly stopped working on the wagon, grabbed his rifle and ran.

Molly never took her eyes from the snake but was aware when Hawk arrived at the bank. The roar of the rifle deafened her hearing as the snake's body exploded in front of her eyes. She watched as the current carried it downstream. And still she couldn't move.

"You are safe now," Hawk murmured quietly from the bank just as Adam reached his side. "Come on out."

She couldn't move. Molly tried to force her legs to carry her toward the promised safety of the voice on the bank but she was frozen by fear.

Adam understood the situation immediately and started to slip out of his boots to go into the river after his wife.

"No," Hawk said softly.

"No?" Adam asked incredulously. "Are you crazy? She's scared to death."

"The danger is past. She has to learn to handle the repercussions of fear."

"Damn it man! I'm sick to hell of your lessons! That is my wife and I'm not going to just stand here and watch her suffer another of your lessons. She is a

43

woman, not a horse you want to break to saddle."

Hawk caught Adam's arm in an unbreakable hold as the man stepped into the water. "Call her to you."

"Let me go!" Adam snarled.

Hawk raised his head, every inch the savage Shawnee warrior. "Call her!"

Molly was unaware of the argument on the bank. She still saw the snake with its bared fangs directed at her. Never in her life had she felt such raw, uncontrollable terror.

"Molly . . . Molly mine, you're safe." He had to force his voice to be calm and soothing. The muscles in Adam's arms bunched as his hands knotted into fists, he had never been closer to hating a person in his life as he did Hawk at that moment. "Come to me, sweetheart. You're safe, I promise."

She heard his voice, the sweet voice of the man she loved and she wanted more than anything in her life to walk to him. But her legs wouldn't cooperate.

"Molly . . ."

"Out of the water, Mrs. Royse," Hawk barked brutally. "Unless it's your intention to tease us with your damp body." He watched as her back stiffened and he knew she was finally hearing past her terror.

"You are aware that wet cotton is no barrier, aren't you? Then you must realize that we have an excellent view of your body."

Adam turned and Hawk read the intention in the other man's face. "Don't do it," Hawk warned softly. "You can try it later, but right now your wife needs you too much. Are you going to stand here on the bank trying to bash my brains in, to protect her honor while she stands in the middle of the river incapable of getting herself to the shore?"

"Let me go in after her, damn it!"

"No." Hawk turned his attention back to Molly and once more began to taunt her. "Your body isn't bad, but I've seen better. Of course, a free look is worth the effort."

Abruptly, Molly lowered herself shoulder deep into the water and turned toward the bank. "Make him go away, Adam."

Hawk looked at her and saw the terror still lingering in her honey gaze. He also knew she could now control that terror enough to walk out of the stream.

"Let her come to you," he said quietly as he released Adam's arm and turned to walk away. His steps were quiet as he listened to the sounds of Molly leaving the stream.

"Molly, oh Molly mine," Adam whispered as he gathered her damp body against him.

Molly started to shake as reaction set in. Tears coursed down her cheeks as she clutched the security of Adam's embrace.

"I hate him! I hate him! I hate him!" she mumbled, burying her face in Adam's sweaty shirt.

Lifting her into his arms, Adam carried her away from the water and sat down beneath a tree. He cradled her against him, lightly stroking her wet hair. He, too, felt a killing fury against the man he had called friend. At this point he was willing to continue their journey without Nathan Morning Hawk's assistance.

"It was so hot," Molly said, her voice picking up volume as fear grabbed her in its clutches again. "I wanted to take a bath, to feel clean. The snake was there and I couldn't move, I couldn't scream."

Hawk had waited in a protected spot behind a tree to see that she was truly all right. His lungs felt as if they would explode as he forgot to exhale.

He had heard her scream. It had been nearly painful in its intensity, the terror had vibrated through his entire body.

She had screamed, he told himself. He had heard it.

Quietly, so that they didn't overhear him, Hawk moved away from the tree. He followed the river downstream, his thoughts overshadowing everything else.

Maybe it had been a screeching noise made as the wheel finally slipped into place on the wagon. Perhaps it had been a bird, shrieking as it flew overhead. It could have been purely coincidence that he had mistaken the sound for a scream and had rushed to the river and found the snake threatening Molly.

He stopped walking and stood staring at the gently rippling water. His thoughts ran chaotically through his mind. It had to have been a noise made by something that had attracted his attention. Since Molly hadn't been in camp it had been natural to assume that the noise had come from her and even more natural for him to grab his rifle and run to the river.

Why, then, if the noise was caused by something else, had the sound thundered through his head? And why had Adam not heard it?

Why had his knees nearly buckled as a terror

unlike anything he'd ever known filled his body?

Something floating in the water caught his attention. Hawk stared at the thing that resembled a floating log. It was the remainder of the snake's body. A shiver travelled through his body, much like one caused by remembered fear.

She had screamed, he reassured himself. He knew she had, because he had heard her.

If it wasn't her scream he had heard then what was it?

He tried to shake off the feeling of something waiting just out of sight around the next bend in the trail. She had screamed, he told himself. He knew she had. In her terror she just hadn't realized that she had screamed and it had been loud enough for him to hear back at camp.

She had to have screamed. After all, he had heard her.

Hadn't he?

Chapter Three

Molly refused Adam's offer to carry her back to camp. After sliding her dress on over her wet underwear and pulling on her shoes she clutched his hand tightly. Commanding her quivering legs to support her weight, she concentrated on taking each step as her eyes jumped from place to place, searching for snakes on the ground, under bushes or in the trees.

When they reached camp Adam motioned to a wooden box and Molly gratefully sank down on its hard surface. After a quick search through his wife's things, Adam found her brush and comb. He returned to her and began to comb the snarls from her long hair. The motions were soothing to both of them and the tension that still held them in its grip slowly loosened its bonds.

In his usual silent way of walking, Hawk entered the camp unnoticed and stood for long minutes watching the scene. He could understand Adam's desire to pamper Molly, since he felt an almost overpowering need to do the same thing. But Hawk knew that the treatment would worsen the condition rather than improve it. There is no place in the wilderness for debilitating terror, no matter what the reason. Someone's life might depend on quick action, and time can't be wasted by long minutes of fear.

"We need to finish with that wheel." His voice broke through the stillness, jarring both Adam and Molly.

The transition is complete, Molly thought to herself as she looked at Hawk. His raven's-wing hair glistened in the sun. His hair was held back by a band around his forehead and it accentuated his piercing black eyes. She had only guessed at his strength before, but now his shirtless body screamed the message. Copper skin stretched sleekly over wide shoulders and a massive chest that rippled with flawlessly defined muscles. Fringed buckskin pants clung low to his hips, disappearing into fringed, beaded knee-high moccasins. He clutched a rifle in his right hand and even in his relaxed stance she had an impression of barely curbed violence, controlled only because it was his choice, not because of some civilized notion of correct behavior.

All trace of the white man was gone. Molly knew he was now unremittingly a Shawnee warrior.

Her back straightened and her chin rose as Adam's hands rested on her shoulders, lightly stroking the sides of her neck.

"We need to talk first," Adam replied quietly.

Hawk nodded his head in agreement and laid the rifle within reach on a barrel. He leaned his shoulder against a tree, his arms folded over his chest. The bark was rough against his naked skin, reminding him that he needed to put his shirt back on.

"So talk."

"What you did back there," he nodded toward the river, keeping both hands on Molly's shoulders, "it was cruel."

"Killing the snake?" Hawk asked skeptically.

"Damn it man, be serious! Molly was terrified and you wouldn't let me go to her. You forced me to stay on the bank while she stood waist-deep in the water and couldn't move."

"She has to learn to control her fear."

"Not that way, she doesn't!" Rage clogged his throat when he remembered the helplessness that had overwhelmed him because Hawk wouldn't let him go to her. "That was just plain cruel. Did you enjoy watching her suffer?"

Hawk's hands fell to his sides as he moved away from the tree. His black eyes narrowed and danger radiated from him.

"Is she going to be so controlled by her fears that it will affect her future? What if someday she walks into the cabin and sees a snake curled up in the cradle with her babe? Is she going to stand there in terror while it sinks its fangs into her child? Is she going to watch her babe die because she's too frightened to go to its aid?

"Or maybe one day while you're chopping wood the ax slips and becomes imbedded in your leg. That's not usually a fatal wound, but it would be if she were too afraid to help you." His voice became mocking, "you'd bleed to death before her eyes because she's scared."

His gaze lowered to Molly and he saw the hate she now felt for him . . . but also her grudging acceptance of his words. "There is plenty of time later to give in to your terror. But while it's happening, while your action could be the difference between life and death, you have no choice but to remain in control.

"Don't let me stop you from falling apart and having a good cry . . . when it's over!

"If teaching you that lesson is cruel," he said, speaking directly to Molly, "then yes, I enjoyed the cruelty. That cruelty may someday save a life. Who knows, it might even be mine!"

As regally as any blue-blooded royal, Molly stood up from the packing box. Her gaze didn't waver as she stared at the man across from her. "You will forgive me, I'm sure, if at this time I am unable to extend my gratitude to you for your lesson, Mr. Hawk. I have never before had a reason to experience true terror as I did today. It was . . . different."

Hawk felt his approval of her climb several notches further as she walked gracefully toward the back of the wagon. She stopped and turned toward him again. "Perhaps, someday, I shall be grateful for today. I hope not. I would rather never again experience such debilitating fright. However, should it happen, I will do my utmost to express my appreciation at that time."

Nodding her head slightly, she lifted her skirt and climbed into the back of the wagon. As Hawk watched her disappear from sight he felt a surprising sorrow for the necessary loss of her innocence. He turned to meet Adam's accusing gaze.

"Perhaps we should continue this trip without your aid," Adam said quietly.

"Do you really think you're ready to be on your own?"

"I don't know what I think, Nathan. But I've seen the way you've changed as we get deeper into the wilderness and I'm not sure that I know you anymore."

"I am the same man that I've always been," Hawk replied. "Perhaps you never looked past the clothes to see who I truly am."

"Perhaps . . . I just don't know." Adam watched a bird flitter from one tree branch to another, his thoughts a tangled web of doubt and uncertainty. "I've always known that you were a Shawnee Indian but maybe I'm just beginning to understand exactly what that means."

Unemotionally, Hawk waited for Adam to arrive at a decision. His stoic countenance gave no hint to the myriad thoughts running through his mind. He knew he had damaged his friendship with Adam, perhaps irretrievably.

"Not surprisingly, I've discovered that I can't bear for Molly to be hurt or abused. I agree that your lessons are a necessity; but I must disagree with your method. It seems to me that there must be a better way to get a point across than the way you did it today."

"It is my way," Hawk stated. "I know of no other. You can tell a child to stay away from a fire or he will be burned. But it's just words that the child hears until he is burned, then he understands. The only thing you can do is watch that the burn is not too severe."

"You would let a child get burned just to teach it a lesson?" Adam asked incredulously. It wasn't necessary for Hawk to reply, Adam saw the answer in his dark face.

"I suppose you'd let it get bit by a snake, too, to learn a lesson!"

"Such lessons would be fatal. Some things must be accepted. You and your wife must learn, one way or the other." Hawk let no emotion show in either his voice or expression. "I killed the snake to protect Molly but I forced her to overcome her fear enough to leave the water. Other lessons will be just as difficult, but I won't deliberately let either of you face death just to learn."

Adam ran a hand through his brown hair then rubbed the back of his neck. "I just don't know you anymore, Hawk. Or maybe you're right, maybe I never knew you.

"We need your help, I'm the first to admit that. I don't know how to go about finding a suitable homesite or how to erect a cabin once I find the place."

Inside the wagon Molly changed into dry clothes and listened to the conversation between the two men. She knew that Adam was speaking more from emotion than from common sense and she feared that he would say something that would force Hawk to leave. Now that she was calm she better understood Hawk's reasons for teaching her to handle her fear.

She still hated him with an intensity that amazed

her, but she accepted his lesson.

Molly climbed from the wagon and walked over to the area designated for the evening fire. Earlier in the day Hawk had killed a couple of rabbits that would be their evening meal. Ignoring the two men—they had stopped talking at her appearance and now watched her every move—she picked up the rabbits, grabbed a knife and headed for the river.

Forcing herself to choose the exact spot where she had bathed earlier, she laid the rabbits on the ground and knelt to begin the process of cleaning them.

"Once we get settled I'll not eat a rabbit again for six months," she mumbled to herself as she deftly cleaned the first one. She rinsed it then reached for the second. When she noticed a pair of moccasined feet beside her, she continued talking to herself and ignored her uninvited companion.

Hawk realized immediately the significance of the spot Molly had chosen and he felt an unexpected flash of pride for her. He knew it had not been easy for her to face the scene of debilitating terror so soon after the event. For her to have done so proved her ability and desire to conquer her fears.

He watched with satisfaction as she cleaned the rabbits. Her every move was calculated and practiced. The skin now came away from the body in one piece rather than small clumps. In fact he had nearly enough skins to make a coat and had planned to show her how that was done when the weather turned bad and there was time enough.

"We can never be friends, Mr. Hawk," Molly said quietly.

"Because I am Shawnee?" he asked but knowing

55

instinctively that wasn't her reason.

"It has nothing to do with you being an Indian." She moved back to the river and rinsed the other carcass. She grabbed both of the rabbits by their hind legs and stood, stretching the kinks from her back.

Her action unknowingly tightened her blouse, making Hawk remember her surprisingly full breasts covered by the wet cotton that had teased instead of hiding. He wondered why he had once thought her too thin and rather plain. Her hair, eyes, and skin all had the golden glow of honey. Hawk forced his thoughts away from wondering if she tasted as sweet.

"I do not like you, Mr. Hawk," Molly continued. "You are unrelentingly cruel and selfish." She paused a moment, then shook her head. "No, that's not fair," she corrected, "you are not selfish, or you would never have agreed to help Adam. However, your cruelty seems to know no bounds."

"It was not my intention to be cruel. It is the only way I know to teach you."

"There must be another way rather than your method. I have several nieces and nephews and I've never found it necessary to resort to torture in order to teach them."

"I'm sure their lives never depended on what you taught," Hawk replied quietly. He watched the lazy flow of the water as he fought to find a way to make her understand and accept his method of teaching. She was the wife of his best friend and he had come to respect and admire her. He wanted her to be as safe in her new home as possible, to know that she wasn't dependent on anyone for her protection.

"If I had killed the snake and then gone into the water and carried you out what would you do the next time it happens?"

Her brow wrinkled in concentration as Molly gave his question serious thought. "I would probably stand there screaming for someone to come help me," she answered fairly.

"What will you now do next time?"

She wanted to smack him on the side of the head with the dead rabbits for forcing her to see his point of view. "I will look for a way to get away from the snake, Mr. Hawk." Her voice was low and full of anger. "I will then wade to the bank and will probably shake for an hour or so before returning to my chores and waiting anxiously for the next life-threatening adventure to come my way!"

"The simplest thing in the wilderness can quickly become life-threatening, Molly. Often you have no one but yourself to depend upon to prevent death— your own death. You have much to learn in the next few months and there is no time to ease you gently through the lessons. If my way seems cruel, so be it. You, however, will benefit."

"Thank you, Mr. Hawk." Molly raised her head and nodded graciously. "I will endeavor to learn as quickly as possible. But that will not change the way I feel about you. As I said earlier, I don't like you!"

"Liking me isn't a necessary part of survival. Knowing how to handle a given situation at a given time, however, is." Hawk folded his arms across his chest in a position Molly silently labeled his "tolerant Indian" stance. She was already beginning to hate it.

"You're moving to a part of the country you've never seen before. You will be faced with decisions that you've had no experience with and you must be prepared to handle anything that comes along. Adam won't always be there at your side. You'll spend a lot of time alone in your cabin—your nearest neighbor will be several miles away. Isn't it better to learn now, while someone is available to teach you, than to have to learn later when it might be too late?"

Molly sighed and nodded in agreement. "Everything you say is true, Mr. Hawk, which makes it damnably harder to accept."

Hawk's stern face gave no hint of the smile he felt lurking just beneath the surface. She had spirit and a sense of justice. She would make Adam an admirable wife. And for the first time in his life, Hawk was envious of a friend.

"Hate me if you must, Mrs. Royse," he said quietly, "but learn everything I can teach you. Perhaps your anger at me will make some of the lessons easier to accept. You can pretend it is my head you are separating from my body the next time you prepare a rabbit for the stew pot."

"What a delightful thought," she agreed soberly. "I may never object to skinning a rabbit again."

"It appears that I would do better not to supply you with more rabbits. Maybe some fish or a wild turkey would make a nice change."

"It's a shame your mother didn't drown you when you were born," Molly muttered to herself as she moved past him.

Hawk let her take several steps before he replied. "My mother died before my birth, but you are free to complain to either of my stepmothers should you ever meet them. I'm sure they'll both agree with you that I am not always easy to get along with."

Blushing with embarrassment that he had over-heard her, Molly slowly returned to camp. She sighed, knowing this would not be her last encounter with him.

It was only much later, after dinner had been eaten and they had settled down for the night, that his words returned to her and she wondered how his mother could have died before his birth. Surely he meant at his birth, not before. It would be many months before she had the nerve to ask him to explain.

As Molly set out the lunch several days later she listened as Hawk patiently explained to Adam how to identify different trees by their bark. He called it "reading" a tree.

"Why learn the difference in the bark when I can always look up and tell what kind of tree it is by its leaves?" Adam asked.

"Winter," was Hawk's one word reply.

Feeling slightly foolish that he hadn't remembered that trees lose their leaves, Adam grinned and nodded in agreement. "Birch makes good bowls and spoons," Hawk continued the lesson. "Your best fence posts come from chestnut, it last forever because it doesn't rot. Use hickory for axe handles,

59

wheel spokes, things that take a lot of stress. The bark can be split for chair bottoms and while you're working you can chew on it. Tastes pretty good in a dry mouth. When you burn it save the ashes, they make the best lye for soap.

"Use maple for furniture. We'll try to find enough good-sized poplar to make your cabin. We'll skin bark off of some elm branches and make waterpipe so that Molly doesn't have to walk to the river for water. Look for—"

"Whoa!" Adam held his hands up and grinned. "I appreciate the lesson, Hawk, but I'm never going to remember all of that."

"It takes time, but you'll learn."

Molly realized that now both she and Adam accepted Hawk's way of teaching. She was relieved to notice that the rift in the friendship between the two men was slowly healing. She didn't want to be the cause for a friendship of long standing to be destroyed.

"How would you like to ride a horse for a while this afternoon?" Adam asked later. He rested against the wheel of the wagon, watching her graceful movements as she cleaned up from their noon meal.

"With you?" she asked dubiously.

"Of course with me, sweetheart," Adam replied with a chuckle. "Hawk'll drive the wagon and I'll ride his horse. I'll saddle mine and you can ride it."

Adam's horse remained tied to the tailgate of the wagon most of the time, since he usually drove the team. Molly was delighted at the idea of freedom from the wagon.

She hurriedly finished her chore while Adam saddled his horse. She saw the two men in serious discussion but ignored them. She was determined to let nothing, including an argument between Adam and Hawk, disturb her day.

Tying the bonnet ribbons firmly beneath her chin, Molly walked to the back of the wagon. She saw instantly what must have been the cause of the latest confrontation.

"Adam, that's not my saddle," she pointed out calmly.

"I know, sweetheart, but Hawk feels a sidesaddle would be too dangerous in the wilderness."

"I wonder if he'll consider a broken neck dangerous when I fall off because of that saddle," she mumbled to herself as she eyed it.

"I've never ridden astride and I don't believe this dress will allow for it," she said to the waiting men as she tried to hide her disappointment. "Perhaps we can have our ride another time."

"Riding astride gives you more grip and better control over your mount," Hawk said as he walked up beside her. Grabbing the sides of her waist he easily lifted her onto the saddle. He adjusted the stirrups to the correct length while ignoring her attempts to protect her modesty as she pulled down her bunched skirt.

Adam's lips thinned into a tight line as he fought not to comment on Hawk's rough handling of Molly. He handed the reins to her and mounted his borrowed horse. He had seen her ride once at a park in Charleston and knew that she was an able horsewoman. However, that had been on a sidesaddle.

Hawk watched her intently for several minutes as she accustomed herself to the saddle. After sliding from side to side several times she seemed to get the hang of it and managed to control herself and her horse. Nodding with satisfaction he turned to Adam.

"The trail forks about a mile ahead, take the right fork. There's a good stopping place beside the river, you can't miss it because it's just after the waterfall. I'll meet you there this evening." At Adam's nod he turned and climbed onto the wagon seat.

Molly rode at a sedate pace until the wagon was out of sight behind them. Once she knew she was away from Hawk's penetrating gaze she grabbed the reins firmly and urged the horse into a gallop. She quickly discovered the advantages of the saddle as the horse twisted and turned through the trail.

Adam stayed just behind Molly, making no effort to stop her or slow her down. Unequal to the force of the wind in her face, the flimsy bonnet blew off her head and tumbled to the ground. At first Adam wondered what Hawk would think when he drove past it, then he realized that his Indian friend would easily read the signs on the trail and think that they had raced the horses recklessly down the path.

But if Hawk could see Molly now he would know that she was far from reckless—in fact, she was in complete control. Watching as her hair tumbled from its pins and streamed behind her, Adam knew that he was in more danger than she. She rode her mount with the grace of a natural-born horsewoman. Adam found himself falling further and further behind as she raced the wind for freedom.

Realizing the danger of being separated from Adam, Molly slowed her horse to a more leisurely pace until he was again at her side. She smiled warmly at him and talked cheerfully as they followed the winding trail through the mountains.

Molly had been raised in the flatlands of the coast, and the views offered by the mountains never ceased to delight her. The huge granite mountain peaks glistened as they disappeared into the clouds. Unexpected views of verdant valleys far below took her breath as she caught glimpses of the winding rivers sparkling diamond bright in the sun.

The mountains were alive with life. Small animals scurried from their path as birds flew overhead, scolding the human intruders. From a distance that made her feel safe, Molly watched delightedly as a black bear and her cub wandered the woods. It was amusing to watch their waddling, rolling gait, but she knew that the humor would quickly disappear if the female decided they were encroaching on her territory. Death would come quickly to anyone or anything challenging the fury of her heavily muscled body.

By midafternoon they found the waterfall . . . and heaven on earth.

Chapter Four

Molly was spellbound, willingly caught by the unsurpassed beauty of her surroundings. Of the many glorious things she had seen thus far on the trip west nothing could compare to this opulence of nature.

"Oh, Adam," she whispered reverently as he helped her to dismount.

"I know," he replied, hugging her tightly to him. "It defies description."

"God must have spent centuries designing this place. Everything is just perfect."

Hand in hand, they walked to the edge of the river. Each direction offered its own addition to the total beauty. Slightly upriver a waterfall tumbled hundreds of feet down the sheer side of the mountain to the rushing stream below. Innumerable rainbows began and ended in its delicate mists as the sun caught the tiny droplets and created a dazzling display of diamond bright beads. Its thundering roar mocked the softer sounds of the forest, forcibly reminding the viewer that there was nothing gentle in its compelling energy.

Giant weeping willows, their flowing branches trailing captivatingly, leaned gracefully toward the gentler current near the place where Molly and Adam stood. Water cascaded around boulders the size of houses then flowed into ponds of cobalt blue and turquoise green.

Huge trout, their rainbow colors glistening in the sun, jumped from beneath the dark surface. On the far side of the river a doe and her spotted fawn lowered their heads and drank from the cool water, the doe constantly alert to the dangers awaiting her offspring.

Birds flew from tree to tree, singing and chattering their cheerful songs while the wind whispered through the leaves in a language unknown and yet familiar.

Molly sat down on a convenient boulder and began unlacing her shoes.

"What are you doing, Molly mine?" Adam asked softly.

"I want to walk to that big boulder over there, sit down and dangle my feet in the water." She pointed to a large rock nearly in the middle of the stream that was easily accessible.

Leaving her shoes where they landed, Molly stood and raised her skirt. She missed Adam's smile of delight when she modestly turned her back to him to remove her stockings.

"Watch out for snakes!" Adam advised as he watched her gracefully move from rock to rock as she headed toward her goal. Chuckling at the look of

66

disgust she threw his way, he quickly removed his own boots and socks and followed her path. By the time he reached her, Molly was sitting on the very edge of the boulder, her skirt raised to her knees and her feet dangling in the water.

"You didn't have to remind me of snakes," she mumbled as he sat down beside her.

"Even the Garden of Eden had its serpent," he reminded her.

"It's so beautiful here," she sighed, "I can't imagine that Eden had anything on this place. You even have the right name."

"Will you be my Eve?" he asked as he wrapped his arm around her shoulders and pulled her snugly against his side.

With a gentle hand beneath her chin, Adam raised Molly's face to his. He lowered his head, lightly nibbling on her mouth until her lips parted. At her invitation, he deepened the kiss, tasting her, devouring her, loving her.

"I don't believe that Eve wore so many clothes." He began to unbutton the back of her dress while teasing her with his mouth.

Anticipation rippled through her as her trembling fingers worked his shirt buttons free. "I know the other Adam never wore a shirt."

As he lowered her dress to her waist, Molly opened his shirt and ran her fingers through the wiry hair on his chest, gently tugging, then soothing the hurt. Adam removed his shirt and laid it behind Molly on the rough rock. He eased her down upon it as he freed the ribbons of her chemise.

Molly closed her eyes and absorbed the feelings

Adam created with his touch. She felt the unfamiliar caress of the sunlight on her naked breasts when he pulled the sides of the chemise apart. His warm lips touched the sensitive peaks but moved quickly away when she arched her back for more.

"Not yet, Molly mine." Abruptly, Adam stood and pulled Molly to her feet. He led her from the rock to the soft spring grass growing beneath the willow trees.

His breath caught at the look of love filling her gentle eyes. Adam quickly removed the remainder of his clothes and then hers before they sank together onto the cool grass.

"Now, sweetheart," he whispered, his mouth teasing the tender skin where her neck joined her shoulders. "I'm going to love you as I've never loved you before. With the sun as our candle and the breeze our blanket, I'm going to make you mine for eternity."

The afternoon was peaceful, a day made for drifting on a daydream. The clumping of the oxen's hooves and the rattling of the wagon wheels on the trail were hypnotically repetitious. A slight breeze rustled through the new leaves on the trees, reminding Hawk of the sound of a lady's petticoat as it slid down her thighs.

Shaking his head, Hawk wondered why he would associate the sound of leaves with something as sensual as a petticoat. It wasn't normal for him to be so inattentive while in the wilderness. He had seen no one since Molly and Adam had left but he knew it was dangerous to become distracted when things were quiet. From his experience he knew something usually happened when things were at their quietest.

The scent of spring flowers drifted around him and he thought of a lady's fragrance as he nuzzled against the soft skin of her neck. With the picture filling his mind, Hawk rubbed the back of his neck as a sense of anticipation wove its way through him.

He slowly became aware that his breathing was more labored and his muscles were tightening with tension. His hands were clenched fists around the reins as his eyes began to scan the area looking for a reason that would explain his odd frame of mind.

Spying something lying on the side of the trail, Hawk pulled the team to a halt. He tied the reins around the hand brake, grateful for a reason to climb down from the wagon. Trying to relieve some of the building tension, Hawk stretched, feeling his muscles bunch and relax at his command. Instead of releasing the tension it seemed to accelerate until his entire body was drawn as tight as a bowstring.

Ever alert for danger, in fact hoping for something to happen to alleviate his growing uneasiness, Hawk walked over to the thing lying in the trail. He recognized it immediately as the bonnet Molly had been wearing earlier.

His knowledgeable gaze traveled the trail, easily reading the signs. The distance separating the hoof marks and the depths of those marks told him the story. Concerned at first that Molly's horse might have gotten out of her control, he carefully studied the trail. Unconsciously sighing with relief, Hawk realized that everything he saw pointed out that

Molly had been in full control of her horse.

Hawk bent and picked up the bonnet, intending to return it to its wayward owner later, but as his fingers closed on the stiff fabric the tension that had plagued him pounded through him. Sweat poured down his brow to drip from his clenched jaw. His breathing was a labored sound hissing through his tightly clamped teeth while his whole body shook from the force of the tension.

Suddenly, without warning, as Hawk fought for control of his own body, the tension receded. Left with a strange feeling of euphoria, Hawk forced his trembling legs to carry him back to the wagon. He leaned against a wheel, head bowed and eyes closed, while he waited for his breathing to return to normal.

Finally, as the sensation ebbed, Hawk raised his head and looked around, almost surprised to discover that everything was normal. Except for him. Right then he would gladly have given ten years of his life to have been able to tell the shaman of his father's people of this. Perhaps the old man's wisdom could explain what had happened.

Hawk climbed back onto the wagon, noticing that his quivering legs were barely capable of accomplishing the feat. He sat for a long time with his elbows resting on his thighs and his head bowed. Never before had such an unexplainable thing happened to him. Even the dreams and emotions he had felt during his Shawnee manhood ceremony could not compare with this. And at least those things were expected and could be explained.

The building of tension and then the sudden rush

of release could only be compared with one thing in his experience, sexual fulfillment. But even his most passionate encounter was tame when compared with the feelings he had just experienced. This feeling went far beyond physical release.

Hawk knew there were many things in the world that had no explanations. From childhood he had been taught to accept such things and perhaps time would offer a reason. The old shaman of the tribe always knew where to find buffalo. Linsey, his stepmother, knew when one of her children was in danger. Hawk, himself, had heard Molly's soundless scream for help. Perhaps this was one of those things that defied a rational explanation.

When he knew he was once more in control of himself, Hawk untied the reins and urged the oxen to move. He refused to let his mind dwell on the one comparison that drifted repeatedly through his thoughts.

He enforced self-discipline to control his wayward thoughts and slowly turn his distress into a towering rage. Rage he understood and accepted, it needed no explanation. Rage blocked out the lingering disappointment that he would never find a love that would create such an overwhelming fulfillment.

Molly adjusted the spit over the fire and turned the meat so that it would cook more evenly. Adam had shot the rabbits and had helped her to clean them while they waited for Hawk to arrive with the wagon.

It had been a perfect afternoon, one she knew she

would cherish forever in her memories. Lightly touching her flat stomach, Molly wondered if they had created more than memories this afternoon. She had no reason to suspect that she carried Adam's child but she hoped that her desire would soon be a reality.

At the sound of the wagon entering the clearing, Molly looked up and smiled at Hawk. His intense, almost savage expression wiped the smile from her face. He pulled the team to a halt, jumped down from the wagon and began unhitching the oxen.

Molly couldn't overhear their conversation, but from the look on Adam's face and the low mumbled of sound, she knew Hawk was angry. And when he reached into the wagon and walked over to her, she thought she knew the reason why.

"You found my bonnet," Molly said, reaching for her hat.

Hawk threw the bonnet at her as if it was something repulsive. He turned to Adam who had walked up beside them.

"You're a bigger damned fool than I thought," Hawk snarled.

"She's a better rider than I am," Adam replied defensively.

"I don't doubt that, but no one gives a horse its head on these trails. You don't know what'll be around the next bend."

"Just a minute, Mr. Hawk," Molly interrupted. "It was my fault, not Adam's. I'm the one who set the pace."

"That doesn't surprise me, Mrs. Royse," Hawk growled, his black eyes burning holes through her.

"You have a normally intelligent man so wrapped around your little finger that he can't tell you no even when he knows better."

"Now, Nathan . . ."

"If you can't control your wife, Adam, then I will!" Hawk knew he was being unfair, making more of the situation than was necessary, but the events of the afternoon still held control over him.

"You and who else?" Molly demanded, stepping past Adam to confront Hawk.

Generations of Shawnee warriors coursed through Morning Hawk's veins. Never before had he looked or felt as savage as he did at that moment. Black eyes burned through narrowed lids, knotted muscles strained at the seams of his shirt and pants while his chest rose and fell with each life-giving breath.

Molly had to force herself not to step back from the man facing her. All he needs to complete the picture of savage Indian, she thought to herself, is a tomahawk in one hand and a knife in the other. She felt intimidated by his intensity but not truly frightened.

"When the time comes, Mrs. Royse, I won't need anyone's help."

Hawk turned, untied his horse and mounted. Wrapping his long legs around the bare body of the animal, he urged it into a gallop, forgetting in his anger that he had just berated Adam for doing that very same thing.

"I never hated anyone before I met your friend," Molly muttered between clenched teeth.

Adam smiled and wrapped his arm around her, nestling her head against his chest. "Don't let him upset you, Molly mine."

"He didn't upset me," she replied. "He made me so mad I could spit!"

"He didn't mean anything by it, it's just his way."

"Why do you always defend him? Why don't you ever get angry at him?"

Adam hugged her tightly then set her away. "You can get angry enough for both of us, sweetheart."

"I hope he gets lost!" Molly muttered to herself as she climbed into the wagon. "I hope he gets lost and his horse throws him." She grabbed the pots and pans necessary to finish supper. "I hope he gets lost, his horse throws him and he breaks his leg!" She banged the pots and pans together to emphasize her words.

"I hope he gets lost, his horse throws him, he breaks his leg and a skunk attacks him!" She climbed out of the wagon and faced her grinning husband.

"A skunk?" Adam asked with a chuckle.

"A whole family of skunks!"

"Isn't that rather much? Wouldn't a broken leg be sufficient?"

Molly couldn't resist Adam's smile. "All right, only one skunk then, but definitely a broken leg!" She walked toward the fire, her righteous indignation soothed.

"If he broke his leg he'd be forced to ride in the wagon every day until it healed," Adam reminded her.

"No he wouldn't," Molly turned and grinned at her husband. "We'll just shoot him!"

Several days later Molly realized that Hawk

rarely returned to camp until after dark and usually left before sunrise. The daily lessons he had insisted on had come to an abrupt halt. He spoke to Adam only out of necessity and he never even looked at her—which was fine with her, Molly decided.

She was surprised when he rode up to the wagon early one afternoon, shortly after the noon meal. She was even more surprised because he had pulled back his hair and tied it with a piece of rawhide. The reason was evident as soon as he spoke.

"There's a family a couple of miles up the trail." He spoke directly to Adam, ignoring Molly at his side.

"Is that the reason you're looking like a white man again?" Molly asked sarcastically.

Hawk acted as if she hadn't spoken. "They arrived a couple of months ago and already have their garden in. It'll be a good place to stop for the night." He gave Adam directions to find the homestead, which was slightly off the trail, then Hawk turned and left again.

"Molly, what's gotten into you?" Adam asked, as he started the team moving again. "Can't you be civil?"

"I can be completely civil to anyone but that man, just looking at him gets my dander up!"

"He'll be gone soon, Molly mine, then it'll just be the two of us."

"I can hardly wait," she muttered, feeling slightly ashamed of her attitude.

They rode in silence, Adam watching carefully for the signs that would lead them to the unknown family. The cleared field was their first indication

75

that they had found the correct location. Red dirt, plowed in neatly paralleled rows, showed the priority given the garden. Several logs had been felled and pulled over to the spot they had selected for their cabin. A wagon was pulled up to the base of a dead tree and as she studied the area Molly realized what she was seeing.

"They live in a tree!" she declared with amazement.

As they drew closer her words were proven true. A woman, with a baby on her hip and several young children hiding behind her skirt, came to the opening in the huge tree. The dead sycamore tree reached more than a hundred feet into the sky and was nearly ten feet in diameter. Its hollowed base made a perfect temporary home for the pioneer family, offering shelter from the elements and an instant home until their cabin was constructed.

Introductions were quickly carried out and Adam moved their wagon slightly away from the tree house to give both families privacy when darkness fell.

Gary and Nora Price and their four young children had left Pennsylvania the previous fall and spent the winter with family members in Charlotte, North Carolina. Knowing the importance of a garden for their own survival, they had headed west before spring arrived so that they would have plenty of time to clear some land and put in their garden.

Molly waited patiently for an invitation to view the tree house but when none was forthcoming she could no longer curb her curiosity.

"Mrs. Price, I admit to being uncommonly

curious," Molly said with a grin. "May I please see inside the tree?"

"Call me Nora," replied the woman who was probably the same age as Molly. "Ain't nothin' wrong 'bout being a little bit nosy. Find out some of the best gossip that way!"

She bounced the baby on her hip and with a wave of her hand motioned for Molly to enter the house. Molly stepped into the interior of the old tree and was amazed by the size. The room was almost ten feet around and nearly as tall. The rough floor was uneven and sank in places, making walking difficult but Gary had laid planks on it to create secure sleeping places.

The necessities of life were neatly stacked on wooden crates and an oil lantern hung from a peg driven into the wall. Molly wrinkled her nose at the overly sweet smell of decay that wafted around her.

"You should be here after it's rained for several days," Nora said with a laugh when she noticed Molly's actions. "It smells so bad you'd rather be outside gettin' wet!" She laid the baby on a bed and gently rubbed his tiny back. "And it gets mighty cold some nights so that we all snuggle together 'neath all the quilts. Can't have no fire in here or we'd burn it down. Don't wanta do that 'cause, bad smell and all, it's better than sleeping out in the open every night."

Nora smoothed the soft curls on her son's tiny head, the humor leaving her face. "We left a good-sized farm in Pennsylvania," Nora continued quietly. "Gary worked it with his pa and older brother, but he wanted somethin' for himself." She sighed softly. "You gotta follow your man when he's

77

lookin' for somethin' even though he don't know what it is. But it sure is hard to say good-bye to everythin' you've always known and head out for someplace you've never seen."

Nora looked up and her eyes locked onto Molly's. "But what choice is there?—'pears to me that if you love him you made your choice when you said 'I do.'" Nora's irrepressible good humor returned with a blink of the eye. "Iffen we hadn't come here I never woulda lived in a tree. Now I ain't sayin' I'd be happy to live here forever, but just think of the stories I can tell my grandbabies. They ain't gonna believe their old granny lived in a tree like a squirrel!"

Molly and Adam spent several days with the Price family. Hawk had returned that first afternoon. He spoke briefly with Adam and then left. Molly wondered if he would return or if he'd decided to leave them with the first family they'd found.

Adam helped Gary fell several trees while Molly and Nora stripped the logs of branches, kept a watchful eye of the active children and cooked the meals.

Nora was always cheerful, and her self-confidence was evident in everything she did. Molly found herself admiring the woman as their friendship grew.

In the evening, after the children had been settled for the night, they all lingered around the fire. Gary spoke of the advantages of the area for homesteading. They were in the foothills of the Blue Ridge Mountains, with rolling land and fresh mountain streams. Several small towns, including Rutherford Town to the south and Morganton to the north, were within less than a day's ride.

"Little Brittain Presbyterian Church is just up the road a piece," Nora supplied. "And iffen you ain't there on a Sunday morning come Sunday afternoon someone is here checkin' to make sure everything is all right. Lordy Moses, a couple of weeks ago we just plumb forgot that it was a Sunday. That afternoon the preacher comes aridin' up checkin' to see why we weren't in church. I was so bumfuzzled when he left that I sat right down and made me a marker to keep track of the days."

"Soon as everybody's garden is in, the neighbors are gonna give us a barn raisin'," Gary said quietly, as the smoke from his pipe drifted around his head. "The people here help each other but mind their own business. It's a good place to set down roots.

"Most of the land around here is already owned but we got lucky. We bought this parcel from Widow Bailey. Her husband died some time back and her only son was killed when his horse threw him. It took near to all the money we had to buy it but me and Nora think it was worth it."

Later that night, snuggled together beneath the warmth of a quilt while the stars twinkled overhead, Molly and Adam discussed the idea of remaining in Rutherford County rather than moving further into the mountains. They liked what they had seen of the area but Adam expressed his concern that it would be easy for Charles Gallagher to find them.

"If Papa comes here we'll just tell him to leave us alone," Molly said firmly.

"He can make things difficult for us, Molly mine." Adam kissed the top of her head and pulled her more

79

snugly into his arms. "I don't want to see you get hurt."

"He can't hurt us if we don't let him," Molly replied. "I like it here, Adam, and if this is where you want to stay, then this is where we'll stay."

As he drifted to sleep, Adam decided to ride into Rutherford Town the next day and check the land office for available homesites. If they could find some land they would settle into this area of North Carolina and begin building their home.

Early the next morning as Molly and Nora prepared breakfast and Gary and Adam discussed the trip into town, Hawk rode in. Nora offered him a cup of coffee. Adam smiled at his friend and Gary greeted him with a handshake. Molly waited apprehensively for the courtesies to be finished.

"I've found your homesite," Hawk said quietly.

Chapter Five

"It's on a good strong creek," Hawk said quietly as he ate the meal Nora and Molly had cooked. Adam and Gary listened attentively while Molly helped Nora settle the children.

"The land's been partially cleared and we should be able to get a garden in without much trouble. There's several good homesites, you just need to decide where you want to build your cabin."

"Are you sure the land's for sale?" Adam asked, excitement threaded through his voice.

"A neighbor said it was, but we'll go into town and make sure. If not, we'll see what else is available, there may be something better than this but I have my doubts."

As soon as they finished their breakfast, the men saddled their horses and headed for town. Molly watched them ride down the trail until they were swallowed by the forest. Trying to hide her disappointment that she had been left behind with Nora and the children, she gathered up the breakfast dishes for washing. She knew Adam would have taken her if she had expressed her desire to go along, but she would have felt guilty leaving Nora alone. Hawk intended to return by nightfall and if the children had gone along, it would have been impossible to make the trip in a day.

It was easy for Molly to stay busy, helping Nora with the numerous chores that needed to be done. They took advantage of the warm spring morning and washed their dirty clothes. The river was just behind the unfinished cabin but it was several feet down a steep hill. Carrying the heavy buckets of water back up the hill was a tiring chore and the two women took turns until they had enough water to complete their wash.

Nora seemed untiring as she completed one chore and went immediately to the next. By midafternoon, Molly was exhausted. She wanted nothing more than to sit down and could only groan when Nora grabbed an ax and headed for the felled logs.

Nora heard Molly's soft groan and turned to the other woman. "You can sit and talk with me while I do this, if you'd like."

"Nope." Molly grabbed an ax and walked over to a waiting log. "I can't just sit back and watch you work."

"You wait," Nora said as she swung the ax, removing the branches from the log. "When it's your cabin and you know the harder you work the sooner it'll be done, you'll be findin' all kinds of energy."

"I'll have to take your word for that," Molly mumbled as she tried to match Nora's ability with the ax.

Nora cleaned three logs for Molly's one while the older children pulled the branches away. Later the larger branches would be cut up for firewood and the smaller pieces neatly stacked for kindling. Even the leaves would be used as mulch for the tender plants in the garden.

Molly sighed with relief when Nora called a halt. They all walked back to the house where Nora soon began the preparations for supper.

"What do you think about me taking the older kids down to the creek and let them play in the water?" The afternoon had grown warm and Molly relished the thought of the cool breeze that would be found down at the stream.

"Sounds good. I'll put the baby down for his nap and get supper cooking. You take your time and have some fun." She admonished the children to behave and waved them off with her usual smile in place.

The water was still too cold for swimming but the children stripped down to their drawers and played noisily at the edge. Molly removed her shoes and stockings and raised her skirt enough so that it didn't get wet as she waded. Her thoughts drifted to the plans she and Adam had made for their future home.

At the beginning it would be a one-room cabin but Adam would add rooms as their family grew. They'd have a big garden and Molly would put up the fruits and vegetables for winter. Someday they'd have a big home filled with lots of love. Her face warmed at the thought of the children her love for Adam would create.

"Molly?" a tiny voice interrupted her daydream.

"What, sweetheart?" Molly asked, looking at six-year-old Wanda.

"There's somethin' behind you."

Her heart pounding with fear, Molly turned slowly. Behind her and slightly uphill, a skunk and her kits were strolling down the trail Molly and the children had used to get to the river. The mother skunk was made nervous by her unaccustomed venture into daylight. The usually nocturnal animal raised her head and sniffed the air.

Molly smelled the distinctive odor that identified the creature, as its bushy black-and-white tail rose defensively. Moving slowly so that she wouldn't alarm the creature, Molly backed into the river and gathered the children with her.

At its deepest point the water rose to Molly's hips. Only Wanda was tall enough to stand on her own while Molly held three-year-old Timmy and four-year-old Charles on her hips.

"It be a polecat," Charles advised knowledgeably. "Pa says the only good polecat be a dead one."

"I think it's pretty," Wanda said.

"You would, you're a girl." Charles replied with a smirk.

"Are you gonna kill it?" Timmy asked.

"What she gonna use, dummy?" Wanda demanded. "She ain't got no gun."

"Well, she could throw a rock, iffen she aimed real good."

"Could not," Timmy supplied. "She's a girl and girls can't throw no good at all."

"Can too," Wanda replied in defense of her sex.

"Can not!" the boys yelled back.

Molly watched as the skunk stiffened, its beady eyes turned in their direction.

"Children, please hush," Molly whispered, her eyes glued to the animal that was the size of a cat.

"Tell him that you can too throw a rock better than he can!" Wanda demanded, her voice overly loud to Molly's ears.

"If you three don't stop arguing we'll all get a lot of practice throwing. Your ma and pa will be throwing your food to you for a good long time if that skunk decides to spray us. No one will want to get any closer to you than absolutely necessary until the smell wears off."

It seemed to Molly that she waited forever for the skunk to move. The water, cold from the spring run-off higher in the mountains, flowed around her legs and pulled at her skirt.

"I'm cold," Wanda whined.

"Me, too," Charles agreed.

"Me be freezin'!" added Timmy, not wanting to be outdone by his older brother and sister.

"I know, children." Molly looked at her charges and saw the shivers rippling through their tiny bodies. "Maybe she'll leave in a minute and we can get out and go home for dry clothes."

Timmy tried to wrap his legs higher around Molly's body but found that his brother was impeding his progress. A fight began to brew as the two boys used their feet against each other, trying to dislodge the other one from Molly's hold.

"Stop it!" Molly demanded as her grasp began to slip. Neither of the boys was large but her arms soon

85

began to ache from holding them. The water swirled around her hips and her feet started to grow numb. At her side, Wanda began to whimper. Finally it became evident to Molly that they would have to leave the cold water, skunk or no.

"Children, I want you to listen very carefully," Molly said as she slowly moved toward the bank. "We're going to try to sneak around the skunk. We won't use the trail to get back home, we'll make a new one."

"Can't," Wanda said with a sniff.

"Why can't we?" Molly again shifted the slipping boys and knew that once they were out of the river they would have to walk on their own. Her arms were too tired to struggle up the hill with them.

"Pa says to stay on the trail."

"I'm sure this time he'll understand if we make our own trail."

"Can't," Wanda again replied.

"Wanda," Molly gritted out the child's name through clenched teeth. "We will make our own trail."

"Mistress Molly, Pa whips awfulsome hard," Charles said quietly.

"Ya," Timmy chimed in. "Awfulsome hard!"

" 'Sides, there's snakes and rats and poison ivy and snakes and . . ."

"I get your point, Wanda." Now knee-deep in the cold water, Molly stared at the three children. She knew the only way she'd get them home was up the trail.

On the same trail, the skunk was on the alert, feet braced, back arched, tail raised threateningly.

Molly took the final few steps to reach dry land and slowly lowered the boys to the ground. All three children shivered uncontrollably and their blue lips covered chattering teeth. She knew she had to get them home so that they could get warm before they became ill.

Molly picked up several small stones and threw them in the direction of the skunk. Unfortunately, Charles had been correct in his assumption that she could not throw. The stones fell far short of the animal.

When the children saw Molly throw the stones they, too, picked some up and threw them at the skunk. Their aim was no better than hers; however, the skunk seemed to realize their intention and its posture became even more defensive.

"Damn!" Molly whispered in frustration.

"Damn!" Charles repeated with glee.

"I'm gonna tell Mama!" Wanda threatened. "You're gonna eat soap!"

"I want Mama," Timmy whimpered, his tiny body shaking uncontrollably.

"Me, too."

"Me, too."

Molly tried yelling at the skunk, waving a stick and even throwing more rocks. Nothing worked. For whatever reasons, the skunk was not going to abandon her place on the trail.

Timmy's sudden sneeze forced Molly to make a decision. Instructing the children to stay together behind the feeble protection of her long skirt, they began the journey back up the hill. As they approached, the skunk moved backward and slightly to the side of the trail. It looked like she intended to let them pass.

Later, Molly couldn't explain exactly what happened. Everything had been going so well!

They drew even with the animal, then slightly past it. Without warning, the children broke away from the protection of Molly's skirt and climbed up the side of the hill with the agility of mountain goats.

The skunk took exception to their exuberance and protected her kits with the efficient weapon granted to her by nature. Molly choked and gagged at the overwhelming smell as the black-and-white creature scurried down the trail toward the river.

Molly's arrival back at camp was announced long before she arrived. She was holding her hand over her nose and trying to breathe through her mouth, and her eyes watered so badly she could barely see to walk.

"God in heaven, I thought the children were teasing!" Nora exclaimed as Molly stumbled to a halt.

"I wish they were," Molly lifted watery eyes to Nora. "Help?"

Nora nodded. "If we were home I'd wash you in tomato juice, but Molly, I just don't know what to use here to cut that odor."

"We've got to try." Molly choked and began to unbutton her dress while Nora ushered the children into the tree with instructions to dry, dress and stay out of the way.

Using buckets of water that they had carried up earlier, Molly washed repeatedly with the harsh lye soap Nora provided. She gave up trying to protect her modesty when she realized her underclothes smelled as rank as her dress. Stripping down to bare skin, Molly handed the clothing to Nora.

"Should I try washing them?" Nora asked, holding the offending clothing away from her on the end of a stick.

"Burn them!" Molly muttered, buried head first in a bucket of water.

An hour and several scrubbings later, Molly's skin burned and itched. Her dripping hair hung in snarls around her face as she sat on a stump with an old quilt wrapped around her.

"It's somewhat better," Nora said from the safety of several feet away.

"No it isn't," Molly moaned and pushed at her hair.

The sun had begun to lower in the sky and the cool evening breeze drifted over her abused flesh. The children begged repeatedly to be allowed to leave the tree and the baby began to whimper for his evening meal.

"What am I going to do?" Molly pleaded, knowing that Nora had no more answers.

As they stared at each other they heard the sound of hoofbeats approaching. Molly moaned and buried her head in the quilt. She couldn't bear to see the looks on the faces of the men when they returned.

Hearing the sound of only one horse, Molly raised her head enough to peek out of the folds of the quilt. She stifled a groan when she spied Hawk.

Hawk spoke briefly to Nora before unsaddling his horse and leading it to the makeshift corral. He rubbed it down briefly before removing the bit and letting it run freely.

Still without acknowledging Molly, Hawk turned and walked into the woods. He returned several minutes later, his arms filled with a variety of weeds and roots. He dropped them on a cutting block and began chopping them into small pieces. Then he dumped the mess into a pot of boiling water. He again spoke to Nora before walking toward Molly.

"Suk àhk wah," he said with a shake of his head.

Though his face remained stern, Molly swore she could see a glint of humor dancing in his dark eyes. Her anger began to build at the thought of him laughing at her. The blanket slid away from her head as she raised her face to his.

"Don't you dare laugh," she warned.

"You are in no position to threaten, *suk àhk wah,*" he said, his dark eyes sparkling.

"What did you call me?"

"Suk àhk wah," Hawk replied this time letting the smile reach the rest of his face. "Polecat."

Molly stood up, clutching the quilt tightly and walked toward him. He backed up with each step she took, stopping only when she did.

"Where is Adam?" she asked with a snarl.

"Your husband and Gary stopped to walk the land he purchased today," Hawk supplied quietly. "If we go to work now we should be able to remove most of the smell before they return."

Molly's eyes narrowed with suspicion. "How?"

Hawk nodded toward the pot of boiling gruel Nora stirred, her hand held over her nose. "The cure isn't much better than the cause but it will wash off once it's done the job."

He picked up the pot and started walking toward the river. "Come on, *suk àhk wah,* let's see if we can make you smell sweeter."

"Don't call me that!" Molly demanded as she reluctantly followed him.

Hawk set the pot into the water for it to cool somewhat before they used the mixture. He turned and saw Molly standing forlornly at the edge of the stream. As a tear slowly rolled down her cheek he noticed how unnaturally red her skin was.

"It smells as bad as the skunk," she murmured, wrinkling her nose with distaste.

"Trust me, it won't burn your skin as the lye soap did," Hawk replied reassuringly, "and I promise the smell will disappear when you rinse it off."

"Seems to me that I don't have any other choice."

"You can always wait for the skunk smell to disappear." Hawk grinned at her burning look. "It shouldn't last more than a month or so."

Keeping the quilt wrapped firmly around her, Molly walked into the water. The afternoon sun had begun to disappear, taking with it the warmth it had offered earlier. She bit her lower lip to stifle a moan as the cold water played against her bare skin and tugged threateningly at the quilt.

"Tell me what to do," she said trying unsuccessfully to hide a shiver.

"Ah, Mrs. Royse," Hawk chuckled, "you could have waited until summer to have a run-in with a skunk. At least then the warm water would have been a pleasure instead of continuing with the punishment."

91

"I'll keep that in mind next time." She wanted to yell at him to get started but her eyes nearly popped out of her head when he removed his shirt and began unlacing his knee-high moccasins.

"What . . ." she had to clear her throat before she could speak when his hands reached for the lacings of his pants. "What do you think you're doing?"

Hawk pushed his pants down his long legs, revealing a breechcloth riding very low on his narrow hips. As he slowly followed her into the river, carrying the smelly pot of boiled roots and weeds, her eyes widened alarmingly.

"What do you think you're doing?" she hissed again.

"I'm not about to ruin a good set of clothes by getting this mess on them." He indicated the pot in his hands.

"You aren't going to wash me!"

His eyes sparkled and strong white teeth flashed as a smile lit Hawk's sculptured face. "Only your hair, Mrs. Royse," he reassured her. "The rest I'll leave to you."

Still unsure of his intentions, Molly nonetheless followed his instructions. She bent and wet her long hair then choked as he worked in the smelly concoction.

Molly was amazed by his gentleness; a characteristic that seemed out of place with his appearance. His thick, sleek hair hung to his shoulders and his copper skin glistened. The modified breechcloth reached only to the tops of his thighs and hung low on his hips. A civilized savage, she thought to herself, the gentleness as much a part of him as the savagery hidden just beneath the surface.

Adam leaned against a tree watching as Hawk carefully washed Molly's hair. He noticed that she held the quilt firmly beneath her chin and that neither of them spoke. Even from his place on the bank he could smell the combined odors of skunk and the potion Hawk was rubbing into Molly's hair. With a grin, Adam decided that Hawk had gone far beyond the call of friendship.

"Having fun?"

Molly raised her head and found Adam on the river bank. She buried her face in the quilt, embarrassed and disappointed that he had returned to find her in such a situation.

"Your wife met the business end of a skunk," Hawk supplied unnecessarily. He pushed her head into the water and rinsed her hair several times before he was satisfied that he'd removed the herbal mixture.

Adam couldn't stifle the laugh he felt building in his chest. "I seem to remember her talking about skunks just the other night."

Molly raised her head. "This is not funny."

"You seemed to think skunks had some merit."

Hawk watched as a silent exchange seemed to pass between husband and wife. He was further mystified when Molly grinned.

"So this is my fault?" she asked cheekily.

"My mama always said to be careful what you wish for, because you might get it."

"This isn't exactly the way I'd planned!"

Shaking his head at their baffling conversation, Hawk slowly left the water. "She's all yours."

"Yes, she is," Adam agreed, love filling his heart for the woman who stood in the cold water, greatly resembling a drowned rat.

Hawk handed the pot to Adam as he climbed out of the river. "Wash, repeatedly, until she can't take the cold water any longer. This won't get rid of the smell entirely, but at least we'll be able to live with her until it's gone." He grabbed his clothes and walked up the trail.

"Thank you, Mr. Hawk," Molly called from the water.

"You are most welcome, Mrs. Royse," Hawk replied with a little bow conspicuously incongruous with his forbidding attire.

Later that evening, Molly snuggled against Adam, her head resting on his shoulder. The odor of skunk, no longer so overpoweringly obnoxious, drifted past her nose.

"I can sleep somewhere else," she volunteered, resigned to many long, lonely nights alone.

"Ah, Molly mine, would you really force me to sleep alone?"

"But Adam, I stink!"

He grinned and hugged her tighter, "I can't argue with that, but sweetheart, I've gotten into the habit of sleeping with you. I don't think I can sleep alone."

"Are you sure? You're not just saying that to make me happy?"

"Molly," his voice lost all signs of humor, "I plan to spend the rest of my life making you happy. I intend to surround you with love until you've forgotten a past life that didn't include me." He raised her head and kissed her gently.

"I love you, Adam," she whispered. "Don't ever leave me."

"I couldn't if I wanted to. You're part of me now."

"Promise? Promise you'll always love me and never leave me?"

"I promise, Molly mine, with all my heart."

Chapter Six

Molly rode Adam's horse beside the wagon, careful to keep a distance between her and the men. Even though the smell had dissipated considerably with the help of Hawk's concoction, she was still conscious of the lingering odor and she continued to be embarrassed. Earlier that morning she had insisted on taking another bath with the remaining herbal mixture. While the men waited patiently, Molly clenched her teeth against the early morning chill of the water as she washed her hair and body again.

Promising to return for a visit, they took their leave from the Price family and headed several miles north to the land Adam had purchased the day before. Molly's excitement was slightly diminished by the encounter with the skunk but she held her head high and waited to see where her new home was to be.

By midafternoon they pulled the lumbering wagon to a halt, and Adam helped Molly dismount from the horse. Taking her hand in his, they walked to a natural clearing.

"This is ours, Molly mine!" he said with a wide grin.

Molly looked around her with new awareness. It was truly a beautiful spot. Huge trees climbed into the sky and wild flowers waved their colorful heads in the breeze. Knee-high grass, so green it vied with the cobalt sky for supremacy, undulated with the wind like gentle waves rolling toward shore. Hidden by the forest of trees, a stream babbled to reveal its presence, and in the distance, as always, the blue mountains held majestic reign.

"Where do you want your house, wife?" Adam asked. "Over there . . . or there . . . or how about there?" He pointed in several directions, all of which looked perfect to Molly. "There's also at least three springs with water so cold it hurts your teeth. We'll build a springhouse over one for you to store things that keep better in the cool."

"Oh, Adam, it's perfect!" Molly wrapped her arms around his neck and hugged him. He picked her up and swung her around and around in a circle until they were both dizzy. When he set her on her feet she pulled free of his hold and stepped back several paces. Looking at each other, they began to laugh with the abandon of small children, delighted by their homesite, their enthusiasm for life and their love for each other.

"The cabin and springhouse will have to wait for a while yet," Hawk interrupted. "We'll start breaking up the ground for the garden tomorrow. Today we'll set up a temporary bush corral for the livestock."

The three people looked at each other, all of them understanding the amount of work that would need to be completed before winter.

"Well, just don't stand there," Molly quipped, hands on hips. "Let's get to it!"

The temporary corral took all afternoon for them to build. Hawk selected a spot with two sides already filled with dense underbrush while Adam began cutting down massive amounts of brush. Molly's job was to ferry the cut bushes to Hawk. He then wove them into a secure structure. He explained to her that the animals would eat the leaves from the branches, but if they were placed correctly the corral would hinder the animals from wandering off. He was emphatic that a permanent corral would be the first thing to be built once the garden was in place.

"You have to protect and care for your animals," he said. "Out here they aren't easily replaced and they could mean the difference between life and death."

At dinner that evening, Hawk carefully laid out the schedule of which things should be done first and which could wait. Neither Molly or Adam disagreed with him, after all, this was the reason they needed him. However, when the cabin came at the bottom of the list, Molly couldn't help questioning it.

"Is there a dead tree around here?" she asked innocently.

"There's a lot of dead trees, Molly mine. Why?"

"I just wondered if there was one big enough for us to live in. With all the work that needs to be done it sounds like it'll be next summer before we get to the cabin."

"You'll have your cabin before winter," Hawk promised quietly. "It won't be fancy but it'll keep the snow off you."

"That's all I need!" Molly replied cheerfully. "Now, if you'll be so kind as to fix some more of that God-awful-smelling stuff, I'll go take a bath."

They worked from sunup to sundown every day, quitting only when darkness made it dangerous for them to continue. A natural clearing on a level portion of the hill seemed the perfect spot to locate the garden. Adam walked behind one of the oxen pulling the plow while Hawk hitched up the other one to remove larger rocks and the stumps of a few trees they had cut down.

Molly's job was to remove the numerous small rocks from the plowed-up dirt and stack them neatly for later use. The first couple of days were filled with pain and physical exhaustion. She was unaware that her strength was slowly increasing. But then one evening she found that she was tired but not extremely so. A feeling of pride and accomplishment filled her at the knowledge that she could be a help rather than a hindrance to Adam.

Even the evenings were far from idle. Hawk's lessons began again. He had Adam chop down a few hickory saplings and make handles for the shovel and ax heads they had brought from Charleston. Molly's job was to clear the smaller branches from small chestnut trees that Hawk intended to use as fence rails for the corral.

Hawk began to make some of the tools that would

be necessary when actual building began. He carefully shaped handles for hammers, hatchets and adzes, axlike tools with a curved blade, used for shaping and smoothing a plank.

The number of tools Hawk created amazed Molly. She had thought that only an ax would be necessary to build their cabin. Patiently, as they all worked on their assigned chores, Hawk explained what each tool was and how it worked. Most of the iron tool heads had been purchased in Charleston without handles to help lighten the load in the wagon.

"How do you know so much about tools?" Molly asked as she laid aside one small fence log and reached for another. "I don't remember anyone ever mentioning that Indians did a lot of wood-working."

"Actually, Mrs. Royse," Hawk replied quietly, "before they moved further west to escape the destruction of whites, my people built permanent settlements with log homes and big gardens." He was quiet for several long minutes as he thought of the stories told to him by Linsey and Luc of the place where he had been born but which he had never seen. "Now my people are more nomadic and their homes aren't built for permanence as they once were.

"However, you are correct, I didn't learn wood-working from them. My stepfather is proficient with woodworker's tools. Some of the pieces of furniture he has built are true works of art. He put those tools in my hands when I was a small child and taught me how to use them."

For the first time in their acquaintance, Molly thought of the difficulties Hawk had faced as a child. "It must have been confusing for you, being raised by white step-parents and Indian parents."

"Not until I ventured into the city," Hawk answered. "I thought it was quite natural to have two sets of parents who lived such disparate lives.

"I would spend months living with Linsey and Luc, sleeping in a feather bed, learning to read and write and how to live as a white man. Then my father would come for me and I'd return to his village and spend months sleeping under the stars, learning to hunt and track, hearing the stories told by the old ones of a way of life that would never be again.

"Don't feel sorry for me, Mrs. Royse," his voice softened as he correctly interpreted the sympathy in her voice. "I had the best of both worlds. Every child should be raised in such a manner, for surely his life would be richer for knowing how others live."

Molly realized she had learned more about Hawk in the last few minutes than she had known in all the months before. His love and pride for both of his families was clearly evident in his voice and she was almost envious that her childhood had not been the same.

Once the garden was plowed, the men began the process of building the corral while Molly planted. Corn, squash, peas and several different kinds of beans were sown in neat parallel rows. When the last seeds were in the ground, Molly sighed with satisfaction. With the grace of God and a little rain, they'd have plenty of food to see them through the winter.

The garden and the corral were both finished the same day, but Hawk, instead of allowing them to rest, insisted they start the next project, and then the next, working methodically until finally the day arrived when they began felling trees for the cabin.

As the two men chopped down one tree after another it became Molly's job to clean it of its branches. She quickly grew adept with the small hand ax and even managed the larger one when necessary.

Once the log was cleaned of its branches they cut it to the correct length, which Hawk told them was called "bucking the log." Next, to protect the log from insect infestation and rot, Hawk made a slit down one side of the log and, using a stick he had sharpened to a blunt chisel point, he stripped the bark from the log. Most of it came off in one piece and was carefully laid aside to be used later as roofing material.

Whenever possible they used the strength of the oxen to pull the logs to the location of the cabin. However, the thickly wooded area sometimes made that impractical. Molly marvelled at the raw strength of the two men as they attached cant hooks to opposite ends of the huge logs and carried them into a clearing where the ox would finish hauling them out.

Slowly, day after day, log by log, the pile grew. It was visible proof of their labors but Molly grew impatient for the actual construction to begin.

"Breakfast!" Molly yelled to the two men who were immersed in conversation at the site they had selected for the cabin. Even so early in the morning the day promised to be a hot one, she thought as she wiped at the perspiration dotting her brow.

"Today's the day, Molly mine,' Adam said with a grin as he took the plate from her hands and kissed the end of her upturned nose.

"The day for what?" She handed Hawk a plate filled with food and turned to fix one for herself.

"The day we begin your new home!"

Molly's eyes grew wide with excitement as she looked from one man to the other. After all the days of backbreaking work, of hands sticky with sap and splinters deeply embedded in tender flesh, after long days of promise that the effort would bear results, she couldn't believe that it was at long last time to begin the cabin.

"Really? Are you sure? When do we begin? What can I do?" Excitement rippled through her voice and she nearly danced with the impatience to begin.

"You can sit down and eat your breakfast," Adam said sternly, his twinkling eyes belying the forbidding scowl.

"I can eat breakfast anytime," she replied with a wide smile. "Let's start building our house."

"Eat, Molly, or two hours from now you'll faint due to hunger." He took his own advice and began eating. "The cabin will take weeks to complete so there's no reason to hurry."

While Molly rushed to clean up the breakfast dishes, Adam and Hawk began laying out the actual position of the cabin. They decided that the windowless back of the structure would face north to provide some protection from winter winds. Even though hostile Indians were no longer considered a problem in the area, Hawk suggested that they build in the open rather than under a strand of trees. It would provide Adam with an unhampered view of the ground surrounding his home and anyone bent on mischief would be unable to sneak up on them.

"What can I do?" Molly asked with excitement as she walked up to the site.

"Stay out of the way," Hawk replied firmly.

Molly placed her hands on her hips and had to force herself not to stamp her foot in vexation. After weeks of waiting to begin construction, she wanted to do something, anything!

"I don't want to stay out of the way, I want to help!"

"Molly mine," Adam said quietly, "staying out of our way will help."

"That's no help."

Hawk looked at her and knew she would continue to plague them unless he set her to a chore. His eyes searched the area looking for something for her to do that would keep her busy and out of their way. He spied the immense pile of bark and knew he'd found the answer.

"You can begin cutting the roofing shingles," he said as he walked toward the pile of bark. She nearly danced with excitement as she walked beside him, and Hawk had to hide a grin. She acted like a small child who'd been given a special treat.

"Cut each piece about fifteen inches long." He took a heavy knife and cut through the tough bark.

"Then lay it as flat as you can. When you have a good-sized stack of cut pieces, find something heavy to lay on them so that they'll dry flat."

He handed her the knife and waited for her to begin. "Any questions?" he asked, surprised by her noticeable hesitation. She had never refused or complained about any chore he had given her, in fact his respect and admiration for her had grown because of her willingness to attempt anything.

"Just one . . . how long is fifteen inches?"

He should have known she wasn't refusing to work, he thought with a chuckle as he looked around for a stick. He broke it to the proper length and handed it to her to use as a guide. He waited until she had completed one shingle and he nodded approval. With the pile of bark nearly as high and wide as he was tall, Hawk knew Molly would be busy for days!

The bark-shingle roofing would only be temporary, needing to be replaced within a year or two, but Hawk wanted the cabin itself to stand for as long as Adam and Molly needed it. He knew that they could build a cabin in only a few days but because of that desire for permanence he chose building methods that would take longer but would hold up to the passage of time.

Adam looked up from his task and watched as Molly struggled to master her new chore. The long sleeves of her linen dress were neatly rolled up past her elbows, and several buttons on the high-necked garment were loose to catch the slightest breeze. She had braided her golden hair and swirled the resulting rope around her head.

The sun had turned her skin to the color of rich, sweet honey, bringing out a wealth of freckles on her nose and cheeks. As he watched he saw her tongue peek out from between her lips as she concentrated on mastering her new task.

Adam's gaze traveled to Hawk and he saw on that stoic countenance an expression that disappeared as quickly as it came. Adam knew he would have missed it had he not been watching at that precise moment.

The expression that Adam had glimpsed so briefly had brought a gentleness to Hawk's face that Adam had never witnessed before. He wondered if Hawk even realized that he was in love with Molly.

He felt a fleeting sadness for his friend, followed immediately by immense pride in his wife. Sadness that Hawk would never know the reality of being loved by Molly and pride that she had given all of her love to Adam.

Adam felt no distress at the knowledge. He knew beyond any doubt that his wife loved him with such intensity that she was incapable of seeing any other man.

Hawk walked back to the cabin site, shaking his head with amusement. The job was going to take her days to complete, and he had no doubt that each shingle would be cut to the same size and then neatly stacked in bundles. Right now she had to concentrate fiercely on each piece she cut, but he knew it was only a matter of time before she mastered the chore.

"She's something, isn't she?" Adam said, his arms folded across the top of the handle of a shovel.

"She's something, but what?" Hawk asked with a chuckle. "I've never seen a woman quite like her."

"Hawk," Adam's voice grew serious as he looked at his long-time friend, "this seems like a good time to ask a favor."

"Ask."

Adam hesitated briefly, "If something happens to me will you see to it that Molly gets back to Charleston? Or if she doesn't want to go there, then wherever she wants to go?"

"You have a premonition of disaster?"

"Nothing like that," Adam replied with a grin. "I intend to hang around loving her until I'm an old, old man. But I want to know that if something does happen to me she'll be safe."

"As you are my brother, so shall she be my sister," Hawk stated quietly. "I'll see to her."

With a nod of mutual understanding they turned and began leveling the ground where the cabin would stand.

By the end of the day Molly had several small stacks of shingles, and the cabin's foundation—sills and the first two rows of logs—had been set in place. Molly marvelled at the fit of the V-shaped notches on the logs. Hawk explained that the shape took a little longer to cut but it would help prevent water from pooling in the logs and causing rot.

Standing inside the structure, Molly realized for the first time exactly how small her new home was to be. Measuring twenty feet by twenty feet, the square, one-room cabin would be smaller than the formal sitting room in her father's mansion back in Charleston.

But it would be filled with love, she vowed to herself, as the lovely, lifeless mansion had never been. It would be a home, never a showplace, and people would feel welcomed for themselves not for their position in society.

Slowly, the cabin took shape and the piles of shingles grew, until the day came when all of the bark was cut and the last log was ready to be pulled into place.

As the men prepared the final log for hoisting into place, Molly walked through the doorway cut in the logs. She could have looked out the sole window set near the doorway but it was unnecessary since the logs had yet to be chinked with mud, leaving her a variety of places to peek out from.

"Come outside, Molly," Adam chuckled as she peeked enticingly through the logs. "We're about to raise the last log."

"Can I watch from in here?"

"Nope, too dangerous. We could lose control of the log and it could land right on top of your little head."

She walked out of the cabin and moved around to the side to watch. There was still a lot of work to be done—chinking between the logs, a fireplace, the roof—but this last log marked the end of the first stage of construction.

A huge log had been split and its sides smoothed to be used as a slide. Hawk and Adam each attached a rope to one end of a log, climbed to opposite sides of the cabin and then hoisted the log up the slide. It was hard, dangerous work and Molly would be glad when it was finished.

The slides were placed so that the slope was as gradual as possible but the men both had to use every ounce of strength they possessed to pull the massive logs up the incline.

"This is it, Molly!" Adam called from his side of the cabin. He sat with his legs wrapped around the top log, a position that helped stabilize him and prevent him from falling.

"Get to it!" Molly called cheerfully. "I've got a big celebration supper just about cooked!"

In deference to the summer heat, both men worked without shirts. Molly watched in appreciation of their effort to raise the log as muscles bunched and strained. Streams of sweat rippled down bodies that surged and swelled with exertion. Arms and shoulders tensed and stretched as they struggled with the weight of the log.

Molly's eyes were glued to Adam as she admired his slick, gleaming body. She felt a tightening of her body as she remembered his capable hands caressing her. Her nipples budded at the memory of his lips tugging and pulling against her breast. Wrapping her arms around her waist, Molly tried to control a surge of desire that flooded through her.

As a team, the two men pulled on the rope that slowly guided the log into place. She admired what seemed to be perfect coordination between them.

Molly's breath caught in her throat when it appeared for a moment that Adam was losing his balance. She began to breathe easier when he righted himself but just as she released a sigh of relief he again started to fall.

Unsuccessfully clawing and digging for purchase on the smooth-sided log, Adam plunged to the ground, landing with bone-jarring impact. Dazed and incapable of moving, he waited for the breath to return to his lungs. Only when he opened his eyes did he become aware of his dangerous situation. By then, it was too late.

Far too late.

Molly watched with horror as the huge log teetered briefly. She was unaware of Hawk's towering struggle to halt its downward slide. But the strength and willpower of one man was not enough against the weight of the log as the rope tore through his grasping hands. She started running toward Adam even as the log plummeted onto his battered body.

"Adam? Please, dear God, let him be all right," she whispered as she knelt at his side. She pushed his hair back from his eyes, noting a darkening bruise on his forehead. She was unaware of Hawk lifting the log from Adam's chest, his fear for his friend giving him the strength to fling it away with effortless ease.

"Adam? Please, Adam?" she whispered, afraid beyond hope. She looked up as Hawk reached her, his chest heaving from his efforts.

Hawk stared with growing dread at Adam. The huge log had landed in the center of Adam's chest, destroying bone and muscle, crushing delicate tissue and leaving his chest cavity concave from its weight.

Hawk's gaze traveled slowly to Adam's face, seeing the faint signs of life that he knew would soon flutter out like the delicate flame of a candle in the winds of a summer storm.

"Adam? Sweet, sweet Adam?" Molly whispered as she sat on the ground and cradled his head in her lap. A spark of hope trembled in her chest as she watched his eyes flicker, then open.

"Molly mine . . ." He coughed at the effort it took for him to talk, and a small stream of blood ran from his mouth and trailed down his chin.

"Adam? Adam, I love you, don't leave me," Molly pleaded, her dry eyes reflecting a pain beyond tears.

His eyes moved lovingly over her features and as she watched, praying desperately to change the inevitable, a look of peace slowly removed the pain from his face.

"Molly . . . Hawk."

She watched as the life fled from his body. Even when the gurgling sound of his breathing had stopped, she refused to acknowledge the utter stillness that surrounded them.

"Adam, you promised," she whispered, tenderly stroking his face, using the hem of her dress to dab at the blood on his chin. "You promised you wouldn't leave me. You always keep your promises, you never lie."

Hawk raised his head to the sky and watched as a cloud briefly covered the sun. He felt an overwhelming need to curse the gods for this needless destruction.

Molly shivered as the Shawnee brave chanted the death song of his people. It felt so right, in this wilderness land, that Adam's death should be announced by the song of a once-mighty people.

Hawk finished his song and slowly lowered his head. He breathed deeply, struggling to control the rage he knew was fighting for freedom. His tortured gaze came to rest on Molly, still sitting on the ground with Adam's head in her lap.

"He chased my bonnet," she said quietly, gently stroking his hair from his forehead. "A storm was brewing . . . the wind was blowing as it can blow only in Charleston . . . it caught my bonnet and pulled it from my head . . . I dropped my basket . . . my skirt was threatening my modesty . . . Adam came from nowhere and chased my bonnet down the street . . . the dust was blowing and the fruit I had purchased seemed to stretch from one side of Meeting Street to the other . . . he handed me my poor battered hat and helped me gather up the fruit . . . said he'd be pleased to escort me home," her voice drifted away to a whisper.

"He laughed," she murmured softly. "When it started to rain he turned his face toward the sky and laughed . . . he said it was the most beautiful day of his life."

Her voice portrayed no hint of the suffering Hawk knew was to come. He wondered how long shock would protect her, and even as the thought formed he had his answer.

"Adam shouldn't have died," she said quietly. Slowly she raised her face to his and Hawk saw the ravages of grief blazing in her honey-colored eyes.

"He didn't deserve to die!" she whispered fiercely, as pain and anger vibrated through her body. "Adam was too kind, too gentle, too young to be lying dead on this hard ground."

Her eyes spit a bone-deep hatred at him as she slowly rocked the beloved body cradled in her arms. Her voice was so quiet he had to strain to hear her words, words that pierced with the agony of razor-sharp knives.

"It should have been you!"

Chapter Seven

Hawk watched Molly's rage disintegrate and her shoulders slump in defeat. He helped her to stand, then bent to lift his friend's battered body. He carried Adam to the wagon and gently lowered him onto a quilt Molly spread on the ground. He watched as she pulled the quilt around his shoulders, tucking him in as tenderly as a child. She smoothed back the hair on his forehead and bent to kiss his lips.

"We'll bury him in the morning," Hawk said quietly as she rose to her feet.

Molly nodded agreement, her eyes moving from spot to spot, looking for the right place for his grave. Her face was unnaturally calm.

"It has to be somewhere perfect," she muttered to herself. "Someplace where he can see the mountains and hear the stream."

"It'll be as perfect as I can find," Hawk replied quietly.

She nodded her head and wiped her hands on her

skirt. "I'll need some water to bathe him. And we'll need a . . ." she raised her head and fought the painful word, "we'll need a coffin."

"It'll be done." As Hawk turned away, Molly noticed the blood dripping from his fingers.

"You're hurt." She reached for his hand only to have him snatch it back. "Let me see your hands."

"It's nothing, just a scratch." He hated the unemotional tone of her voice but dreaded the time when she would begin to feel. The short outburst of anger was only a minute showing of the pain to come.

And he knew it would come. All of the steps must be taken before she could begin to heal. The numbness could shatter abruptly, without cause, or it could slowly crumble like a rock turning to sand by the pounding of water. The rage, the tears, the denial, the sorrow for dreams that would never be, the regret for tomorrows that must be faced alone, each step painfully taken before she could find her way back.

She was strong, he knew she would survive. But would she ever be the woman she had been? Or would this change her in some way as yet unknown?

Unaware and unconcerned by his thoughts, Molly grabbed his hand and held it firmly. She looked at the deep, bloody trails across his palm. A quick glance at his other hand confirmed that it was in equally appalling condition.

"Good Lord above," she whispered, "what have you done?"

"The rope," he replied, trying to pull from her grasp.

116

"What rope?"

"Rope burns, from holding it too tightly."

As she looked at the cuts, Molly realized the extent of his effort to save Adam. She stared at his abused flesh and an unwanted thought drifted through her mind . . . it shouldn't have been Adam who died.

"What?" Hawk asked, hearing her mumble too softly for him to understand the words.

"He shouldn't have died," she replied. She felt anger begin to grow, replacing the numbness that had protected her. "He shouldn't have died!"

Hawk searched for words to console her, but found none. He agreed with her that it shouldn't have happened, but it had, and nothing could change it.

Molly dropped his hands as if they suddenly burned her flesh. She took several steps away from him, her eyes widening with rage.

"It should have been you!" she said softly. "You're the one who should have died, not Adam. Adam was kind and gentle and loving. You're a savage who doesn't deserve to live." Her voice grew stronger until she was nearly screaming. "You should have died! You! Not Adam! You!"

She barely noticed as he straightened his shoulders and proudly lifted his head. The stoic expression, once so familiar to her but now rarely seen, returned to his face.

"I hate you," she snarled through clenched teeth. "I hate every breath you take. You should be the one stretched out on that ground, slowly turning cold!"

Again, as quickly as it had come, the rage left. Her

shoulders slumped and she pressed her hand to her eyes. Slowly, with footsteps older than time, she walked to the bucket of water. Lifting it, Molly set it on the table near Hawk and motioned for him.

When he stood beside her, Molly gently bathed his injured hands. She rubbed a salve into the cuts and abrasions then carefully wrapped them in clean cloths.

"They're going to be pretty sore for a few days," she said quietly.

"I've suffered worse." Pulling away from her, Hawk walked to the wagon. He gathered together various pieces of planking, some that had been boxes for storage, others that had been the bed of the wagon, and carried them away from camp.

Molly could hear him hammering as she walked back from the river, carrying a bucket of water in each hand. There was one final chore she could do for Adam. But it wouldn't be a chore, it would be a final act of love. To prepare his battered body for burial.

By the time Molly had washed Adam and dressed him in his best suit of clothes, Hawk returned with the coffin. Molly lined it with her best quilt, and from her favorite silk gown she made a pillow for Adam's head.

Throughout the long, lonely night, Molly sat beside Adam, occasionally reaching out to touch his face or smooth his hair, knowing that all too soon even that small thing would be denied her. Hawk sat beside the fire, now and then sipping from a cup of coffee, his dark eyes rarely leaving Molly's face.

She never slumped, holding her shoulders up, her

eyes glued to Adam's face. She didn't speak. In fact, since his return with the coffin they had exchanged no words. It was almost as if she were unaware of his presence, wrapped so deeply in her grief that nothing else could enter.

And she didn't cry. Hawk worried that she would bury herself in grief so deeply that she wouldn't be able to return to the world. He had seen it happen before at the Shawnee camp. A warrior's woman would grieve so deeply at the death of her husband that she seemed to will herself to join him in death.

At last the morning sun lighted the sky. Hawk picked up a shovel and walked up the hill, past the cabin that glistened with the light of a new day, beyond the garden with its neat rows of green leaves pushing through the ground. He walked to the very crest of the hill and with the mountains as his witness, Hawk dug the lonely grave for his friend.

"Shall I ride out to find a preacher?" he asked when he returned to camp. He noticed that she had taken the time to dress in the gown he remembered her wearing at her wedding. Her hair was neatly combed and a small hat with a tiny veil rested on her head.

"No," Molly replied without hesitation. "We don't know the people around here and I couldn't bear to listen to them mouthing false platitudes as people seem to do at a funeral.

"We'll bury him ourselves. His wife and his best friend, seeing him to his final resting place."

One last time, Molly ran her fingers through Adam's hair and gently kissed his cold lips. She stood back and watched as Hawk fitted the lid in place and nailed it firmly down.

Without help, he hefted the heavy box onto his shoulder, carefully balanced it and then began the walk up the hill. Molly didn't concern herself with the formidable display of strength he revealed, carrying the coffin by himself. To her it was the thing for him to do.

Molly watched as Hawk slowly lowered the wooden box into the rich ground. She ignored the signs of life around her, concentrating instead on each shovelful of dirt hitting the lid, forever separating her from the man she loved. Her world had come to an abrupt halt and yet birds chirped in the trees, unaware of the human tragedy beneath them. The wind blew sweetly against a face dry of tears and the soothing gurgle of the water went unheard by ears straining to hear a beloved voice.

When the hole was filled and the prayers had been recited, Hawk turned away to give Molly time alone. She knelt and placed a handful of wild flowers on the new earth. Words of farewell drifted through her thoughts but none left her lips. It was too final to say those words aloud.

She slowly rose and backed away from the grave. "I'll be back," she whispered softly. "I won't leave you alone. I'll come to visit and tell you of the things that go on."

Turning slowly, Molly moved toward Hawk and walked silently beside him back to camp.

"I'll have a noon meal prepared shortly," she said quietly, breaking the silence.

"We need to talk, Molly."

She nodded, unaware that he had called her by her

120

name for the first time. "We'll eat first."

In a surprisingly short time they had changed into everyday clothes and were eating the meal she had prepared . . . or rather Hawk ate and Molly pushed the food around on her plate.

"You need to make some decisions," he said quietly when he realized she wasn't making any effort to eat.

"Decisions?"

"Not today or even tomorrow," he reassured her, even though she had shown no evidence of alarm or concern. "You need to be thinking about what you want to do."

"I have no intention of changing any of the plans Adam made."

"If you want to return to Charleston I'll take you."

"No! I will stay here."

"Molly, I'll be heading north before winter sets in and you can't stay here alone," Hawk replied, trying to hide his exasperation at the thought.

"I will not return to the life my father had planned for me. I escaped him once, he wouldn't let it happen again nor would he ever let me forget that I chose to defy him." She stood and carried her still-full plate to the slop bucket. She scraped it clean, grabbed Hawk's plate from him and scraped it.

"I wasn't finished," he said quietly.

"Now you are!" She dropped both plates into the bucket of wash water and began scrubbing them. "And I don't want to hear another word about me going back to Charleston. I will not leave my home."

Molly found ways to keep herself busy for the remainder of the afternoon. She was aware that

Hawk was using the ox to pull the final log into place but she kept her back turned until the activity was finished. She wanted to ask why the ox hadn't been used before. Why he had chosen the more dangerous method that had cost Adam his life, instead of employing the strength of the ox. But she felt the brittle rage begin to grow and she knew it would consume her if she began to question him.

She didn't fear the rage but it led to other emotions, ones she wanted, needed, to control. Now she walked around in an indifferent haze but freeing the anger would also free the pain and the torment, and Molly doubted she could survive the agony.

Far too soon, the lowering sun turned the sky into a tapestry of colors, apricot and mauve swirled over aqua while cobalt blue faded into the gray of night. Oblivious to the beauty of the sunset, Molly wrapped her arms around her body and tried to control a shiver racing up her spine. Wishes and prayers were futile as she fought to hold back the night. The first of many nights that she would be forced to sleep alone, without the comfort and security of Adam's arms.

She prepared Hawk's evening meal but refused even to pretend to eat. As he sat on a stump, Molly slowly walked toward the setting sun and the lonely grave on the hillside. The wild flowers had been scattered by the wind and already the summer sun had started to dry the dirt so that small cracks were appearing on the surface.

Long after dark, Molly returned to camp. She noticed that Hawk had moved his bedding nearer but it didn't help to ease the loneliness as she settled into the bed she had shared so willingly with Adam.

With the star-studded sky as witness, Molly groaned as memories tormented her and pain filled her heart. Slowly one tear, quickly followed by another and more, fell from her brimming eyes and her muffled sobs floated through the darkness.

Hawk listened to the sound of her heart breaking and felt her torment pierce through him with the sharpness of an arrow. He had thought he could leave her alone in her grief but her anguish and pain were threatening to destroy his own heart. When he could no longer force himself to remain away, Hawk rose and walked over to her.

Hawk knelt beside her, his big hand gentle as he smoothed the hair from her face. Cheeks glistening with tears, Molly went willingly into his arms. He sat down, gathered her onto his lap and slowly rocked her back and forth. She clutched a fistful of his shirt, and buried her face in his shoulder as her tears dampened the fabric. Each silvery drop tore at his heart even as he acknowledged that they were a necessary part of healing and that many more would flow before the process was complete.

Words would have been an unnecessary violation of the moment, as she sought comfort and he offered solace. Finally her tears slowed and her body-racking sobs eased. He felt her relax as sleep offered its own form of escape.

Hawk gently lowered her down onto her bed and covered her with the quilt. When he was sure she wouldn't awaken, he stood and moved back to his own bed. It was a long night, with only the wind and his memories for company.

*　　*　　*

Adam smiled softly, his eyes sparkling with love. The rising mist swirled and twirled in a mystical undulating dance, threatening to hide him from her view, and Molly began to run to catch him before he disappeared. He turned and slowly walked away from her until the terror in her voice seemed to reach out to him and stop him in his tracks.

"Wait for me, Adam!" she pleaded, but each step she took seemed to move her farther away from him instead of toward him. Finally, realizing the futility of movement, Molly stopped and watched as he turned toward her again.

"Please, Adam, please?"

"Ah . . . Molly mine," his voice whispered through the mist. "How much I love you, girl!"

"Don't leave me, Adam."

The gentleness of his smile nearly broke her heart. He reached out and she felt his tender touch against her cheek, bringing with it a tranquility that caressed her soul. When he lifted his hand the feeling was gone and once more she was surrounded by panic, knowing he was leaving without her.

"I love you, Adam," she pleaded tearfully. "Don't leave me."

"Molly mine . . ."

"Wake up, Mrs. Royse!"

Molly fought the all-too-human voice calling to her. She knew that if she answered it, she would forever lose the misty covered place where Adam now dwelled.

"Come on, Mrs. Royse. You can't sleep forever."

"No . . . leave me alone," she pleaded. Too late, the dream was gone.

"Time to get up, breakfast is ready."

"I want to sleep." She rolled onto her side, her back toward him.

"You've slept for two days," he replied, pulling the quilt from her and ignoring her startled protest. "Out of bed, Mrs. Royse."

"No!" Molly grabbed for the quilt as he threw it beyond her reach.

"You have a choice," he said as he stood, his black gaze unreadable. "You can get up and dress yourself or I'll do it for you."

"Go to hell!"

"After you're up and dressed. I'll enjoy your company on the trip." Hawk turned and walked away but he listened for any movement that would indicate that she was complying with his demands.

"You've got till the count of three, Mrs. Royse," Hawk stated quietly as he knelt by the fire and poured a cup of coffee, "then I'm coming back."

"Go to hell!"

"You're repeating yourself. Remind me to teach you how to cuss, that part of your education has been sadly neglected," Hawk replied.

"One . . ."

Molly sat up, threw a defiant look in his direction, grabbed the quilt and lay back down. She pulled the blanket up to her chin and closed her eyes. She would return to that dream! He couldn't stop her. She wouldn't give in to his demands!

"Two . . ."

His deep rich voice vibrated through her, promising that his threat wasn't a bluff. The smell of the freshly brewed coffee didn't help, either. It drifted invitingly past her nose, and her stomach growled in reminder that she hadn't eaten in several days.

Hawk set his cup on a convenient rock, stood and slowly approached Molly. Her eyes were tightly closed, her hands knotted into protective fists on the edge of the quilt.

"Three."

At the sound of his voice directly overhead, Molly's eyes flew open, her startled gaze connecting with his determined one. She had concentrated so hard on returning to the dream that she had been unaware of his approach.

"Up, Mrs. Royse!" Hawk grabbed the quilt and easily jerked it from her grasp. With the same sure movement, he grabbed her hands and pulled her to her feet.

"Go to—"

"You might try saying 'you bastard!'—it would be much more effective than continuously repeating the same tired phrase."

"You . . . you . . ."

"Bastard?"

"Bastard!" Molly hissed.

"Very good," Hawk nodded. "Now that you're awake and out of bed you can get dressed. Or do you need my help?"

Molly's eyes spit defiance as she stood toe-to-toe with her antagonist, his black gaze never wavering from hers. She stubbornly held her ground until he reached for the buttons on her nightdress.

"I can dress myself!" she snarled through clenched teeth.

"Be quick, breakfast is ready." Hawk turned and walked back toward the fire while Molly cursed him, his family, past and future generations and the very ground he walked on . . . as she quickly dressed herself.

When she finally stumbled to the fire, Hawk forced a plate into her hands. A snake curled to strike could not have brought a more repulsed look to her face.

"I'm not hungry."

"Yes you are."

"You're telling me that I'm hungry?" she asked with astonishment.

"You haven't eaten in three days. You're hungry."

"And I suppose you're going to force me to eat?"

"You learn quickly." Hawk sat down and began eating his own breakfast, his gaze never leaving her.

"I hate you," she said quietly.

"Good, hate is a healthy, honest emotion. Now eat."

After the first couple of bites Molly discovered to her surprise that she was starving. She tried to eat slowly, to foster the impression that she was simply yielding to his demand, but when she cleaned her plate and requested another helping she gave the lie to that notion.

"Did you ever play in the mud when you were a child, Mrs. Royse?" Hawk asked, satisfied when she cleaned the plate a second time.

"No, Mr. Hawk, my father would have been appalled."

"Well, then, today will be a first for you."

"I beg your pardon?" Molly lifted her nose slightly. "Why would I wish to play in the mud?"

Hawk nodded with satisfaction at her expression of disdain. She'd make it, he decided. Her sorrow was far from soothed but her spirit had not deserted her.

"After you wash the dishes come down to the creek. I'll have the mud ready when you get there."

In spite of herself, Molly was curious. She lingered over the dishes, trying to find ways to occupy herself other than joining Hawk at the river. Finally, knowing he would respect her grief, she slowly climbed the hill and stood beside Adam's grave.

Hawk watched Molly as she sat down beside the grave. He waited for her to leave and come to him, knowing it might be necessary to force her to do so and dreading the idea. When he knew he could wait no longer, she surprised him by rising and walking toward the creek.

"You are about to learn the fine art of playing in the mud, Mrs. Royse," Hawk said as he finished filling a bucket with the dark red mud that lined the riverbank. "Fill that bucket with water and follow me," he instructed as he grabbed two buckets and walked away.

Molly filled the bucket as instructed and started to follow, but her steps slowed when she realized he was heading for the cabin. Hawk emptied the mud into a trench he had dug earlier, added some gravel and grass, then turned to reach for the water. His eyes narrowed when he saw the look of dread that covered her face.

"I need the water, Mrs. Royse," he said.

"I . . . I can't."

"Can't what?"

"The cabin . . ."

Hawk stood with his hands on his hips, his dark gaze enigmatic. "Have you decided to return to Charleston?"

"No!" she hissed through clenched teeth. "I won't go back to Charleston!"

"Then you need somewhere to live, we have to finish the cabin."

"Can't we build another one somewhere else?" she asked hesitantly.

"Bring the water, Mrs. Royse."

Molly moved slowly toward him, her eyes glued to the cabin. "You can't bend an inch, can you?"

He took the bucket from her hands and poured most of the water onto the mud in the trench. With a heavy branch, Hawk slowly began to stir the mixture of mud, small stones and grass.

"Building a new cabin wouldn't involve bending, Mrs. Royse," he said quietly as he worked. "It would mean starting over, doing work that has already been done once. Why waste everything we've already accomplished?"

"This cabin will always remind me of . . . Adam."

"There will be a lot of things that remind you of him. I could tell you that someday your memories will be sweet but that would be a waste of breath because you'd never believe me," Hawk replied as he handed her the limb. "Stir, Mrs. Royse."

Sweat soon beaded Molly's brow as she fought the weight of the heavy mixture. When Hawk decided it was mixed enough he filled two of the buckets then covered the trench with a piece of canvas to prevent it from drying out.

"This mud will be the chinking between the logs." He took a handful of the mixture and packed it firmly between two logs. He worked quickly, tightly stuffing the mud into the holes, smoothing as he worked.

"I've already finished the upper logs." Hawk turned and pointed to the bucket. "Get busy, Mrs. Royse, you've got a lot of work to do."

Molly looked at the rows of logs forming the walls and knew his comment was a vast understatement. It would take weeks for her to finish her assigned task. She opened her mouth to object, but a look in his eyes had her biting back her words. He was waiting for her to protest, to refuse to work. Without a doubt, Molly knew he would use it as the reason to return her to Charleston.

She bent, grabbed a handful of mud and began chinking the logs. Somehow Hawk had made it appear easy. His rows were neatly smoothed, one continuous progression, while it quickly became evident that hers was not.

"You're not using enough mud." Hawk demonstrated the procedure again. "Pack it in tightly. It'll shrink as it dries and if it's not tight enough you'll discover all kinds of holes this winter when the wind comes in."

Molly worked diligently throughout the day,

stopping only to mix more mud. She was aware of Hawk's presence but she ignored him except when he spoke directly to her. The physical labor was exhausting but it left her mind free and she fought to control the unwanted memories that flooded her. More than once she had to wipe away uncontrollable tears as memories of Adam threatened to destroy her brittle composure. Even her increasing hate for Hawk was no deterrent to the ever-threatening heartache.

"Go get cleaned up," Hawk said. "I'll see to supper."

"Get up, get dressed, eat, work, take a bath," Molly hissed. "I'm getting sick and tired of your orders!"

"Fine," Hawk replied mildly. "It doesn't matter to me if you take a bath or not, I'm not the one covered from head to toe in red mud."

Molly looked down at her mud-splattered dress and at her arms, covered to her elbows in the rapidly hardening muck. A trickle of sweat rolled down her brow and she used her forearm to wipe it away, realizing that she had to have left some of the clay on her face as well. Protest be damned, she knew that she would be the only one to suffer by refusing to bathe. Muttering beneath her breath, Molly walked back to camp, grabbed clean clothes and headed for the creek.

The cool water felt good on her heated skin and in spite of herself, Molly enjoyed the bath. Her once-smooth hands stung in hundreds of places from the abrasive effects of the mud, and calluses had already begun to form from her unaccustomed labors.

She unwillingly remembered the kisses Adam had placed in the palm of her hand and the feel of his skin beneath her fingers.

"Supper is waiting, Mrs. Royse!"

Pulled abruptly from her memories, Molly walked out of the river and began to dry herself. A cool evening breeze trailed across her skin and she rushed to dress.

Deep shadows darkened the stream and Molly shivered as she noticed the position of the lowering sun. Night, and the pitiless loneliness it brought, was rapidly descending.

Chapter Eight

"Finish your supper."

"I am finished."

"Eat!"

"Then will you leave me alone?"

"That's a possibility."

"You mean you won't badger me to go to bed?"

"You can sit up all night, if you wish."

"You're kidding! You won't insist that it's time to go to bed?"

"If common sense doesn't tell you to go to bed then I think your tired body will. You've worked hard all day and before long it's going to insist on rest."

Stubbornly, Molly raised her chin. "I think I'm the best judge of whether or not I'm tired." Defiantly she dropped her full plate on the ground. "Or hungry!"

"Then, by all means, stay up." Hawk grabbed her plate, scraped off the food, and quickly dispatched the evening dishes. Without another word he turned and walked away from camp.

Molly keenly felt his absence, as the night sounds grew threateningly closer. Only the crackle of the fire sounded familiar, but it seemed sinister rather than soothing. She pulled her shawl more firmly around her shoulders, sighing silently with relief when Hawk returned to camp.

Tiny drops of water sparkled with a silver sheen on his midnight black hair, revealing the reason for his disappearance. She watched with faint disbelief as he unrolled his blankets, added more wood to the fire and then stretched out on his bed.

"Remember that morning comes early and you still have logs to chink." With those final words he rolled to his side, pulled the blanket over his shoulder and closed his eyes.

Molly watched as the new logs caught fire and she waited for Hawk to demand that she go to bed. The night noises, no longer threatening with him in camp, drifted slowly past her ears. In the distance an owl called its eternal question and katydids chirped in a rhythmic cadence. A cool breeze played with tendrils of hair lying on Molly's neck as a whippoor-will's plaintive song echoed poignantly through the darkness, needlessly reminding her that she was alone.

Wrapping her arms around her bent legs, Molly rested her chin on her knees. The fire burned low until only glowing embers lit the darkness. Night, once so welcome, was now an enemy to be held at bay. It brought sleep and the promise of dreams, but dreams that were granted only after suffering the nightmare agony of reality.

"Adam," Molly whispered as her eyes brimmed with tears. She wrapped her arms around her waist as sobs tore through her body. Her shoulders shook with the force of her anguish and she was unaware of making soft whimpering sounds.

Molly went willingly into the powerful arms that tenderly enfolded her. She welcomed the strong beat of his heart beneath her ear as her head leaned against his chest. Hawk neither encouraged nor discouraged her tears, only holding her tightly and offering her whatever comfort she could find from his embrace.

He gently stroked her back, and his breath fell softly against her brow. As her sobs lessened she thought she detected a quiet chant that she more felt than heard. His voice seemed to vibrate through his chest and she became quiet, trying to hear any words that accompanied the tuneless song. Never increasing in volume, it slowly drifted away until it merged with the sounds of the night.

"Once, when I was about five or six, I fell and cut my knee," he said softly, inviting Molly to share in his memory. "I was living with Luc and Linsey at the time and ran crying to Linsey. She picked me up and held me and dried my tears. Then she bandaged my knee and offered me a cookie to help me forget the pain." With her head nestled beneath his chin Molly didn't see Hawk's gentle smile at the memory.

"Several months later my father had come to get me and I lived for a time at the Shawnee camp. I again fell, this time breaking my arm. I remember crying from pain and fear as I walked back to my father's lodge. When I got there he ignored the tears and spoke harshly when I cried out in pain as they set my arm.

"When the process was finished and my tears had dried on their own, he informed me that tears were for women. Warriors learned to hide the pain and fear.

"I never cried again," he added softly.

"But you were just a baby!" Molly gasped indignantly. "How could he have been so cruel and heartless?"

"Ah, Molly, the Indian way is sometimes so different from the white man's. When a boy reaches the age of six or seven he is taken away from his mother. He still lives in the same lodge with her but she suddenly treats him differently. He is no longer considered a baby, he is on his way to manhood."

"But a boy of six is still so little," she interrupted.

"Maybe a white child, but not an Indian. By that time he is expected to bring in food of some kind. At that age most boys are pretty proficient with a small bow and can kill birds and rabbits. It's not unheard-of for a boy of eight to kill a deer."

"When did you kill your first deer?" she couldn't resist asking.

"Seven," he replied with a shrug, then continued his story. "The time I broke my arm, the Cub and I stayed with the tribe for nearly a year before Luc came and got us."

"The Cub?"

Again Hawk smiled. "Luc and Linsey's oldest son. Luc is known as Bear Who Walks Alone. His first son was called the Cub until he outgrew the name," he answered with a chuckle. "He's only a few months younger than me and when we were growing up we were inseparable. When my father came to get us we'd spend several months at the village. Finally, usually when Linsey couldn't stand the separation any longer, Luc would come and get us and we'd stay with them until my father returned for us. We spent our entire childhood first with one and then the other, but always together."

"It must have been difficult living in both worlds."

"At times it was confusing, but looking back, I wouldn't have had it any other way."

"You miss them."

"I miss them," he agreed quietly. Moving carefully, Hawk stood with Molly in his arms and carried her to her bed. He gently lowered her onto the quilts but she grabbed his hand when he started to move away.

"Don't leave me," she pleaded softly, the glimmer of tears still painting her cheeks.

"Not yet, Molly, just let me sit down." He made himself comfortable beside her, holding her hand in both of his.

"Tell me more."

"A bedtime story?" he questioned, then proceeded to do just that. "An Indian changes his name several times through his life. At birth he is usually given a name by his grandmother or an aunt. As he grows, his name often reflects his maturity, or lack of . . . sometimes a boy will do something stupid and the other boys will start calling him a derogatory name that will, unfortunately, stick with him for years.

"He selects his true name after the ceremony of manhood. That is most often the name he carries with him throughout his life."

"I can't imagine being called anything but Molly!" Interest in a way of life so different from her own was obvious in her voice. "What were your names?"

Hawk was quiet for so long she began to wonder if she had inadvertently asked a question that was disrespectful to him or to his culture.

"That's a story for another time," he finally replied.

"I didn't mean to offend you."

"You didn't," he offered with a smile. "But this bedtime story is about a bear and his cub, not a hawk.

"Luc is one of the largest men I've ever seen, well suited to his name of Bear. The Cub's name never changed because it suited him, too, though sometimes it was not used as a compliment. Then one summer he grew taller than the Bear. I thought I'd never meet anyone bigger than the Bear but it seems like the Cub just plain forgot to stop growing."

"Big, huh?"

"No, he's more than just big," he replied with a chuckle and a shake of his head. "When we went to the tailor in Philadelphia the poor man's eyes nearly

138

popped out of his head. He'd never made clothing for someone of the Cub's size.

"Dressed in the clothing of the frontier, the buckskins and moccasins, the Cub was intimidating to strangers. But in city clothing he attracted attention like a runaway buggy. People tripped over their own feet staring at him and the women . . . ah, the women made complete fools of themselves vying for a chance to arouse his interest."

"He sounds awful," she murmured, intimidated by just the thought of the unknown man.

"No, Molly, if you met him you'd quickly realize that the Cub is a man who honors you when he calls you friend."

She decided to reserve her opinion on that statement. "You said his name changed. What's he called now?" Molly asked, her eyes growing heavy in spite of her desire to stay awake and listen.

"At his birth his mother named him Daniel, but my people called him Mountain with Voice of Thunder."

"Well at least the mountain part sounds appropriate," she whispered drowsily.

"So is the voice of thunder."

Molly smiled and rolled to her side, pulling Hawk's hands until her cheek rested against them. The position was awkward for him but he maintained it as he watched her drift in the nether world before sleep.

"More."

"Another time, Molly," he murmured. He freed one hand and gently rubbed her back. "Sleep now."

139

Once again the sensation of a wordless chant enfolded her in its embrace. She drifted to sleep with the comfort of his hand beneath her cheek and the rhythmic movement of his other hand on her back while the unspoken melody enveloped her in its magic and soothed her spirit.

Molly worked unceasingly from dawn to dark every day. The thought remained in her mind that perhaps, if she tired herself enough, then sleep would come without bringing with it the torment of reality.

Her goal was never achieved.

In spite of bone-weary fatigue, as soon as the sun lowered in the sky, Molly was painfully reminded of Adam's death. The darkness brought the tears that she successfully controlled during the day.

And the tears brought Hawk.

Each night he would come to her, gather her within the comfort of his arms and hold her until her tears dried. A stranger could be forgiven for thinking they were bitter enemies during the day but as darkness descended he was there with her, sharing her sorrow, offering a part of himself that was unknown to anyone but Molly.

"You never told me what your other names have been," she commented one night as she wiped the visible traces of tears from her face. "You told me about Bear and the Cub but not about yourself."

Hawk carefully released her from his embrace and lowered her to her bed. It had become their custom

140

for him to sit beside her and tell her tales of his childhood until she drifted to sleep. She was unaware that he often remained beside her long into the night, soothing her when she cried out in her sleep, watching her with a freedom denied to him during the day.

"Linsey named me Nathan Morning Hawk," he began, his strong hand carefully holding hers.

"Why? I thought a grandmother or aunt named a new baby."

"I was born during a measles outbreak in our village. My mother died, as did my grandmother and several aunts."

"All of them died at the same time?" she asked, appalled.

He nodded in affirmation. "There were over six hundred people in my village, less than a hundred survived the disease."

"My God . . ."

"My people cannot tolerate the white man's diseases. I've been told that at my birth Linsey and Bear rushed me away from the village. My father asked her to give me a name and after much thought she decided on Nathan Morning Hawk. Nathan meaning 'Gift of God,' Morning was in honor of my mother, and Hawk was chosen because one seemed to guide them to their cabin when they were escaping from the destruction of my village."

"But I thought Indian names changed?"

"They do, but I never felt a need to change the one Linsey had given me. When I was about sixteen I went through the manhood ceremony. A man

141

usually changes his name at that time, selecting something that has great meaning to him because of the visions he sees during the ceremony.

"I fully expected to return to the camp with a different name. But as the sun rose on the morning of the third day it revealed a hawk resting on a rock near my feet. It sat there for the longest time, showing no fear of me.

"When it finally flew away it headed to the east and I watched it until it disappeared from sight. A short time later it returned, circled above me several times, then flew away again, this time in the opposite direction.

"It told me of my destiny and allowed me to keep Linsey's choice of names as my own."

"Told you of your destiny?" Molly smiled a sleepy smile. "How can a hawk tell you anything?"

"That is something, Miss Nosy," Hawk gently tapped her button nose, "that you will forever wonder about. No warrior ever tells of the things he experiences during his manhood ceremony."

"You're only a warrior during the day." She closed her eyes, holding firmly to his hand with her own.

"What am I during the night?" he asked with amusement.

"My friend . . ."

Minutes become hours; hours become days; days become weeks. So marches the slow progress of time.

142

In the process of days, weeks and months, pain lessens. Memories become things to cherish instead of a tortuous agony. The sorrow still hovers in the background but it is more easily controlled.

Molly cherished her precious memories of Adam but the dark no longer brought a nightly bout of tears.

It did, however, still bring Hawk to her side, to sit with her until she slept. The midnight Hawk, so different from the one seen by the light of day.

"Up, Mrs. Royse!"

"Oh, God," Molly moaned, burrowing deeper beneath the quilt.

"Breakfast is ready!"

"Go 'way, leave me 'lone."

She wasn't surprised when she felt him grab the quilt and pull it from her grasp. Before she knew it, Molly was standing beside her bed, staring belligerently at her antagonist.

"Have you always been cruel or is this a new trait you've recently developed for my benefit?" she asked as she pushed her sleep-tossed hair from her face. "Just once, just one morning, couldn't you let me sleep until I wake up on my own?"

She could have sworn she saw a smile lighting his dark eyes as he turned and walked away. "Get dressed before your breakfast gets cold," he called back over his shoulder.

"Get up . . . get dressed . . . eat . . . ," she mumbled as she hurried into her clothes. "All the man can do is give orders."

She conveniently ignored the memory of solace

freely given, and so achingly received, in the haunting hours of dark. The compassionate man who offered her a shoulder to cry on and held her until she drifted to sleep was someone totally different from the tyrant who bossed her from sunup to sundown. Sometimes it seemed to her that two separate men occupied the same body.

"Garden needs to be weeded." Hawk handed Molly a plate and waited for her reaction to his statement. She didn't keep him waiting long.

"Weed it yourself!" Resentfully, she took the plate and sat down to eat. She would have loved to refuse the food, and she was disgusted that her stomach wouldn't cooperate with her desire.

"I did it the last time." Hawk reached for the hoe with a handle fashioned from a dogwood limb. "I assume you know how to use this?"

Molly chewed a piece of fried meat and tried to pretend to an ability she didn't possess.

"I'll show you when you've finished your breakfast," Hawk said, accurately reading her face. "Clean up the dishes then come over to the cabin, I'm going to finish up the roof and start on the chimney." He leaned the hoe against the wagon and walked away.

Molly cleaned her plate and drained her cup of coffee to the dregs on the bottom of the tin cup. Hawk had thoughtfully left a pot of hot water for the dishes and more quickly than she wished, her first chore of the day was completed.

When she walked up to the cabin she found that Hawk was on the roof. The back half of the building

144

now boasted a roof of bark. The pieces had been laid on like shingles, each overlapping another, then each was fastened in place with one of the precious nails brought from Charleston.

She watched him work for several minutes until he finally noticed her on the ground. With the agility of a mountain lion he climbed down the rafters which were still waiting for shingles and he lowered himself to ground.

Hawk's instructions on the use of the hoe were simple and thorough. When he returned to complete the roof, Molly worked out her frustrations by hacking at the weeds, which appeared to be the only things growing. Even with her inexperienced eye, she knew that the garden wasn't doing very well. So far the summer had been very dry. Without rain, she feared, the garden would produce very little food.

Wiping sweat from her brow, she stretched her aching back and let her gaze drift to the hill and the marker Hawk had painstakingly carved for Adam's grave. In the weeks since his death, Molly had discovered a strength she had never known she possessed. She still missed him, and knew a part of her always would, but the pain was no longer an acute tearing of her soul.

When she wasn't utterly disgusted with him, she freely acknowledged that Hawk was responsible for helping to ease the pain. During the daylight hours he was a demanding tyrant, never giving her time to dwell on anything but the current chore or the next one waiting to be done. At times she hated him with an intensity that frightened her. Never before in her life had she felt such an overwhelming hatred for another person.

But at night, during the lonely hours when darkness invited sorrow, he was a friend who held her while she cried, and he never berated her for those tears.

Gradually the tears came less often, but Hawk was still there at night, holding her and talking to her until she drifted to sleep. Molly refused to dwell on the day when he would finally leave her to return to his family. He never mentioned Charleston anymore, but summer was nearly finished and she knew he would leave when autumn turned the leaves to red and gold.

"Morning, ma'am."

Startled out of her thoughts, Molly turned to the voice behind her. The stranger's approach had either been silent or she had been more distracted than she had realized.

"Good morning," she greeted hesitantly, her eyes drifting to the cabin for a reassuring sight of Hawk.

" 'Pears to me that you be in need of a rainseed to reckly or you ain't gonna have a slew of greens, come barnin' time."

Not quite sure exactly what the man meant, Molly was reluctant to reply. She continued to search for Hawk and she wondered desperately when he had disappeared. All morning long she had been aware of his surveillance from the roof and now, when she needed him, he was nowhere to be seen.

The stranger walked several steps closer and

Molly backed away. He was hardly a reassuring sight. A scraggly, matted beard hung nearly to his chest and it was obvious that his buckskin pants and cotton shirt had never seen a scrubbing. Black, broken teeth peered out as he smiled at her. She fought an overpowering urge to gag as his ripe odor drifted toward her.

"Where be yore man, little lady?" he asked, as his red-rimmed eyes studied her. "You be all 'lone out here?"

"No . . . no, I'm not alone."

"You ain't be asoundin' too sure of thet." After thoroughly studying Molly, his gaze turned toward the cabin. "Don't be alookin' to me like thar's anybody but you and me here."

"Look again, friend."

Molly turned, filled with relief by the familiar sound of Hawk's deep voice. He had walked up the slight incline from the creek, a stringer of trout in one hand and his rifle in the other.

"Here's our supper, sweetheart." He held out the fish and grinned as Molly's eyes opened wide at the endearment. "Take them on back to the cabin. I'll be along as soon as I hear what our visitor has to say."

Molly took the fish and walked several steps away before she stopped and turned back. The familiar impassive expression was in place. She had seen that look before and knew he would answer her questions only when he was ready to do so.

Hawk waited until Molly was nearly back at camp before he turned his menacing gaze back to the

147

stranger. He had seen his type before, a man who made his living from the pain and suffering of others. A man who followed no rules except those governed by his own greed.

The stranger's gaze was nearly on level with Hawk's and yet he felt a premonition of impending doom as he met those fierce black eyes. This was not someone who would be moved or even concerned by threats.

"I'm Junior Wilson, up from Columbia way. Been hired to find a woman and return her to her father."

Hawk remained impassive and Junior Wilson found himself fidgeting under the unwavering gaze. "She done run away and he's awantin' her back. I done followed her this far and I be aknowin' that she's here somewhere."

"What has that to do with my woman?" Hawk asked in a voice made more threatening because of its softness.

"You ain't her man."

"How did you arrive at that conclusion?"

"You ain't white! You be an Indian." Swallowing hard at the fierceness contorting the savage visage, Junior Wilson continued. "She fits the description of the woman I'm alookin' for. I'm atakin' her home and collectin' the reward that's rightly mine."

"Listen well and remember, you'll not be told a second time," Hawk said in a quiet voice that thundered with pitiless brutality. "She is mine and no one takes what is mine."

Occasionally letting her gaze drift toward the garden and the two men deep in discussion, Molly

148

cleaned the fish with the dexterity of long practice. It appeared to her that the stranger did all of the talking while Hawk stood with his rifle resting across his folded arms. She knew the kind of look that would be on Hawk's face, stern and forbidding, and thought that the old man was either very brave or a fool to confront him.

After putting the fish on to fry, she mixed up a cornmeal batter and poured it into a dutch oven and set it in the coals. Beans had been slowly cooking since the noon meal and Molly tasted them to make sure they were ready.

Hawk finally returned to camp, alone, just as the meal was ready to eat. Molly filled plates and coffee cups for both of them. Her impatience grew as Hawk began to eat without mentioning his discussion with the stranger.

"Well, what did he want?" she was forced to ask when Hawk remained quiet.

Hawk lifted his dark, penetrating gaze to her but he continued to eat without comment. Deciding it would be easier to get blood out of a turnip than information out of him when he chose to be obstinate, Molly quietly finished her meal.

"All right, don't tell me," she mumbled as she stood up. "I'm sure it had nothing to do with me."

Hawk's eyes narrowed slightly. "We'll sleep in the cabin tonight."

"Really? Do you mean it?" Molly temporarily forgot their strange visitor, in her excitement. She longed for a roof over her head again and for several days she had been asking when they could occupy the cabin.

In other circumstances, Hawk would have enjoyed the pleasure radiating from her face. "The fireplace won't be finished for several days yet, but I don't see any reason why we can't start sleeping in there."

"I don't know what to carry in first!"

Hawk stood and handed his plate to her. "Just bedding. There's still work to be finished inside and we don't need to be tripping over things."

"Just bedding," she agreed reluctantly, "but at least we'll be inside!"

Hawk picked up his rifle and cradled it in his arms. "Stay in camp. If you need help fire the gun."

Turning from her contemplation of a night under a roof, Molly looked at him. "Where are you going?"

"To see that our visitor has left."

A chill ran up her spine and she was no longer sure she wanted to know what the man had wanted. "You'll stay close?" she asked quietly.

"I'll hear you if you fire the gun."

Deciding it was better to be sure than to sit and wonder, Molly raised her chin with determination. "What did he want?"

"Not what," Hawk replied quietly, "but who. He's a bounty hunter and he has been offered a pound of gold if he finds a certain woman and returns her to her father."

Molly knew, without asking, that she was the woman. "What did you tell him?"

Like a stormy cloud covering the bright sun, Hawk's expression changed to the familiar stoic countenance. Only this time, as never before, Molly realized that his dark eyes were readable. The emotion that filled his black gaze made her breath catch and her heart begin to pound with an erratic rhythm.

"What did you tell him?" she asked again, her voice barely a whisper of sound.

"I told him you were my woman."

Chapter Nine

The afternoon dragged by with the speed of a snail crossing a meadow. In the sky, dark clouds piled like feather pillows upon each other, promising much-needed rain and a break from the steamy heat, but disappearing without fulfilling that promise.

Dust rose in its own stifling cloud as Molly worked with a vengeance and finished weeding the garden. Her gaze constantly searched the surrounding woods for a sight of Hawk.

At dinnertime, when he still had not returned, she ate a solitary meal of leftover fish. fighting to keep the growing fear from taking control, she quickly dispensed with the dishes, then carried the bedding into the cabin and carefully made up two beds on the dirt floor.

She took as long as possible to spread out the blankets, placing her own bed on the opposite side of the room from Hawk's. He had slept within touching distance of her for weeks but suddenly she felt strange about sleeping close to him. What had seemed right and natural in the open suddenly seemed wrong within the confines of walls.

She didn't let herself dwell on the expression she had read in his eyes. Surely it was her imagination that placed the possessive emotion there? He had never made any move toward her to indicate that he saw her as anything but an encumbrance, an unwanted liability.

And she still loved Adam, didn't she? Molly closed her eyes and tried to bring his beloved face into focus. The warm blue eyes were overshadowed by a penetrating black gaze. The gentle grin was blurred by a mouth that rarely smiled, but when it did it threatened to take her breath away.

Molly slowly straightened the quilt that made up her bed. She ran her hand over the patchwork pattern and sighed softly. With her final chore of the day complete, she reluctantly returned to sit by the fire, Adam's gun within easy reach. She watched as the greedy flames slowly consumed the wood, and she wondered when Hawk would return. Surely it was too dark for even an Indian to track someone effectively.

With no chore left to occupy her hands and loneliness her silent companion, Molly's thoughts turned to the stranger. There was no doubt that he had been sent by her father or her father's agent to find her and return her to Charleston. Charles Gallagher was not a cruel man—just one whose self-centered ambitions had long ago caused him to forget that other people didn't always share his opinions.

She knew, if she returned to Charleston, that he

would berate her for leaving him. He would use guilt to control her future actions and would wrap a web of humiliation so tightly around her that she would never again be free.

The fashionable home on Tradd Street, with the piazza facing the lovely gardens and the library filled with books and priceless treasures, would become a prison. The captain's walk on the roof of the house, a childhood hideaway with its view of the wharf and the ever-changing Ashley River, would be her only means of escape—an escape that would last only until Charles Gallagher demanded her presence for whatever whim needed attention.

Adam had been both a means of escape and a fulfillment of a dream. He had taken her from an elegant cage that offered every known luxury and he had carried her into the wilderness of North Carolina, offering only his love as a replacement for the grandeur she had left behind.

Molly rarely thought of the beautiful belongings she had abandoned in Charleston. She had made the better part of the bargain, trading them for Adam.

Suddenly, guilt crawled with needle-sharp claws through her heart. Had Adam been only a way to escape an intolerable life, she wondered. She had loved him, she had! She would have loved him for the rest of her life if death hadn't taken him away. Then why, only a few short weeks after his death, her relentless mind asked, was she having trouble picturing his face?

"Oh, Adam," she whispered in agony, "I did love you. Why did you have to die and leave me alone? We were supposed to share our life, grow old

155

together and sit on our porch and remember our youth."

Dry-eyed, Molly stared at the glittering flames and felt the guilt slowly release its fists as the warmth of memories replaced it. Their time together had been so short, the memories so few. She knew that eventually they would become like a dream. She felt a melancholy sadness different from her lingering sorrow. A sadness for what should have been but never would be, a sadness for what was.

Underlying the sadness was an awareness of a growing anger. Unreasonable as her rational mind knew it to be, Molly wondered if Adam had fought to live or if he had just accepted his death as inevitable. Self-pity threatened to overwhelm her as she fought the anger and sadness and the inflexible knowledge that her life had altered irrevocably.

Now everything had changed. Adam was gone, his loving touch a gently fading memory. The cabin that was to have been their haven seemed to loom forbiddingly in the light of a half moon. The half-finished chimney rose in an eerie skeletal framework while the door and window opened into the black nothingness of the interior. For all her earlier excitement at the idea of sleeping inside, she was strangely reluctant to enter it alone.

A yawn caught her unaware and with a tired sigh she rested her head against her bent knees. It seemed to her that she was always tired. But, she reasoned with herself, her days were so filled with work it was no wonder that as soon as darkness fell she was ready to sleep.

She closed her eyes as fatigue fought a winning

battle with fear. She wouldn't sleep, she promised herself, until Hawk returned. She'd just sit here by the fire and rest for a while.

With darkness concealing his presence, Hawk watched Molly. It alarmed him that he was so close and yet she was unaware of him. Anyone could silently walk up on her and attack before she could protect herself.

In the four months since they had left Charleston she had learned much, but not nearly enough. She still had so much to learn but so little time left in which to learn it. Hawk knew that if he was to reach home before winter set in and made travel hazardous, he had only a few weeks before he must leave.

She was a vision of gold in the sparkling firelight. Her hair was unbound and lay in rivers of honey gold around her shoulders and down her back. The light accentuated the warm color the sun had given her skin and he knew if he were close enough he would be able to see the freckles that danced across her cheeks and the bridge of her button nose.

Staring at her now, Hawk tried to remember when he had thought her plain, too tall, too thin. She had a beauty and spirit matched by few women. True, she was tall, she'd look like a giant beside petite Linsey. But he had discovered that he liked a woman who could match him in height—one whose head came to just beneath his chin.

He forced his wandering thoughts away from the memories of her in the river, her wet chemise clinging to her like a second skin, proving that she was far from thin. He closed his eyes at the memory of her shapely body, then quickly opened them when the vision became uncomfortably clear.

She was the widow of a man who had been a good friend. Circumstances had placed her in a position that she was unprepared to handle. He was proud of her ability to adapt to any situation, but the desire to learn could not replace experience. And only time would give her that experience—time he didn't have to give her.

He refused to consider his reasons for not staying with her through the winter. His life was his own— he didn't have to return home at a specific time. And yet he knew that he wouldn't change his plans. He *couldn't* change his plans.

Soon she would be forced to make a decision, one that he would refuse to help her make. Until that time came he would continue to be her teacher and friend.

Silently, Hawk moved through the darkness until he entered camp behind Molly. Kneeling beside her, he grabbed a handful of hair and jerked her head back. Startled eyes met his own and a scream was stifled at its birth as recognition replaced fear.

"Had I been an enemy you would have been dead before you knew I was in camp," he snarled.

"You bastard!" Molly screamed as she pulled her hair from his grasp.

"Very good! You can now say that with almost no effort."

"You did that on purpose!" she hissed as she stood.

Hawk leaned his rifle against a tree. Grabbing his

tin cup he hunkered down beside the fire and filled the cup with coffee. His black, ambiguous gaze never left hers as he drank deeply of the dark, rich brew.

"If it was your intention to scare me to death you very nearly had your wish." Molly paced beside the fire, the shawl wrapped protectively around her shoulders.

"If that had been my purpose I would have succeeded." He stood but stayed in the glow of the fire. The light played over his features, lovingly sculpturing his high cheekbones and his square jaw. He didn't need the shoulder-length, jet black hair to proclaim his ancestry. It was clearly visible in his face, in every inch of his majestic body.

"What would you have done if I had been a stranger, intent on harming you?"

"Oh God, not another lesson at this time of night," Molly moaned.

With disgust Hawk threw the remains of his coffee at the fire. It popped and sizzled at the invading liquid then seemed to glow brighter.

"Answer me, woman!" he demanded. "What would you have done."

"Screamed?"

"And?"

Molly rubbed a hand over her face wondering what answer would satisfy him. "Wait for you to come?"

"It's not a game, Mrs. Royse," Hawk growled as he approached her. He grabbed another handful of hair and pulled her head back until she was looking into his face. Stopping just short of causing pain, he wrapped the silken strands around his hand.

"Do you have any idea of what a determined man can do to a defenseless woman?" He held her body against his until she was forced to accept the knowledge of his superior strength.

"Have you ever heard of rape, Mrs. Royse?" he snarled.

"You're frightening me, Hawk."

"I won't always be here, Mrs. Royse, and some men get pleasure out of making a woman scream."

"Stop it!"

"He'll abuse your flesh in as many ways as he knows how, getting satisfaction from your fear, thriving on your screams. He'll hold you to the ground and grind his body into yours. You can scream and bite and scratch, but that won't stop him. And when he's done, if he doesn't kill you, you'll wish you were dead.

"There might be several men. They'll each take a turn on your soft, white body; maybe more than one turn. When they're done, there won't be an inch of your flesh left unmolested. The degradation won't stop when they do, you'll never again feel clean. You'll never be able to trust anyone again. You'll always wonder if some other man is just waiting his chance at you."

"Stop it!"

Hawk saw the fear in her eyes and with a snarled oath he released his hold on her hair. He turned and walked away from her, standing in the shadows of the fire, staring into the darkness.

"Your father has sent a man to get you," he said quietly. "He is the first but he won't be the last. He

160

may even still be around here somewhere just waiting for an opportunity."

Hawk bit back the threatening rage at the thought of a father who would so callously send a stranger after his own daughter. Did he give no thought to the treatment the stranger might inflict upon his helpless daughter on the return journey? Was his only goal to have her back, regardless of the means?

Turning, he stared at Molly, seeing the fear on her face and knowing it was as much for him as for the unknown man.

"Go to bed, Molly," he said quietly.

"Hawk . . . I . . ."

"Tomorrow we'll start working on some self-defense. We'll practice with both the rifle and a knife."

"Hawk . . ." Not sure what she wanted to say, Molly stuttered into silence.

"Go to bed."

Nodding silently, Molly turned and walked toward the cabin. She hesitated at the doorway, turning to look at Hawk. His unreadable gaze did not invite her to return to the fire, so she slowly entered the dark structure.

Hawk cursed himself silently: for his harsh treatment of her—for her inability to provide for herself. He knew he could have chosen a different way to show her the dangers she faced. He didn't have to scare her to death to prove a point.

And now she feared him more than some unknown man who might or might not be intending to harm her.

Hawk leaned against the wagon and watched as

the fire slowly burned to embers.

Changing into her nightdress, she listened for the sound of his footsteps, anticipation changing to disappointment when he didn't come. Since Adam's death, she had not fallen asleep alone. Each night Hawk had held her until sleep claimed her. She quickly discovered that she missed him, his quiet strength, his gentle understanding. She stared through the darkness, ignoring the unfamiliar creaking and groaning of the cabin and as her eyes adjusted she found that the blackness was far from absolute. The unfinished windows and door, as well as the spaces between the logs that still needed to be chinked, all allowed the moonlight to filter into the room.

A long time later the moon gave her more than enough light to see Hawk as he soundlessly entered the cabin.

"Hawk?" she whispered, sitting up, the quilt falling to her waist.

He had known she wouldn't be asleep. He had put off coming into the cabin as long as possible, hoping she would be. He was afraid to discover if she now feared him to the point of terror. But that one word, his name whispered in a voice that was unknowingly seductive, answered his questions.

Hawk walked to the far side and lowered himself to the floor. He leaned against the wall and gathered Molly into his arms.

"I shouldn't have—" he began only to be interrupted by gentle fingers against his lips.

"Tomorrow," she said softly. "I'll yell at you for scaring me to death, you'll boss me, as always. We'll solve our differences in the light of day."

Tempted to kiss the fingers against his mouth, Hawk reached up and captured her hand in his. With a sigh he held it next to his heart and leaned his head back against the wall. Aware that only the thin cotton of her nightdress and his own shirt separated her flesh from his, Hawk sighed deeply and fought to control his natural urge to caress her.

"Have I told you about Kaleb Smith?" he asked quietly.

Molly snuggled against his strong, hard chest and shook her head. "Is he another one who lives with Bear and Linsey?"

"You could say that Kaleb introduced them," Hawk said with a smile. He adjusted her into a more comfortable position on his lap and found long strands of hair wrapped around his hand. Unconsciously, he stroked the clinging tendrils as he told his story.

"Kaleb spent many years searching for the men responsible for his wife's death. When he found them he also found Linsey. They had kidnapped her and intended to sell her. To shorten a long story, he took her away from them, deposited her at Bear's cabin and then went back for the two men."

"Did he get them?" Molly asked.

"They'll never bother another woman," Hawk replied. He realized that he was playing with her hair and reluctantly unwound the strands from his hand.

"Is that all?"

Hawk chuckled at the childish disappointment so evident in her voice. "No, that's not all, *ó-wès-sah skwài-tha-thàh.*"

163

"What did you say?"

He lifted her from his lap and gently placed her on her bed. "Do you want to hear the rest of Kaleb's story or not?" he asked, tapping the end of her nose.

"Of course, but I want to know what you said, too!"

"I said that you were a pretty little girl who is incorrigibly nosy."

"Oh, is that all." Disappointment was evident in her voice. "Can you say my name in Shawnee."

"Sure."

"Say it!"

"Molly," Hawk replied, a grin tugging at the corners of his mouth.

"Funny, very funny!" She pulled the quilt up to her chin, looking even more like a child to him. "Tell me your name."

"Then can I get on with my story?"

"Yep."

"Kwa-lah-wah-pàh-kee m̀-shkol-àh-nee, Morning Hawk," he said, his deep, rich voice flowing around the fluid Shawnee words.

Hawk settled beside her, gently taking her hand in his. "Kaleb is the grandfather I never had. He settled down in a homestead near Bear and adopted their family. When we were little, the Cub and I followed him everywhere."

"He never remarried?"

"No, Mary had been his whole life. I guess he just never found anyone else he wanted.

"Bear met Kaleb shortly after the Iroquois had . . . ah, removed his hair."

"They scalped him?" Molly asked, horrified.

Hawk smiled at her response. "Fortunately for Kaleb, the Iroquois did a poor job of it. They sort of lost interest in Kaleb when Bear arrived on the scene. It was a small raiding party, though to hear Kaleb describe the incident it was the entire Iroquois nation.

"Bear managed to get Kaleb free and spent the winter nursing him back to health. They parted in the spring and didn't see each other again until Kaleb left Linsey in Bear's cabin. Kaleb always says that she was a thank-you present."

No longer able to resist temptation, Hawk reached out and wound a long strand of hair around his hand. "Bear says she's the best gift he ever received."

Aware of his hand tangled in her hair, Molly remained very still. "And what does Linsey say?" she asked quietly.

Ebony eyes sparkled in the sparse moonlight. "She's never said anything, but I think she must agree. She named her second son Kaleb."

Long minutes passed in silence as Hawk stroked her hair. He let the silken strands waterfall through his fingers only to chase after them and capture them before they were truly free.

"Hawk, what am I going to do?" she asked softly, her voice reflecting her despondency.

He let the strands of hair fall one final time through his fingers and watched as they landed in a golden pool on her shoulder. His dark gaze found the sparkle of her golden one through the darkness. He didn't pretend to misunderstand her question.

"You have to make the decision. I won't tell you

what to do with your life."

"Do you realize that I've never made a decision in my life? First my father and then Adam decided what I'd do. Even the decision to elope was Adam's. Now I'm being forced to make a decision and I don't even know how to go about it. Do you have a lesson on how to make decisions?"

Hawk raised his hand and traced a gentle path down her soft cheek. Following the line of her jaw, his fingers caressed her stubborn chin and moved up to her other cheek. Her skin held the warmth of a summer day, the softness of a spring morning.

"*Pel-áh-wee skàwi-tha-thàh,* Summer Woman, the answer will come." He let his touch slip down her nose and whisper past her lips.

"Hawk . . ." Lost in the sparkling sensation of his touch, Molly was hard-pressed to create a coherent sentence.

"Sleep, *pel-áh-wee skàwi-tha-thàh,*" he murmured. "Search for your answer in your dreams."

His hand once again firmly holding hers, Molly obediently closed her eyes. After the fears she had felt today she was almost afraid of the contents of her dreams.

In the silence of the night, the wordless chant reached out to enfold her in its beguiling magic. Swirling around on a whisper of breath, it teased, invited, enchanted, caressed. It offered an ethereal haven from earthly cares, a sanctuary from fear. In the sound was a pledge of security, a promise of safety.

Molly felt sleep enfold her in its tranquil arms. Her last thoughts were of Hawk, of the gentleness so thoroughly concealed from casual observers by his savage intensity.

Hawk was aware of the instant she fell asleep. He felt the gradual release of her grasp on his hand, the slow softening of her body. Maintaining the soothing chant long after she slept, he watched the rhythmic movement of her breathing. His gaze, both fierce and tender, roved hungrily over her slumbering features.

"Sleep, my Summer Woman," he whispered. "You will find your answers, and when you are ready they will lead you to my waiting arms."

Chapter Ten

As the rain pounded the thirsty earth, Molly watched, unconsciously rubbing her right shoulder. Bruised by the kick of the rifle, her shoulder ached continuously, a dull pain that was more irritating than painful. Since the incident two weeks earlier that had proved her lack of ability to protect herself, Hawk had spent a couple of hours each evening teaching her to use the rifle and a small-handled knife.

The knife proved easier to control than the rifle, though she knew she was far from a master with the weapon, even though it fit snugly in the palm of her hand. She began to fear that her accuracy with the rifle, which was nearly as long as she was tall, would ever improve enough for her to be able to put food on the table or even to provide minimal protection. Perhaps if she could convince her attacker to stand perfectly still at point-blank range she could manage to hit him, but she knew she'd miss if he took a deep breath.

With a sigh, she moved away from the door. She feared that the rain had come too late to save her garden. And any plants that had survived the drought were now threatened with drowning. This was the third straight day of rain, and rivers of mud flowed freely down to the creek.

"Restless?" Hawk asked. He sat on the floor near the fireplace that he had finished just days before the rains began. Even though warmth was not needed, a small fire burned to give them light, and heat for cooking their meals.

"I'm tired of the rain," she complained quietly. "Three days is two days too many!"

"It'll soon stop." His agile fingers moved confidently over the piece of leather he was fashioning into a sheath for her knife.

"Yeah, probably a week after I start to rust!" She pushed her hair out of her face and walked back to the door.

Hawk's eyes narrowed with thought as he watched her restless pacing. It was unlike Molly to be impatient or irritable, but for the last week her moods had swung as freely as a pendulum on a clock. He had watched with amazement as she laughed happily one minute only to turn teary-eyed the next. She had snapped at him for the slightest reason then tearfully apologized with the next breath.

"Want to tell me what's wrong?" he asked.

"Nothing's wrong!" she snapped, moving away from the door. "I'm just tired of the rain. I want to go for a walk. I want to work in my garden. I want to look at something other than these four walls!"

"Then go for a walk," Hawk suggested.

"Are you out of your mind? In case you haven't noticed," she continued sarcastically, "it's raining!"

"It's warm, so you won't catch cold and I doubt that you'll melt. Haven't you ever walked in the rain?"

"You have to be kidding. Why would anyone want to walk in the rain?"

"Ah, *ó-wès-sah skwài-tha-thàh,* you have missed some of the finer treats of life."

"Don't speak in Shawnee. Since I don't know the language, it is extremely rude. And I'd hardly call getting drenched in a downpour one of the finer treats of life!"

"I called you 'pretty girl,'" he said as he laid his leather work aside and began to unlace his knee-high moccasins.

"I'm hardly pretty when I haven't had a bath in three days," she mumbled, oddly pleased by his compliment.

"Another reason to walk in the rain." He placed his moccasins beside the unfinished sheath and rose to his feet. Like a stalking animal, he began to walk toward her. "Take your shoes off, Mrs. Royse."

"Oh dear God, not the Mrs. Royse routine. I know every time you call me that that I'm not going to like what comes next."

"You'll like this, I promise."

"And if I don't?"

"Shoes, Mrs. Royse." He stopped in front of her,

looking down at the toes of her black shoes peeking from beneath her dress.

"I don't want to walk in the rain, Hawk."

"Yes, you do." He knelt and began to unlace her shoes.

"No, I don't!"

He ignored her, untying the laces and pulling her feet free. When he discovered the white cotton stockings covering her feet his gaze rose to hers.

"You remove them or I will."

"Hawk . . ."

His hands moved beneath her skirt and Molly jerked away from his touch. "I'll do it!"

She turned her back to him, missing his quick smile of amusement. When the stockings had been rolled down her legs and safely placed in her shoes, Hawk grabbed her hand. Before she could protest further, he pulled her outside and into the pouring rain.

Hawk turned his face to the sky and opened his mouth to catch the drops. "Taste it, Molly. There are few things sweeter than the taste of falling rain."

Molly was too fascinated by the feel of the mud at her feet to raise her face to the rain. It felt different from the sandy dirt at the river bank. It was cold and slick and oozed between her toes as her feet sank deeper. She raised her skirt and wiggled her toes, enjoying the soft trickle of water.

When she didn't respond, Hawk turned to her and noticed her raised skirt. She lifted dancing eyes to his and he was captivated by her innocent enjoyment.

172

"It tickles!" she giggled.

The rain was pulling her hair from its pins and Hawk smiled as he reached up and freed the remaining strands from their anchor. Her hand closed willingly in his as he walked away from the cabin. She snickered when his feet slid in the slippery mud and he tumbled to his knees in the red ooze.

Hawk turned to her, his fierce expression belied by his merrily dancing ebony eyes. "So you think it's funny, do you?" he asked wickedly.

"Hawk, you wouldn't," she said, reading the intention in his gaze. "Would you?"

Molly backed slowly away as he rose from the ground. "Of course I would, Mrs. Royse."

"No!" she shrieked as she turned to run. The slippery mud worked in conjunction with Hawk. She slid to the ground even as he reached for the skirt of her dress. She squealed as the cold mud met the warm flesh of her legs.

Hawk knelt over her, his white teeth sparkling in his dark face. "Lesson number one, Mrs. Royse," he said with a chuckle, "never run in mud!"

"Lesson number two, Mr. Hawk," she replied with an answering chuckle as she rolled over and forced a handful of slime down the open neck of his shirt. "Never delay in telling a lady lesson number one!"

She felt fully vindicated when he yelled as the cold muck slid down his smooth chest.

Mud covered her hair and dotted her face. The front of her dress, whose color was no longer discernible beneath its layer of mud, was plastered to her body. She seemed unaware that her skirt was bunched up past her knees, but Hawk had to force his gaze away from the inviting crevice delineated by the wet fabric.

She had never appeared more beautiful to him and he knew that she'd taste sweeter than any rain.

"Lesson number three, Mrs. Royse," he replied, a handful of mud held in her sight, "never, ever, throw mud at a Shawnee warrior."

"I'm sorry." Molly's feeble apology was totally destroyed by the giggle that accompanied it. Her eyes grew huge as she watched the threatening mud move slowly closer to her face.

"No you're not."

"No, really," she said earnestly, her hand locking onto his wrist, "I am sorry."

"You're only sorry that I'm going to take this mud," his arm moved in spite of her efforts to prevent it, "and drop it here." It landed with a wet plop onto her belly.

"Oh, uck!" she giggled merrily. "Now I'm all dirty."

"Not to mention wet!"

"Whose dumb idea was this, anyway?"

"Yours?"

"Huh! I was perfectly content to sit in my nice cozy, *dry* cabin and watch it rain."

"You said you wanted to take a walk." He stood and pulled her to her feet. "So let's walk."

They slipped and slid down the paths that had become so familiar in the past weeks. Molly occasionally stepped on a stick or small rock that hurt her tender feet but Hawk seemed impervious to such afflictions.

Heading toward the sound of the rapidly flowing river, Hawk intentionally walked away from the hill where Adam's grave rested. He didn't want to chance changing her mood by inadvertently reminding her of the loss. Her childish pleasure in walking through the pouring rain told him more than words ever could of the simple things she had been denied as a child.

Three days of rain had turned the gently flowing creek into a cauldron of raging water, overflowing its shallow banks and obliterating the boulders that normally rose above water level in the center.

Leaning against a tree, Molly watched the bubbling water flow past her feet. The rain wasn't as heavy beneath the canopy of leaves. It dripped almost gently, washing the mud from her face.

"What makes it rain?" It was more of a spoken thought than a question.

"My people believe that rain is the tears of Mother Earth." A raindrop hung suspended from Molly's matted eyelashes. With an infinitely tender touch, Hawk caught it on his finger. "Mother Earth is crying because she has seen the damage done by man to her trees and flowers, her creatures great and small, her rivers and oceans."

His deep voice wove around her, cocooning her in the magic of his words. His finger had caught the raindrop and had stayed to caress her damp cheek softly. "She cries for hours or days, until she sees that her trees reach to the sky, begging for sunlight. Or that her birds sit huddled in misery for lack of warmth. Then she dries her eyes so that the sky clears.

"Sometimes, in remorse, she will paint the sky with a rainbow."

"Mother Earth is the Shawnee god?"

"No, their god is called Manitou. He is like the white man's God, only more so. The Shawnee feel that not only did he create everything on earth he *is* everything on earth. He is the trees and grass, the earth and sky. His voice is the breeze that whispers secrets through the trees, his breath the wind that blows violently before a storm. The sun and moon are his eyes, all the creatures that walk or crawl or slither are his ears.

"Some would say that Manitou made you from honey and stardust." His hand moved to her hair and he raised the sodden strands to her face. "Your hair is the color of the sun shining on a honeycomb, your eyes share that color and have the added sparkle of golden stardust."

He let the hair fall to her shoulder and he ran a gentle finger across her cheeks, tracing a path over the countless freckles. "Where the sun has kissed your face it has left proof of its approval."

Mesmerized by his voice, Molly watched as his face moved closer to hers. Her lips parted in anticipation, her breath caught in expectation. His ebony eyes blazed as his hand moved to the back of her neck.

With a visible shudder, Hawk suddenly released

her and moved away. "Someday, when we have a lot of time, I'll explain Shawnee religion to you. It's quite involved." He breathed deeply several times to regain control, then offered his hand to her. "Let's walk back to the cabin."

Hand-in-hand they returned to the cabin. Molly fought the conflicting emotions that raged through her; disappointment that he hadn't kissed her clashed with relief that he had moved away. She wondered about the texture of his mouth—would it be soft and gentle or hard and demanding—then she berated herself for having such thoughts.

She had been a widow for only a few months, surely it was wrong even to think about another man. Molly didn't stop to consider that she had now been a widow longer than she had been a wife.

"Fetch some soap and I'll help you wash your hair," Hawk offered at the door.

"In the rain?"

Hawk chuckled at her startled expression. "You're soaked to the skin already, a little more water won't hurt anything. And the mud's so caked in your hair you're never going to get it out alone."

After digging out her precious bar of scented soap, Molly stood patiently in the pouring rain while Hawk worked soap into her hair. The rich, fragrant lather filled the air with a flowery essence and she closed her eyes with pleasure as Hawk's strong fingers massaged her head.

"Is it possible to sleep standing up?" she asked, her voice almost purring with delight.

The effect on Hawk was completely different.

Teeth tightly clenched, eyes closed, he struggled against his growing desire to take her into his arms and make her his. He silently cursed the restraint imposed upon him by Linsey's teachings. If he had been raised in the Shawnee way he would have taken her, without concern for her own desires.

Hawk knew in that moment that it would take little inducement for him to become the Shawnee warrior that coursed through his feverish blood.

To wash the soap from her hair, but mostly to cool himself off, Hawk picked up a bucket of water and poured it over her head. He handed her another bucket of water and motioned to the cabin.

"Go on inside and get dry." He grabbed his bow and quiver of arrows from the inside wall near the door.

"The true Shawnee warrior, heading off to provide for his family in spite of weather conditions," she teased.

Her teasing bordered too close to his earlier thoughts. "Be glad I'm not a warrior or I wouldn't be leaving you right now even if we were threatened with starvation," he said cryptically as he strung the bow and slipped the quiver over his shoulder. With a look that said far more than words, he turned and disappeared into the rain.

With her still-damp hair tied at the nape of her neck, Molly finished cleaning up from the evening meal. Hawk had returned empty-handed from his hunting but his expression made her refrain from teasing him. He had been quiet throughout the meal and again he sat on the floor adding some finishing touches to her knife sheath.

"Where's your knife?" he asked, suddenly breaking the silence.

Molly pulled the knife from her stack of belongings and carried it to him. As he slipped it into the sheath he said a silent prayer that she would never have to use it. From one end to the other it measured just a couple of inches longer than his hand. Wielded by an expert it could become a deadly weapon. In the hands of a novice it could be little more than an irritant to an antagonist.

"Try it on."

Molly took the sheathed knife from him. A long, narrow strip of hide at the top was matched by a short, equally narrow strip at the bottom. She started to tie it around her waist when his cold voice stopped her.

"Under your dress."

"What?"

"Wear it under your dress," he repeated with exaggerated patience.

"Why?" Molly asked in a whisper.

Because of his years spent in a white man's environment, Hawk was not surprised by her horror at his suggestion. Of the many things that still had the power to amaze him, the way white women hid their bodies had to be among those at the top of the list. The layers of clothes in even the hottest of temperatures were a mystery he knew he'd never solve.

179

"If the knife is under your dress then no one will be aware that you have it, and no one will be able to take it away from you. Surprise will be on your side and if your opponent is larger or faster than you, then surprise may be the only thing that saves you."

"I can't wear it under my dress!"

"Why not?"

"Because . . . because it's indecent!"

"Being raped is indecent, Mrs. Royse," he replied viciously. "Having no way to protect yourself is indecent. Being murdered is indecent! Wearing a knife under your dress is self-preservation."

"That may be true, but . . ."

"This is not a game, Mrs. Royse," Hawk interrupted. "You're in the wilderness, not on some civilized city street." He rose from the floor and pulled the knife from her trembling hands.

"This thing just might give you enough edge to save your life. I've told you about the men who would use your delectable body to satisfy their own lust, but there are others."

Kneeling in front of her, Hawk grabbed the hem of her skirt and pulled it up out of his way. Molly instinctively grabbed the material as it was thrown in her face. Her face turned a deep scarlet when he threw the two layers of petticoats up, exposing her lace-trimmed drawers and a good portion of shapely leg. Despite the temptation, she didn't dare let her skirt drop. Hawk was not someone to trifle with when he was determined to see something through to the end. And he was determined to see that

180

the knife was strapped to her waist beneath her skirt.

Hawk quickly tied the thong around her waist. "There are some who would cut your finger from your hand for that gold band you wear." He tied the matching thong low on her thigh, checking to make sure it was snug but not tight.

"There are those who would steal anything that might appear to have some value and they won't be polite about it. There are wild animals who will attack simply because you're walking on their territory. And let's not forget snakes, Mrs. Royse." His smile was merciless as he reminded her of the encounter with the snake. "You might just run into another snake and be grateful that this knife is there.

"You'll learn to raise your skirt and palm the knife as quickly as possible." He pulled the skirt from her hands, ignoring her red face, and settled it about her ankles.

"Lift your skirt and go for the knife."

"Hawk, really . . ."

"Do it, Mrs. Royse!"

Molly wasn't brave enough to defy him when he used that tone of voice. Swallowing her embarrassment at so wanton a display, Molly raised her skirt and reached for the knife. Hawk's eagle-eyed gaze did nothing to ease her discomfort as he watched her actions. He readjusted the knife slightly to the front of her thigh, then pulled her skirt free.

"Again!"

Once more Molly raised her skirt, her hand

reaching for the weapon. "Better," he mumbled. "But not nearly fast enough. You have to learn to raise that skirt in seconds and get that knife in your hands. It'd be better if you didn't have those petticoats to contend with."

"I will not go without undergarments!" Molly didn't think her face could get any more flushed as it did at his casual mention of her intimate apparel.

"No one is telling you to run around undressed, Mrs. Royse," Hawk replied roughly. "By all means, wear as much clothing as you deem necessary. But I want you to practice retrieving that knife over and over again until it becomes swift and natural.

"And wear it in the same place each time. It's at the end of the natural extension of your arm. It'll be easier for you to grab it there."

"Hawk, I really don't think this is necessary," Molly stated as she settled her dress around her ankles. "It feels very strange to have it strapped to my leg."

"Only a fool goes through life unprotected. I never figured you for a fool, Mrs. Royse." Hawk stood and moved back. "Get your knife."

"Hawk, really . . ."

"Now!"

Gritting her teeth, Molly lifted her skirt. Right hand, left hand, right hand, the skirt was raised enough to expose the knife. Grabbing the fabric in her left hand, she unsheathed the weapon.

"Use your left hand first," Hawk instructed. "Left, right, left, then your right hand is free to grab the knife without readjusting the fabric."

182

Muttering beneath her breath about dictatorial men in general and one overbearingly arrogant man in particular, Molly practiced raising her skirt until Hawk was satisfied that she had the movements down, if not the speed.

"Practice every chance you get," Hawk said as he turned away. "Eventually you'll be capable of reaching your knife before someone knows what you're doing."

"Does Linsey wear a knife strapped to her leg?" Molly asked, the disdain in her voice conveying her doubts that Bear would insist that his wife wear such a weapon.

Hawk turned to her, his intimidating countenance breaking into a grin. "He made her sheath himself."

"Of course he did," she muttered, defeated. "I think you must take after him more than you know."

"Thank you." His grin spread to a full smile.

"That wasn't a compliment!" Molly walked to the door and stared through the darkness at the falling rain. Men! Their arrogance knew no bounds!

"I liked that bit of lace," Hawk said casually as he added wood to the fire.

"What lace?" Molly tried to ask in a casual voice, glad for the darkness that hid her once-more flaming face.

"An Indian woman would never hide something so delicately pretty. She'd wear it someplace so that everyone could see." He banked the coals for the night then stood. "Of course, an Indian woman doesn't wear underdrawers and wouldn't understand why you'd wear anything beneath your dress."

Molly's cheeks flamed with color even though she realized it was exactly the reaction he'd hoped for. "What, exactly, do Indian women wear beneath their dresses?" she asked without thinking.

"Why nothing, Mrs. Royse. Absolutely nothing at all." He thought of the feminine bit of lace that had teased his hands as he'd tightened the knife sheath. "But is is a shame that a warrior will never know the delight of discovering the bits and pieces of lace and ribbon so seductively sewn on a delicate bit of fabric.

"There's a lot to be said for an unexpected peek at a slender ankle or a lacy petticoat. Or knowing that a slight tug on a piece of ribbon will free it from its anchor. An Indian warrior will never know the heightened anticipation brought on as each piece of feminine clothing finds its way to the floor."

"Mr. Hawk, I believe this conversation should be terminated." Molly stared into the darkness, hoping that he wasn't aware of the need he was arousing in her, a need that she couldn't satisfy.

Hawk picked up his rifle and walked to the door. A smile crossed his dark face as Molly moved quickly out of his way. He could almost smell her feminine awareness of him.

Stepping into the darkness, he turned once more to her. "I've always been fond of pink ribbon, Molly." His velvet voice was a shadowy well of soft seduction, a promise of paradise beyond the simple words he spoke. "I particularly like the way it slides free from its knot."

His eyes burned with a fiery intensity, barely distinguishable in the glow from the fireplace. Every feminine cell in Molly's body urged her to take the few steps necessary to put herself into his arms. Common sense told her to step back, to deny the attraction.

"I can't," she whispered so softly she doubted he could hear her.

"You will," he replied firmly. "Never doubt that for a moment, Molly Royse. You will."

Chapter Eleven

In spite of the blistering late-afternoon heat, summer was nearly at an end. The breeze was cool and the air had lost its sweet, flowery fragrance of summer and was instead filled with the spicy, woodsy scent identifiable with autumn. Even the shadows had a different appearance, not quite as defined or as deep as the shadows cast by a summer sun, as if they, too, were preparing for the short, bitter days of winter.

Nightly, the temperatures dropped to near freezing, and every morning Molly expected to find the first frost of autumn. She knew that at any time the temperatures could turn cold. Already the trees were beginning to show some early signs of color change.

Molly pushed her damp hair back from her forehead as she stretched her aching back. One leg was braced at an awkward angle to prevent her from sliding off the uneven stump she sat on. She looked at the dismally small pile of ground corn in the bowl at her feet and tried not to feel discouraged when she compared it to the huge pile of the dried kernels still waiting.

Hawk had carved a concave slab of wood for her to grind the corn in—using the manner employed by the women of his tribe. A flat, fist-sized rock completed the mortar and pestle and a lot of elbow grease supplied by Molly eventually produced the meal. It had appeared easy when Hawk had showed her how to do it. Somehow, it wasn't quite as simple when she did it herself.

Her corn crop was too small to warrant the daylong journey to the grist mill. In fact, she would have to be diligent in her usage in order to make the corn meal last all winter.

The small amount of edible produce from Molly's garden had been dried, canned or ground. She hoped, with only herself to feed, that it would be enough until spring planting.

Hawk had dried or smoked some meat that would provide a welcome change for her when winter cold, and her own lack of skill, made it impossible for her to kill fresh meat.

Molly tipped the meal into the waiting bowl and added fresh corn. Sighing, she picked up the rock to begin the process all over again, but her attention was diverted from her task by the rhythmical sound of the ax biting into wood.

Utterly fascinated by a scene that should have become commonplace after this length of time, Molly watched spellbound as Hawk chopped a huge log into fireplace-length pieces. Later he would split each length into several smaller pieces that would burn better and be easier for her to handle.

His movements were a study of masculine grace as he chopped smoothly at the huge log. Legs spread for balance, Hawk lifted the ax above his head. Muscles bunched, rested suspended in a moment of time, then hardened like the finest steel as he brought the ax slamming down. Barely breaking pace when he finished with one piece, he kicked it out of his way as he moved down the log and began again.

Neatly stacked and split logs were piled just outside the door, nearly to the rooftop. Hawk was determined to double the size of the pile before he left.

Molly's breath caught at the back of her throat when she acknowledged what had yet to be spoken by either of them.

He was leaving.

He hadn't mentioned it in so many words, but for the last couple of weeks he had worked methodically at one project after another.

Explaining that she would have no need for the wagon and that the oxen would be an added burden to feed during the winter, he'd taken them into town and sold them. The money from their sale could be saved until spring when she could use it to buy a mule to help plow the garden or even pay one of her neighbors to turn the soil.

At his insistence, all of her supplies had been stored in several different containers. The corn she had already ground filled two bags and by evening she hoped to have the final one filled. Her precious supplies of salt, sugar and tea were divided into at least three boxes each.

Once again Hawk's reasoning could not be faulted. It was possible for something to happen to one box or even two, but she was almost assured of staving off starvation with her foodstuffs well divided.

Early that morning he'd looked at the woodpile and decided it wouldn't be enough if the coming winter should be severe. He'd been at it most of the day and the woodpile was nearly double its original size.

His thoughtfulness and hard work could mean the difference between life and death during the harsh winter months.

So, Molly thought to herself, she'd be warm and well fed, but what would keep loneliness at bay during the long winter nights? It deeply saddened her that she only thought of Adam at rare times now. When she pictured the long, endless nights, her thoughts were of Hawk and his comforting presence.

She clenched her teeth and lowered her suddenly watery gaze to the mortar. With fierce determination, she ground the corn.

He was leaving. She would stay here and make a home for herself. She'd be lonely, she reasoned, but hadn't she always been lonely? Her sisters had husbands and children to keep them busy while she'd had only a selfish, self-centered father to occupy her time.

Hawk had shown her the contentment two people could find sharing the necessary but tiring everyday chores. He'd given her satisfaction from a job well-done and laughter at her own human foibles. He'd given her a peace that she had never before known existed. And he was leaving soon to return to the life she'd briefly interrupted.

She'd always known he'd leave, but somehow she had managed to pretend that it wouldn't happen. It wasn't as if he was just abandoning her. Several times he'd offered to take her back to Charleston. He'd even suggested that she consider moving into Rutherford Town and making her home where she'd have close neighbors. When she'd refused all of his offers, insisting stubbornly that she'd stay in her cabin, he'd gone out of his way to visit with the Prices and inform them both of Adam's death and his own leaving.

Molly's thoughts were bleak as she finished grinding the corn and placing it securely in the canvas sack. Climbing wearily to her feet, she entered the cabin and hung the sack from a hook in the ceiling where it would be safe. A berry pie sat temptingly in the middle of the table but her bleak thoughts prevented her from eyeing it in anticipation.

The rhythmical sound of the ax provided a warming comfort as she prepared their evening meal. The chopping stopped just as she finished placing the food on the table, and Hawk entered the room at precisely the time she would have called him to come in.

The food was eaten in near silence. The one-room cabin now boasted a sturdy table, with two bench seats at one end of the room, and a rope bed at the other. Several hooks and shelves provided storage space for foodstuffs and clothing. It was as snug as a mud-chinked log cabin could be, with stout shutters for the window and a heavy plank for barring the door.

Molly was inordinately proud of the dirt-floored structure but as she sat at the table trying to force food past her constricted throat, she knew she'd scream if she didn't leave its confining walls.

Nausea threatened to overwhelm her best intentions. Without a word of explanation she slid off the bench and grabbed her cape as she opened the door and stepped outside. A nearly full moon provided ample light to guide her away from the cabin. She wrapped the wool cape tightly around her shoulders as a cool breeze drifted past.

She listened as the cabin door opened and closed. Her gaze turned toward the moon as she counted footsteps. She didn't turn when he stopped at her side, seeing him was not necessary. Knowing that her time was limited and memories would be all she'd have to keep of him, she'd already memorized every nuance of his face.

"You're leaving." It was a statement, and Molly was proud of the quiet, serene tone of her voice.

"Yes." Hawk could only admire the strength he read in her poised manner. He knew her well enough to know that what she was attempting to hide would bring a lesser woman to her knees in feminine tears.

192

TO GET YOUR
4 FREE BOOKS
MAIL THE COUPON BELOW.

FREE BOOK CERTIFICATE

GET 4 FREE BOOKS

Heartfire Romance

Yes! I want to subscribe to Zebra's HEARTFIRE HOME SUBSCRIPTION SERVICE. Please send me my 4 FREE books. Then each month I'll receive the four newest Heartfire Romances as soon as they are published. Free for ten days. If I decide to keep them I'll pay the special discounted price of just $3.50 each; a total of $14.00. This is a savings of $3.00 off the regular publishers price. There are no shipping, handling or other hidden charges. There is no minimum number of books to buy and I may cancel this subscription at any time. In any case the 4 FREE Books are mine to keep regardless.

NAME

ADDRESS

CITY   STATE   ZIP

TELEPHONE

SIGNATURE

(If under 18 parent or guardian must sign)
Terms and prices subject to change.
Orders subject to acceptance.

HF 109

GET 4 FREE BOOKS

HEARTFIRE HOME SUBSCRIPTION
SERVICE
P.O. BOX 5214
120 BRIGHTON ROAD
CLIFTON, NEW JERSEY 07015

"When?"

Since he hadn't decided on a definite day for his departure, Hawk hesitated briefly before he answered. He wondered if it would be easier for him to stay a few days longer or if he should make a clean, swift break and leave immediately. Either way wasn't going to be easy—for either of them.

"Tomorrow," he finally answered.

Molly's swift breath was audible in the silence that suddenly seemed almost overwhelming.

"So soon," she whispered. "I thought it might be longer."

"I can still take you back to Charleston, Molly," Hawk said quietly. "Or at least help you get settled in town."

"No, Hawk," Molly replied, quickly getting a firm grip on her wayward emotions. "This is my home. I may be making a grave error in judgement, but I intend to stay here."

Hawk forced himself to bite back his invitation to go with him. He could offer her nothing but the ridicule and contempt that many would feel it necessary to display if she were to link herself to an Indian. He had been raised white, was university-educated and well traveled but he could never change the fact that he was a full-blooded Shawnee Indian and many people looked at him with disgust and hatred because of it.

But she was the only woman he'd ever known that could make him regret, if only for a brief moment, that he was an Indian.

The moonlight brought a softness to the usually

angular planes of her face, accenting her button nose and a chin he knew could be exceptionally stubborn. He studied her face as an artist might study a subject, forgetting that he'd ever considered her too plain, too thin, too tall.

Molly shivered in the breeze that whispered of winter. Feeling as deep-down cold as winter, she pulled the cape tightly around her shoulders and buried her face in its warm folds.

"You're cold, Molly," Hawk said quietly. "It's been a long day for both of us. Let's go in and I'll help you clean up from supper."

Molly wanted to hold back time, to force it to stop its relentless march onward. Maybe if she didn't move, if she didn't clean up the dishes or comply with his suggestion, maybe time would stop. Snorting at her own imagination, Molly turned and headed for the cabin. Maybe pigs could fly, she thought sarcastically.

Hawk was leaving and nothing could change that.

Dishes were soon washed and stacked on their shelves. Molly tried to fight the knowledge that tomorrow night there would only be one place at the table instead of two; one cup, one plate, one fork. Somehow, the image of the single place setting was more depressing than the knowledge that she'd be the lone person using it.

"There should be more than enough feed and hay for the horse if you use it sparingly." Hawk knelt to add some wood to the fire. "On clear, warm days you can hitch him to a tree branch and let him graze on whatever's available."

"He'll be fine," Molly said firmly, using the damp towel in her hands she took another swipe at the already clean table. She wouldn't let him leave thinking she was helpless. "If necessary, I can always ride to town and buy some supplies."

He stood and turned his back to the fireplace. "When I stopped at the Prices', Gary said he'd come by occasionally to see if everything was all right."

"I'll be fine, Hawk," she reassured him. "I'm not the first woman to homestead alone. I know I'll make mistakes but I'll manage."

Hawk again bit back the invitation for her to accompany him. He grabbed his coat and rifle and opened the door. "I'll take a final look around before I turn in."

Molly watched him leave, knowing already that she'd miss the nightly routine that they'd established. Soon after dinner, Hawk would always leave for an hour or so to give her privacy to prepare for bed. When he'd return she'd be in bed, the blanket pulled to beneath her chin, waiting patiently for him. He'd check the fire that she'd already banked, and he'd put out the candles and come to her. Gathering her into his arms, Hawk would hold her and tell her stories of his past and the people who'd been a part of it.

Fearing that this night would be different, Molly waited for him to return. She expelled a silent sigh of relief as she watched him check the fire and blow out the candles. She went willingly into his arms as he sat on the edge of her bed.

Molly rubbed her face against the softness of his

shirt wanting to memorize the clean, smoky, masculine smell that was Hawk. So much to remember, she thought sadly, for so many lonely nights.

"Tell me about Linsey," she asked quietly, trying to maintain hold on her threatening tears.

Gathering her more firmly in his hold, Hawk leaned against the wall, his chin resting on the top of her head. He knew he'd also miss these quiet times they had come to share—as much as he'd miss her teasing smiles and rare displays of temper.

He'd miss her.

"Linsey is my mother," Hawk complied softly. "Bear says she's small enough to fit into his pocket but he knows she wouldn't stay there so he's never tried it. She's tiny and fiery and full of fun. She can cuss in Gaelic like a Scottish lord but she has no idea what she's saying and her singing is always a half key off. She has hair the color of autumn leaves and a temper to match, but she never yelled at any of us kids when we were bad or spanked us or sent us to our beds without supper. She didn't need to, she'd just give us one of her disappointed looks and we'd never again do whatever it was we had done to cause her displeasure.

"She'd romp in the snow or climb a tree or wade in the river but she is one of the most innately feminine women I've ever known. She adores Bear but is more than a match for his temper. I've never seen her show any fear of him. And believe me, when he is angry a wise man would back away, but not Linsey. She knows that he would cut off his own right arm before

196

he'd hurt her, even with words."

"You love her," Molly interrupted.

"With all my heart," Hawk confirmed. "She had raised me from the moment of my birth and I must have been five or six before I understood that I wasn't her son. Even though I had spent time with my father I didn't really understand the difference until a traveling missionary stopped at the house and bluntly asked who the little Indian brat belonged to." Hawk could smile now at the memory of the incident that had caused so much pain and confusion to the child he'd been.

"Linsey put her hands on her hips, drew herself up to her full five feet of height and claimed me as her oldest son. When she was done with that man he couldn't leave fast enough.

"Later that evening we had a long talk. I'd always known that my mother had died when I was born and I'd even felt guilty that I'd caused her death. Linsey explained in a way that a six-year-old could understand, that the only difference between me and the Cub was that God had given me to her a few months before he'd given her the Cub.

"I was, and am, as much her son as the seven sons she gave birth to."

"I think it's a good thing I'll never meet her," Molly said. "I'd probably be intimidated by someone that capable, that perfect."

Hawk's warm laugh filled the room. "She wouldn't let you feel anything even close to intimidation. And believe me, Linsey would be the first one to tell you she's far from perfect."

"You miss her."

"I miss them all." Hawk closed his eyes and thought of the brothers who had grown to manhood with him and the ones who had still been children when he'd left home. "It's been four years since I've been home, and letters have been few and far between."

"Do you have any Indian brothers," Molly asked, then squirmed with embarrassment when she realized she could have phrased the question better. "I mean, did your father remarry, or whatever, and have more children."

"Your question was all right the way you said it," Hawk chuckled. "And yes, I have one older brother, who is now known as Quiet Otter, even though Linsey insists on calling him by his childhood name of Chattering Squirrel. My father has married twice more and the last I heard I have four brothers and three sisters."

"How tragic that he's lost two wives," Molly stated.

"He's only lost one wife, my mother. His other two wives are perfectly healthy."

"Two wives!" Shock brought Molly away from Hawk's chest and she turned to look at him. "Are you telling me he's married to two women at the same time?"

A grin played across Hawk's noble features. "Molly, it's not uncommon for the warriors of my tribe to have more than one wife."

"That's . . . that's . . ." she stuttered, trying to describe her shock.

"Life is hard. It takes a lot of time to provide just the basic necessities of living. Two wives, or even three or four, make life simpler."

Leaning back against the security of his embrace, Molly tried to understand, but found it difficult. She had been raised in a society that practiced monogamy, anything else was incomprehensible. Suddenly a new thought had her sitting up and turning to look at him again.

"Do you plan to have more than one wife?" she asked in a voice filled with dismay.

Hawk looked at her shadowed eyes and knew they were a warm, honey color that could sparkle with mischief or anger. He studied her silky honey-colored hair and knew it shone golden in the sun and was as soft as anything he'd ever touched. His gaze moved to lips he had never tasted and he knew the answer to her question.

"Molly," he replied quietly, his deep voice velvet soft. "I'll never have even one wife. I can't have the one woman I want. I won't settle for anyone else."

"Why?" Her heart nearly stopped beating when she thought of some woman somewhere who had refused the love of this man.

"Why, what?"

"Why can't you have the woman you love? Doesn't she love you?"

Hawk pulled her back into his arms and softly nuzzled her hair with his chin. He resisted the urge to lift her face to his and cover her mouth with his own.

"Why?" she asked again, aware of his soft caress.

"She is white," he finally replied quietly. "And

I am Indian."

"I don't understand."

"I know . . . I know."

"What difference does that make? You are a fine man, any woman would be proud to call you husband."

Hawk closed his eyes as heat pounded through his blood. When had he fallen in love with her? He couldn't remember it happening. It seemed so natural, so right, as if it had always been.

He was tempted, so very tempted. Then, unexpectedly, the memory of that missionary so long ago vibrated through him and he found the strength to resist.

"A white woman would be condemned to ridicule, among other things, if she married an Indian. I won't put the woman I love through that."

"Have you given her a chance?" Molly wanted to find this unknown woman and make her suffer the agony she could hear in his voice. At the same time she was femininely pleased that he belonged to no one.

Hawk looked at the fire dancing in the fireplace and wondered if that flame could come close to matching the heat of his blood.

"She'll never know, sweet Molly. The decision is mine."

"But . . ."

Abruptly, Hawk slid her onto the mattress and stood. He pulled the quilt up to her chin and allowed the backs of his fingers to linger on her soft cheek.

"I won't let her be hurt by something I can prevent."

"Maybe you're causing a bigger hurt by not telling her."

"If I thought that were true, nothing could stop me." He gazed with longing into honey-gold eyes that held a promise he knew he'd never find again. "God help me, I love her."

Chapter Twelve

Molly opened her eyes and glanced around the cabin. The morning sun filtered through the cracks in the shutters dimly lighting the room. The fire was out, but it would come quickly to life once she dug through the ashes to the embers waiting beneath. The chilled air teased her nose and she pulled the quilt more tightly around her neck.

Somewhere outside a bird chirped cheerfully and she had an overwhelming desire to find it and wring its neck so that it could be as miserable as she was.

Sitting up, she wrapped the waiting cape around her shoulders, disgusted with her glum mood. This was the third morning since Hawk had left and she couldn't help wondering, if she felt this unhappy after only three days, what would she be like in a week?

Glad that she had worn her stockings to bed, Molly slipped her feet into her shoes and walked to the fireplace. Bringing the fire back to life took mere minutes and soon a roaring blaze was offering warmth and light.

She tried not to think about the morning, three days earlier, when she'd awakened to a similar blazing warmth. She had lingered in bed, hoping to delay the inevitable only to discover that it had already happened.

It had quickly become apparent to her that Hawk's things were gone. A simple note on a small sheet of paper had said it all.

"Aim carefully and you might hit your target. Plant after the last frost in spring. Watch for snakes and spiders in the woodpile." Hawk's unsigned note offered only one other thing. "It is better this way. Partings are never easy and I think this one would be harder than most."

She had wadded it up, thrown it into the fire and watched with satisfaction as it was consumed by the flames. Tears had flowed as it turned to ash.

Molly put water on to boil for coffee and began preparations for a breakfast she wouldn't eat. She dressed for a day that promised nothing but loneliness and she wondered when she would begin to accept what couldn't be changed.

She had mourned Adam's death, but each stage had offered its own healing. Hawk's leaving was worse than death. She knew the stages of mourning; first sorrow, then anger and finally acceptance. They would never heal the open wound his departure had caused. Death was final, irreversible. This felt like desertion, and Molly fluctuated between pity for herself and towering rage at him.

By midmorning, the sun had finally begun to warm the air. Molly left the cabin door open as she mixed the dough for a batch of biscuits. She was distracted from her chores by the sound of footsteps. The hopeful, expectant expression left her eyes, to be replaced by one of fear when she recognized her visitors.

Junior Wilson grinned evilly as his offensive odor fouled the sweet smell of the cabin. But Molly's fear was not caused by the bounty hunter. In fact, she was barely aware of him. Her eyes were glued to the thin, older man immediately behind him.

Hawk spent his first day on the trail determined to put as many miles between him and Molly as possible. He argued continuously with himself that leaving her was the only thing he could do. But somehow, no matter what defense he used, he never seemed to get close to winning the argument.

The morning of the second day, Hawk spent sitting by a fire. The argument continued. He was no longer confident that he was right. If Molly would indeed be safer and happier living without him, why was he starting to feel that he had abandoned her? By afternoon he was again in the saddle but this time his progress was minute.

Long before sunrise on the third morning, Hawk was heading back to her. He no longer knew or cared what was right; only that leaving her was wrong.

By midmorning he was less than a mile from the cabin. He stopped at the river and watched its never-ending flow. He was so close to her that if he breathed deeply he could detect the smell of smoke. And still the argument continued.

His reasons for leaving were still as valid as they had always been and he felt self-disgust at his inability to accomplish his decision to leave. Nathan Morning Hawk had never before been controlled by his emotions. And he was far from ecstatic to discover that he was as susceptible as any man.

He raised his head to the sky, his hands knotted in fists at his side. With a barely controlled violence, Hawk tore the white man's clothing from his body. He plunged into the cold water and scoured his skin and hair with sand from the bottom until every smell associated with civilization was washed away. His breath was coming in short gasps when he left the river and stood on its banks.

From his saddlebags, Hawk found the strip of cloth that formed a breech-clout. It rode low on his hips, exposing the raw power and strength of his masculine body. Hair blacker than a raven's wing hung without wave or curl onto his shoulders. Tying a band of red cloth low on his forehead, Hawk carefully placed sacred feathers behind his left ear and felt their reassuring touch on the side of his neck.

A necklace of sacred beads hung on his chest. The meaning of their special form of protection was known only to their wearer.

He was Shawnee. A warrior.

A tension began to build in him that had nothing to do with the coming confrontation with Molly. A feeling of dread, so compelling it caused him to shake, filled every cell of his body. Something was wrong, very wrong. He knew, as well as he knew his own name, that Molly was in danger.

He could have sworn that he heard her voice pleading with him to hurry, to save her from whatever threatened.

As he sprang onto his horse, he could only pray that he wouldn't be too late. He made a solemn vow that if he was, whoever had caused her pain would not live to see the sun set.

"Father," Molly greeted the older man with a slight nod, her chin raised with determination not to falter in his presence.

"Where be yore man?" Junior Wilson asked belligerently.

"I beg your pardon?" Molly replied.

"I'll handle this, Wilson," Charles Gallagher said firmly, never doubting for a moment that the inferior man would step out of the way.

"Think I'll take me a little looky-see around," Wilson muttered as he stepped out of the cabin. He didn't care for the way Charles Gallagher treated him, but the man's money made it acceptable; for now.

"Have a seat, Father. I'll fix you a cup of tea." Molly put the biscuit dough to the side of the table and lifted the heavy pot of hot water from its hook over the fire.

"This is far from a social call," Charles Gallagher

replied harshly. "I am extremely disappointed in you, Mary Helen. You have cost me a severe inconvenience, not to mention a vast amount of money. It will be some time before I will find it easy to accept your apology."

"I don't remember offering an apology, Father," Molly stated quietly. Her hand shook as she poured tea into the pot, giving the lie to her confident voice.

She jumped when his hand slammed down on the table, making her spill some of the boiling water onto the front of her dress. The heavy fabric protected her tender skin but she needed both hands to hold it away from her until it cooled.

"I have never allowed insolence from any of my daughters," he yelled as he walked around the table and grabbed her by both shoulders. "And by God, I do not to intend to start now!"

"Then I suggest you either treat me in a manner that does not cause caustic replies, or leave. The choice is yours."

His open-handed slap surprised her as much as did the savage snarl from the doorway. Before either of them knew that they were no longer alone, Molly felt herself being ripped out of her father's grasp.

There could be no doubt that he was a full-blooded Shawnee warrior. He was stripped to the waist, and his copper skin gleamed as it stretched over rippling muscles. Shoulder-length blue-black hair was held back from his face by a red band across his broad forehead. Two feathers, that she knew instinctively were from a hawk, came from behind his ear to rest on his shoulder.

If his body was impressive, his expression was terrifying. Savagery tightened every carved line. Black eyes held pure hate for the man who had dared to inflict pain on Molly.

She had never felt so safe.

"Hawk, please don't hurt him," she requested softly. "He's my father."

Hawk's snarl was not reassuring to the man who was being held by the compassionless warrior.

Looking at her reddening cheek, Hawk was tempted to teach the older man a lesson he'd never forget, but Molly's gentle pleading stayed his hand. He turned his gaze back to his captive.

"Never, ever," he stressed each word as he spoke it, "hurt her again."

"Hawk, behind you!" The fear in Molly's voice gave him all the warning he needed. Instinctively, he turned, using the older man as a shield. The bullet intended for his heart struck Charles Gallagher instead.

Seeing his error, Junior Wilson dropped his rifle and ran. Hawk lowered the older man to the floor, checked to see that he was still breathing, then headed after the assailant.

Molly knelt beside her father and attempted to stanch the flow of blood. The old man's eyes glared hatred at his daughter and he moaned in pain as she applied pressure to the wound.

Hawk quickly returned and examined the wound. The ball had entered and exited, leaving a clean injury. It would be painful for some time, but it wasn't life-threatening.

"Get your hands off me," Charles moaned, trying to roll away from Hawk.

Ignoring the order, Hawk made a thorough examination and applied pressure to the holes on both sides of the older man's shoulder. He used the salve Molly handed him, before he applied a bandage.

"You'll live," Hawk pronounced as he stood. "There's a stage stop just outside of Rutherford Town. I suggest you recuperate there. Take as much time as you need before you start the trip back to Charleston."

"And if I don't?"

"It's up to you." Hawk folded his arms across his naked chest and looked down at the older man. "Just make sure you stay away from Molly and this cabin."

"She is my daughter. I intend to take her home where she belongs."

"She belongs here."

Molly wanted to remind the two men that she was capable of making her own decisions, thank you very much, but Hawk's next words stopped her breath, as well as all thought.

"She belongs with me!"

"He's an Indian!" Charles Gallagher exclaimed, catching his daughter's attention.

Molly raised her chin, her eyes sparkling with anger. "He is a man, Father. He is university-educated and has traveled throughout Europe. He's dined with kings and danced with their daughters."

210

"That doesn't change what he is!"

"Thank God for that. If more men were like him there might be less greed and hatred in the world."

"If you stay with him you will cease to be my daughter. I'll disinherit you!"

Molly's eyes clouded with pain. "I will always be saddened by losing your love, Father, but that won't change my decision."

Rejecting help from either Molly or Hawk, Gallagher rose from the dirt floor. He stumbled as he made his way to the door.

"You'll regret this, girl, and come running home to me. Just remember to use the back door. Maybe if you beg and plead long enough I'll allow you to sleep in the stables." He stood for a moment longer at the door and eyed his daughter. "Don't bring any of his bastards home with you. I won't have a half-breed in my house. I'll take it to the market and sell it as a slave!"

Molly's breath caught at the bitterness in his voice. Pain filled her chest as she watched him stumble from the cabin.

Snarling beneath his breath, Hawk followed him outside. He watched as the old man pulled himself onto his horse. Hawk threw Junior Wilson's unconscious body onto his horse, tossed the reins at Gallagher and issued a final warning.

"I could easily kill you for the pain you've inflicted today, old man. I'd feel no regret or remorse. Don't look back when you ride out of here. She's mine and I won't let you hurt her again."

He slapped the horse on its rump and watched with satisfaction as Charles Gallagher had to fight to stay on the animal.

Hawk returned to the cabin, expecting to find Molly in tears. He was surprised to find her leaning against the table, quietly sipping a cup of tea.

"That is only a mild sample of the ridicule you'll face," Hawk stated as he stood just inside the door. His legs were spread for balance and his arms crossed over his chest just below the beaded necklace.

"I'd hardly call total rejection by one's own father, mild," Molly replied. She continued to drink the tea though she barely tasted it. She was torn between wanting to throw herself into his arms in tears because of his return or throw herself into his arms in tears because of the scene with her father. In either case, she wanted badly to cry. Almost as badly as she wanted to be in his arms.

"I am an Indian."

She drank in the sight of him. "Yes, but that's nothing new. You always have been."

"White man's clothing will not change me into anyone's idea of a civilized man."

"Thank God for that."

"I can be autocratic."

"Don't blame that on your Indian heritage!" she said with a snicker. "You can also be inflexible, obstinate and downright stubborn!"

"I will expect obedience."

"We'll discuss that at length later."

"Make your decision carefully. There will be

far too many years to regret if you choose incorrectly."

She raised her chin and he nearly smiled at her obstinate expression. "There will never be any regret."

"You will be my wife."

Molly felt tears well in her eyes. "Your only wife!"

"My only wife," he agreed quietly. "Come to me, sweet Molly."

She dropped the teacup and flew to his arms. Burying her face in the sweet-smelling skin at his neck, she let the tears flow.

"I was so lonely," she sniffed.

Hawk held her tightly. "Be very sure this is what you want, Molly. Don't let loneliness be the deciding factor."

"Loneliness was the deciding factor when I married Adam, but I never regretted that decision. And I won't regret this one. I need to be with you; to work and play, argue and tease."

Her cheeks were silvered from tears. She pulled away from him. "There is something you should know. Maybe it'll make you change your mind."

Reaching up to dry her face gently, Hawk shook his head. "There is nothing that could make me do that."

"I'm pregnant," she stated bluntly.

"I know."

Her expression of shock brought a smile to his face. "How could you know? I've only just started accepting the idea myself the last few weeks."

"You'll have to blame Linsey for that. The last month or so you've been acting differently and it confused me until I remembered how she acted at the early part of each pregnancy."

"Well I sure wish you'd told me!"

"Besides which, you are starting to expand."

Molly looked down to where her wet dress clung to her rounding stomach. "Can you be a father to Adam's child?" she asked quietly.

Hawk rested his hand on her stomach, gently caressing the slight swell. He had never touched her so intimately before and Molly felt her cheeks turn red with embarrassment.

"Adam was my friend. As Luc and Linsey accepted me as their son, so shall I accept this babe as my son."

"And if *he* is a *she?*" she asked, her eyes twinkling with mischief.

Hawk moaned as he bent slightly to rest his forehead against hers. "Don't do that to me, Molly. I know nothing about raising daughters. I would surely spoil her rotten and scalp any potential suitors by the time she is crawling."

"I'll try my best to see that it's a boy," she said seriously. "I don't think the neighbors would appreciate us if you were to start scalping their toddler sons."

Hawk nuzzled her nose briefly with his own, then he stepped away. "I tied my horse down by the stream. I need to get him and do a few other things, then we need to do some serious talking." He turned toward the door. "There are more decisions to be made, Molly. Some of them will probably bring you grief."

Admiring the sunlight reflecting on his skin, she watched as he disappeared out the door. She knew he was wrong, the only major decision had finally been made. As long as she was by his side nothing could cause her grief.

Chapter Thirteen

"When I went to town the other day to sell the team, I saw several families arriving," Hawk said quietly as he finished his meal.

"Aren't they getting here kind of late? They'll never get a cabin erected before it snows."

"They had some kind of trouble on the trail," he replied with a shrug. "Most of them will winter wherever they can and will start building and planting before the last snow has melted."

Molly chased the hominy stew around on her plate with a golden-brown biscuit. Once again dressed in his buckskins, Hawk had returned to the cabin after putting his horse out to graze. He had yet to mention her father or the decisions to be made but she began to feel that this was the beginning.

"What are you suggesting?" she asked, hoping to get the conversation started. The sooner started, the sooner finished, she decided, knowing that the decisions had already been made in his mind and she had only to agree with them.

Which didn't mean she had to agree readily, she decided.

"One of them might have the money to buy you out," he stated.

Giving up all pretense of eating, Molly pushed her plate away before sliding off the bench seat. She walked to the open door and leaned against the frame.

The first stars were beginning to glitter in the rapidly darkening sky. As the sun disappeared, the air quickly began to cool. Molly shivered and wrapped her arms around her waist. The decision to leave had already been made in her mind, but her heart ached at the thought of leaving the cabin.

In the short time she had lived in it, the cabin had become a home, a place of laughter and security. The stumps of many of the trees used in its building stood eerily in the growing darkness, waiting for their turn to be wrestled from the ground.

If she tried hard enough she could almost hear the sounds of the axes chopping rhythmically as the two men had brought down one giant tree after another. Their voices and masculine exhilaration were overpowered by the cracking thunder of the towering goliath as it gave up its life with an earth-shaking collision against the ground.

If she breathed deeply enough she could detect the rich aroma of the earth as it had smelled when it was plowed with the steel blade and exposed to the sunlight for the first time in eons. She could feel the weight and silky texture of the dirt that had provided sustenance for her first garden.

Memories piled one upon another in such rapid

succession that she had only a brief time to feel each; the laughter and tears, the joy and pain; the long, hard days, the even longer, lonely nights; the sweat of honest labor and the taste of rain on her tongue; burnt stew and sweet berries ripe from the bush; poison ivy, mosquito bites and love bites.

The memories came to a brief, bittersweet halt as the love she had felt for Adam floated gently around her. She knew now that it would always be there, her tender feelings for the man who had given her so much. But it no longer caused her pain to remember him.

Someday, when his child was old enough to understand, Molly would tell him of the man who had given him life. But by then the child would know another man as father, another man who would provide both love and protection.

Molly placed her open hand on her growing stomach and felt no guilt or remorse for admitting to herself that she had fallen in love with the man her child would call father.

Hawk watched her from his place at the table, knowing that it wouldn't be easy for her to leave this place. She had made it a home and he was aware of her attachment to it. He also reluctantly admitted to himself that it would be difficult for her to leave Adam, particularly with his child growing in her.

It struck him as ironic that the only woman he had ever wanted to claim for his own had first belonged to another man; another man who had happened to be his best friend.

"How long do you think it will take to sell this place?" Molly turned and walked back into the room, closing the door behind her.

"I can go into town tomorrow and ask around," Hawk replied. "If there's someone interested, it shouldn't take more than a day or two."

"A day or two," Molly whispered. "So quickly . . ."

"I can't stay here, Molly." Hawk stood and walked to her. "My home is to the north, in a place called Shawnee Town. I've been gone far too long."

"How long will it take us to get there?"

"Six, eight weeks, depending on the weather and how well you travel."

"I traveled here without problems," she defended herself.

"You rode a horse or in the wagon. We'll only be able to take the horses part of the way before the trail gets too rough. From there it's on foot or by canoe." Seeing the lingering sadness in her face, Hawk could no longer resist touching her. His fingers were gentle as he cradled her cheek.

"And you weren't pregnant then, Molly," he reminded her needlessly. "You carry a precious bundle beneath your heart. I won't do anything to endanger him."

Touched by his words, Molly rested her hand against his. "Do you care for my baby so much?"

"Our son." He lowered his hand to her stomach, lightly caressing the slight mound.

The decision wasn't difficult to make, she realized, as she said the words that would change the course of her life.

"Find a buyer, Hawk. But be sure it's someone who wants a furnished cabin. I don't think we'll be taking much with us on the backs of our horses."

He drew her into his arms, holding her with infinite care. "You won't regret your decision, sweet Molly. A whole bunch of loving people are just waiting to make you a part of their family."

Doubt, of a different kind, clouded her thoughts. "Maybe they won't like me," she mumbled, burying her face in his shirt.

Hawk's shout of laughter brought her face up. "Molly, they're going to be so delighted with you that you'll wonder why you ever worried. Linsey has said for years that I needed a good wife to keep me in line. And Kaleb will be rubbing his hands in glee that there is a new generation of babies he can spoil."

"What about your father? Your Indian father?" she asked.

"Limping Wolf will accept you and welcome you—if for no other reason—because you are my choice." He gently pushed the hair from her eyes, his hand remaining at the side of her head. "My people are little different from what you know of white families. They squabble with each other at times. They tease and argue and help each other. Their ways will seem strange to you, at first, but you'll quickly accept them as they'll quickly accept you."

Her honey eyes showed her apprehension even as she squared her shoulders. "And my baby? Will he accept my baby?"

"Our baby, Molly," he corrected firmly. "Our baby will be so spoiled by all of his grandparents that we may have to move to Canada to keep him away from them."

221

"Too cold." Molly smiled as she pulled away from him.

"Then we'll just have to give them a bunch of babies to spoil so that no single child gets all of the attention."

Molly's breath caught in her throat at the thought of conceiving Hawk's child.

"Would you like that, sweet Molly?" His voice deepened and his eyes burned with question. "Would you have my children?"

He slowly pulled her toward him until she rested lightly against his chest. His head lowered until she could feel his warm breath on her face.

"Can I plant my seed in the warmth of your body and watch you swell with my child? Will you let me feel him as he moves in the crowded space of your body? Does the thought of having my baby, a half-breed child, disgust you or thrill you?"

"Hawk . . ." Mesmerized by his voice, as well as by the thought of his children, Molly had to struggle to speak in a whisper and then all she could say was his name.

It may not have been an invitation, but Hawk chose to take it as such. His eyes gleamed with earthy sensuality as his mouth closed over hers.

It was delicious, like the first soft breeze of spring. It was sweet, berries and cream on a warm summer day. It was distant thunder warning of a building storm. It was over far too soon but a moment too late. Molly began to crave more just as his mouth lifted from hers.

Slowly, slowly, Hawk reminded himself. His friends at the university had told him that ladies did not like any form of sex and submitted because it was a wifely duty. They had advised him to visit the women in taverns if he wanted to satisfy his needs.

Even though Hawk had met several ladies who had proven his friends wrong, he was concerned that Molly might have definite ideas about such intimacies. He was determined to take it slowly, to teach her the pleasures of her own body and of his.

He gritted his teeth as desire speared through him. Because of her pregnancy he realized it might be several months before he shared her bed. He studied the look in her eyes and knew he could wait. Gentle caresses and soft kisses could be liberally, and frequently, given to shorten the waiting and strengthen the desire.

Molly wondered why Hawk had drawn away so quickly. With the experience of a married woman, in spite of the short duration of the marriage, she knew what to expect. And the thought of sharing that with him made her toes twitch.

Deciding she might have to encourage him, Molly smiled softly and turned away. She couldn't believe that the intimidating warrior was bashful about sharing a bed, but her eyes didn't lie. It would be fun to be the teacher, she decided, instead of the student. She had no doubt that with a few lessons Hawk would quickly catch on.

Molly paced the limited confines of the cabin, waiting impatiently. In a corner, piled neatly in small bundles, were the things she had decided were necessary to take on their trip.

After he had returned from town yesterday, Hawk had gone through the stack, pleased to note that she had selected carefully. It was a pitifully, small bundle, but he had assured her that everything they would need to set up housekeeping was waiting in Shawnee Town.

Molly hated to appear like a beggar, without even the smallest household item, but right at this moment her concerns were centered on something else.

Hawk had ridden into town early the previous morning and he had returned well before dark. He had found a family who were very interested in buying the land and cabin. They had just arrived in Rutherford Town and were afraid that their late arrival would prevent them from settling in before winter.

Hawk had given them directions on finding the cabin and now Molly paced impatiently, waiting for them to come and look over her home and decide if it was good enough for them.

The rattling of wagon wheels just outside the door alerted her to the arrival of her guests, and Molly carefully smoothed her hair into place and tried to shake some of the wrinkles from her dress as she approached the door. She tried to remind herself that it didn't matter if they liked her or not, it was the cabin and land they had come to see.

Opening the door, Molly was greeted by the couple and their five children. Abel and Mabel Harris climbed from the wagon and walked to the door. Wondering where Hawk had disappeared to, Molly was forced to introduce herself.

"Yore hired hand told us yore place were fer sale," Abel said in way of greeting. "Done told Ma that I ain't sure but what we've wasted our time, him bein' an Injun and all. Never did trust me no Injuns."

Molly felt the first flash of anger begin to simmer at the man's attitude. "Yes, Mr. Harris, my place is for sale. Mr. Hawk made the trip to town on my behalf and I assure you, I trust Mr. Hawk beyond all else."

Mabel Harris walked into the room and her nose immediately elevated several degrees. "Why, there ain't no floor. Why, I've never . . ."

"Sure you have, Ma," Abel interrupted. "The cabin back in 'Ginie din't have no floor either."

If looks could kill, Abel would have been withering in agony on the floor from the scathing look his wife sent his way. Noting that he ignored the look, Molly tried to smother her own escalating temper.

"Our home in Virginia was temporary," Mabel explained needlessly to Molly. "I intend for this move to be permanent and I ain't livin' in no cabin without a floor."

"With winter breathin' down yore neck, you'd better be happy with a roof over yore head!" Abel commented firmly. "A floor ain't gonna do you no good iffen yore freeze yore unders off."

"Really!" Mabel exclaimed in an appalled voice, her hand placed dramatically over her chest.

"You be excusin' my wife, ma'am," Abel said with disgust. "She met a real lady on the trip out here and now she's athinkin' she's better than ever'body else. Kinda embarrassin' but she's the ma of them kids out there in the wagon and I guess I'll just have to live with her til she gets this bee outta her bonnet."

He looked at his wife as if daring her to make another comment. "Now, by my way of thinkin' y'all done a lot of work gettin' this place ready fer winter. I seed there ain't no barn fer the animals?"

His tone of voice was halfway between a statement and a question, and Molly chose to answer with an explanation. "We ran out of time, Mr. Harris. The barn was the next thing to be built, but my husband was killed before the cabin was finished and Mr. Hawk completed the work mostly by himself."

"He done a good job."

"You poor thing," Mabel murmured sympathetically. "Now you'll be returning to your family."

"Well, actually, I'm . . ."

"Ain't none of yore business, Ma," Abel interrupted.

"Certainly it is!"

"Ain't!"

"I'm not going back to my family!" Molly interrupted before the argument could get out of hand.

"Then just what will you be adoin'?" Mabel asked, her nose tuned for juicy gossip she could pass on to her new neighbors once they were settled.

"Ma, I'm awarnin' ya, mine yore own business."

"I'll be traveling north with Mr. Hawk."

"Yore goin' into the wilderness with an Injun?" Abel asked before his wife had a chance. "Now, ma'am, I cain't be lettin you do such a thing."

"Yore right, Pa. She'll live here with us 'til we can

find her a nice, upstanding man to marry."

"You have got to be kidding," Molly muttered but she was ignored by the two people who had suddenly invaded her life.

"It'll be tight, but we can squeeze a bed in fer her in the corner near the fireplace. That way she can keep it going at night when it's really cold. And she can help me with the young'uns when she ain't doing the wash or cooking."

"I can use her help fer plantin' come spring," Abel replied, nodding his head in agreement with everything his wife said. "Well, it's settled then, we'll move in here and she can stay until we find her a husband. Get the young'uns off their butts. Tell 'em to start unloadin' the wagon."

"Wait a minute," Molly said firmly as they moved toward the door. "Don't hurry to unload that wagon. Nothing is settled."

"Why, dear, I know yore upset with the passin' of yore husband," Mabel said kindly. "Don't you worry about a thing, we're here now and we'll take good care of you."

"Listen very carefully," Molly replied, carefully enunciating each word as she fought a valiant battle with her temper. "This place is for sale. I do not now nor will I ever, intend to live here with you. I will not cook, wash and tend your children while you search for a husband for me. I do not need a husband!"

"Why course you do, deary." Mabel moved toward Molly as if intending to take the younger woman into her embrace. "I know you are heartbroken by the death of your husband, but we'll open our home to you for a while."

Molly backed away from the woman. "If you aren't interested in buying my cabin and land then I'll have to ask you to leave."

"Yore tellin' us to git?" Abel asked with bewilderment. "Woman, you must be outta yore mind iffen you think yore goin' to go off with an Injun!"

Unseen by the three combatants, Hawk slipped silently inside the door. He stood with his arms folded across his powerful chest and listened. His expression became forbiddingly severe as he began to understand the argument, but he noticed with pride that Molly wasn't giving an inch to the meddlesome couple.

"Mr. Harris, it is none of your business what I do or do not do." Molly narrowed her eyes at the two. "Are you interested in buying or not."

"Just how long has it been since your husband died?" Mabel asked bluntly.

"My husband was killed less than a month after we moved here, approximately five months ago." Molly waited, knowing exactly what was coming next.

"You mean you been living alone since then?"

"I have not been alone."

The implication was not lost on the two people. Mabel stuttered, Abel muttered and Molly waited. It was a short wait.

"You've lived here, in sin, with that Injun!"

"It's indecent. I thought you were a grieving widow!"

"That Indian," Molly stated firmly, "is a full-blooded Shawnee with more generosity in his little finger than both of you have in your whole bodies.

228

He is honest to a fault, caring about others and will go out of his way to help a friend. Without him I wouldn't have this cabin or the food in it. He cared for me without asking for reward when my husband died. He not only knows the true meaning of friendship but practices it.

"Before too much longer he will be my husband." She placed her hand on her stomach and knew a moment too great to resist. "He will be the father of my child." She patted her tummy so that they couldn't mistake her meaning.

"Wicked!" Mabel said, scandalized to the bottoms of her feet, but making a mental note of everything that had been said. This was too good to take a chance on forgetting any of it. Surely her new neighbors would be appalled when they heard the truth. And she firmly intended to make sure they heard the truth.

Molly finally looked up and saw Hawk at the door. Never before had his look been quite as intimidating, but she could have sworn that she saw humor dancing in his black eyes.

"I am sorry that I can no longer help you. I find that I must lie down and rest. A woman in my condition tires easily. Now, if you're still interested in buying my place, you will have to discuss it with Mr. Hawk." She nodded in his direction and noticed Mabel's face whiten. "He is not my hired hand. He is, however, my solicitor and has full power to make any arrangements necessary to transfer the title into your hands."

Molly turned her back on the couple and listened to their mutterings as they made their way out of the cabin. She sat on the edge of the bed and rested her head against the wall. True to her words, she did feel exhausted but she knew that her pregnancy had nothing to do with it. She wondered how anyone could be so unfairly prejudiced against someone simply because of his race.

She closed her eyes and gave in to the fatigue. She could hear Hawk's deep voice through the open door but made no attempt to understand his words. She knew he was well able to handle the situation. She unknowingly slid into a light sleep as the sound of his voice eased her tension.

"Molly." Hawk gently stroked the soft skin of her neck and studied the smooth lines of her face. He had felt an anger greater than any he'd ever known, when he'd listened to the Harris's degradation of her. He knew now exactly how savage he could become. Whenever Molly was threatened in any way, he all too easily reverted to the brutality of his ancestors.

"Are they gone?" Molly open her eyes to gaze sleepily into his.

"No, they're going to spend the night camped in the pasture."

"Small-minded, stupid dimwits," she murmured as she stood and stretched.

Hawk bit back a grin. "They aren't too pleased with us spending another night here but I told them you needed a good night's sleep and we'd be leaving at first light."

"Oughta go take a bath in the stream just to watch the shocked look on their faces!" She unhooked a sack of corn meal and slammed it onto the table.

"Wanted me to be their maid while they sat back and did nothing." Unsatisfied by the thump of the bag, she grabbed a bowl and slammed it down.

Hawk waited to see if the clay bowl broke from her rough handling. A smile lingered in his eyes as he watched her work out her anger.

"She can sleep by the fire," Molly mimicked as she looked for something else to slam around. "This place is sadly lacking in drawers!"

"Drawers? Why do you need a drawer?"

"So that I can slam it! When I get mad I like to slam drawers or doors or anything that makes a good, loud bang!"

"I'll remember that." Hawk let the smile slide from his eyes to his mouth. "If you start slamming things around I'll know that you're mad."

"I'd appreciate something to slam!"

"I'll make sure there are several doors, drawers and window shutters available."

"They're idiots," Molly stated, changing the subject.

Hawk lost all signs of humor. "You'll face many people like that if you become my wife, sweet Molly. They profess to be good Christians but most don't practice what they preach." He folded his arms across his chest, his face stern and intimidating. "They will make your life hell because you have an Indian husband and half-breed children."

Molly placed her hands on her hips and matched him expression for expression. "If they don't like it then they can go suck skunkweed!"

Chapter Fourteen

The breeze was a softly whispered melody drifting through the trees. It offered a sweet invitation to linger awhile, to decipher the mysteries of nature readily revealed in its song to anyone willing to listen. Leaves, some still green, others showing red, orange or vibrant yellow, quivered with a mellow crinkling rustle.

On a hill beneath the trees, within sight and sound of the gently rippling stream, the lovingly carved wooden cross showed signs of weathering. Someday, after time and the elements had been at work, it would no longer be there to mark the solitary grave.

Molly knelt and spoke quietly to the gentle memory of the man who had brought her to this place. With only a small amount of guilt she accepted the knowledge that, without her staying to tend the grave, time would soon eliminate all traces of the man buried there.

She rested her hand against her growing stomach.

She would never forget the man with the laughing blue eyes and gentle smile. She would have the most precious gift he could have left her, his child. Behind her, the noise of the Harris family as they took possession of their new home, vividly reminded her that she no longer belonged here.

She belonged with Hawk. To Hawk.

Whispering a final farewell, Molly stood and turned to face her future. Hawk's black gaze burned with understanding as he offered his hand.

He would be gentle, she thought, but only when it suited him. His laugh, indeed his smile, would be so rare that each would be a gift to treasure. He would expect absolute trust. He would demand unwavering loyalty.

He could give arrogance a new meaning, she decided as she watched his eyes narrow. She thought of his ability to intimidate with a look, his boldness, his self-assurance that bordered on insolence.

She remembered his compassionate gentleness when she had been so lost and bewildered that she didn't know which way to turn, the days when he had forced her to work through her grief, the nights when he'd held her to keep away the nightmares.

He would not be an easy man to live with—or to love. But he would never desert her or abuse her trust. He would protect her and provide a safety she had never felt before in her life. And he would love her child as his own.

And she loved him. She hadn't intended it to happen. In fact, had she been asked, she would have said she could never love a man like him. But that was before he had allowed her to see the man he really was.

She knew there were many things about him she still didn't know, but she trusted him above all else. Time would show her anything else that might be important for her to know, but it could never change the trust he had gained by his actions.

Chin up, shoulders squared, Molly met him more than halfway. The decision was made. Her life was now intertwined with his. She reached out until her hand rested in his.

"Be very sure, *nèe èe kwài wàh,*" he said firmly. "There will be no turning back."

"I am sure, Hawk." Molly's confident voice confirmed her decision. She walked to her horse and waited for him to help her to mount. "When can I start learning Shawnee?" she asked with a small grin. "I want to know what you're calling me."

"Nèe èe kwài wàh, my woman." With the ease of a strong man, Hawk lifted her onto the saddle. He had insisted that she ride astride and that she wear trousers, decisions that Molly accepted without argument.

Adam's trousers, altered for her shorter legs, fit snugly around her waist. They felt strange but she already enjoyed the freedom they allowed. She wondered if they would fit at all by the time they finished their journey. Every day the baby seemed to make his presence better known by adding inches to her middle.

Hawk mounted his horse and turned toward the north. Even though he had insisted on keeping their supplies to the minimun, the reins to a packhorse were tied to his saddle. This early in the journey the trail was wide enough for a wagon, making it possible for Molly to ride by his side. Later on they'd have to go single file, at times walking the horses through narrow passes.

"So," she asked, resisting the urge to look back at the cabin one final time before it was out of sight. "Where are we headed?"

"Home."

The arduous journey over the mountains was made easier because of the horses but it was still a long, tiring venture. Hawk allowed Molly to have plenty of time to rest during each day, stopping as soon as he saw any sign of fatigue. He knew it would add time to their trip but he estimated that they would still reach their destination long before the first snow. He hoped, after a few days on the trail, that she would be able to ride for longer stretches of time.

Each night, when they made camp, he insisted that she gather wood for the fire. She was unaware that the chore had been specifically assigned to her for the sole purpose of helping her muscles to stretch. Uncomplaining, Molly gathered several armloads of wood, moving easier by the time the chore was finished.

As long as the nights stayed clear, Hawk didn't bother to put up any kind of shelter. He had a large oilcloth tied to the packhorse that he had brought just for the times when it rained. For himself, he could have found adequate shelter to wait out a storm. But Molly needed the protection the cloth would provide.

Molly had thought it would be difficult for her to sleep on the trail. But she had forgotten to allow not only for her condition but also for the unaccustomed exercise.

Each night, as soon as the evening meal was dispensed with, she snuggled down on the bed Hawk had made for her. Two separate beds, side by side. He held her until she slept, chanting the familiar, wordless tune.

She never knew when he eased her from his shoulder, gently tucking the quilt beneath her chin. She didn't see him slip from his own bed, every instinct alert, as he scouted the area around their camp. It never entered her mind that he slept so lightly that even the slightest change in sound would bring him fully awake and alert to danger.

She was protected and secure.

Hawk headed almost due north toward the eastern Tennessee town of Jonesborough. A friend from university days, John Childers, was from the area. He was the son of a Presbyterian minister, and Hawk hoped to enlist John's help in persuading his father to perform a marriage ceremony.

Most people frowned on marriages between an Indian and a white person. In some places such unions were actually illegal. But Hawk had met the Reverend Childers several times and knew the man was accepting of his Indian heritage. He just hoped

237

he would be as accepting when Hawk presented Molly to him and made his request.

By midmorning of the fourth day, they came to the home of William and Barsheba Cobb. The farm, called Rocky Mount because of the huge rocks at the front of the house, was a two-story log cabin with several outbuildings. Slaves and indentured servants kept the former home of territorial Governor William Blount in perfect condition.

"It's lovely," Molly exclaimed as they approached the house.

Hawk reined his horse to a stop and waited for her to come up beside him. He studied her with such intensity that Molly had to fight the urge to fidget.

"I intend to make a short stop here and then go on to Jonesborough," he finally stated. "This is your last chance to avoid a life that might bring you more pain than happiness."

"Are you trying to avoid marrying me?" Molly asked, anger burning in her gaze.

"Our marriage will never be easy. It will cause you to be ridiculed by some and scorned by others."

"Our marriage will be made more difficult because you can't resist reminding me exactly how difficult it will be! If people don't like it that's their problem. I will not live my life to the satisfaction of someone else's irrational hostility. If I had intended to live by someone else's plan I would have remained in Charlestown at the beck and call of my father.

"If you don't want to marry me, fine. But that is the only reason I want to hear, *not* that it will be difficult!"

"Molly Royse, remind me not to anger you and then turn my back," Hawk said, a noticeable smile creasing the corners of his mouth. "You might decide that a little physical retribution is warranted."

"Turning your back won't be necessary!"

"Are you implying that you'd attack face-to-face?" His full-blown smile showed exactly how humorous he found the entire idea.

"That is exactly what I'm saying!" Fighting an overwhelming desire to swoon at the awesome virility revealed by that smile, Molly turned her horse toward the house and hoped she wouldn't make a fool of herself before she could regain her composure. Perhaps it was a good thing that he seldom smiled. She wasn't sure she could stand frequent displays of such magnitude.

Since visitors were usually few and far between in the wilderness, and they were welcomed simply as a break from the monotony of the everyday routine, Molly didn't fear rejection when their presence was noticed by a small child in the front yard.

She soon discovered that Barsheba Cobb was an amiable and gracious hostess who totally ignored Molly's unsuitable attire. Even though she did not know Hawk personally, she did know Luc and therefore welcomed members of Luc's family into her home.

The main room, laughingly called Mrs. Cobb's sewing room by their hostess, was comfortably furnished with all the modern conveniences of a house situated in town. They had obviously interrupted Mrs. Cobb's work on a colorful quilt that was stretched on a frame and hung from the rafters.

The pattern was unlike any Molly had seen before and she longed to question her, but Mrs. Cobb, a midwife of considerable talent, quickly noticed Molly's condition and insisted that she rest for an hour or so before the noon meal.

"This really isn't necessary," Molly commented as she followed Mrs. Cobb up the narrow stairs to the second floor.

"Certainly it is!" Leading Molly into one of the two bedrooms, Mrs. Cobb folded back the quilt from the bed. "You rest for a short while and I'll have one of the girls wake you in time for you to bathe before we dine. Once you're rested you'll feel more the thing and we can share some harmless gossip!"

"You have a lovely home," Molly said as she sat on the edge of the bed to remove her shoes.

"Why, thank you, dear." Mrs. Cobb helped Molly to remove her outer clothing. "Mr. Cobb has provided well for me. He has even brought in a necessary chair." She pointed to a large, square chair in the far corner of the room. "It is such a pleasure not to have to visit the outside convenience in the winter time. I'm afraid I am in danger of being spoiled!"

Molly was more interested in the bed than in the chair as she stretched out and sighed with pleasure. The rope bed with its straw-filled mattress felt heavenly after her nights on the hard ground. She gave a brief thought to Hawk and wondered what he was doing, then she fell into a deep sleep.

Molly was awakened by the lilting Irish voice of a young girl. Lilliann was an indentured servant, who said she had only a few months left and then she'd be free. She was cheerful and good-natured as she assisted Molly.

The visit was over too quickly for Molly. Mr. Cobb, busy with the last of the harvesting, had not returned for the noon meal. She enjoyed being around the gracious Mrs. Cobb and she prayed that Linsey would be as welcoming.

Mrs. Cobb invited them to stay for several days but Hawk insisted that they leave when the meal was finished. He explained that he wanted to travel the fifteen miles to Jonesborough before dark.

"Would you like to sleep in a bed tonight?" Hawk asked as they rode toward Jonesborough.

"I didn't realize how much I missed a bed until this afternoon," Molly replied. "I think I could have slept for a week!"

"We don't have time for a week, but there is a way station outside of Jonesborough. We'll get a room for tonight and you can sleep late in the morning while I go into town and try to locate John." He had explained to her earlier that he hoped John's father would agree to marry them.

Heaven must be to sleep in a real bed the night before your wedding, Molly decided, glad she didn't have to confess which prospect filled her with more anticipation.

*   *   *

"We don't 'llow Injuns or their—"

"Don't say it." Hawk's voice was made more threatening by its very softness.

The innkeeper wisely swallowed back the rest of his comment and squirmed beneath Hawk's penetrating stare. His eyes drifted to the rifle held confidently over Hawk's arm.

"As I was saying, I need a room for the lady, for the night."

"We don't take Injuns," the man insisted, in spite of his fear.

"I require only one room. It will be for the lady." Hawk bit back the need to wrap his hands around the man's throat and squeeze. It was because he had feared this exact type of reaction that he had insisted that Molly stay outside with the horses.

"She'll hafta share. I only got three rooms and they're filled."

"She can share . . . with another lady." The man motioned toward two ladies sitting across the room and Hawk nodded approval. It wasn't unusual for strangers to share sleeping quarters, in fact he would have been surprised had she had a room to herself. But he wanted to be assured that the other women were ladies of quality, not river trash looking to make money with their bodies or by going through someone else's things.

"I'll bring her inside in a minute," Hawk stated in the same quiet voice. "But first you can give me directions to the Reverend Childers."

"What you be wantin' with him? Reverend Childers is a good man who won't accept any trail-trash Injun."

Hawk's level stare forced the man into silence. "His direction?"

Stumbling in his haste, the innkeeper gave Hawk detailed instructions for finding the Childerses' residence.

"I will be back for Mrs. Royce in the morning," Hawk informed the man. "I might even stop in later this evening to assure myself that she is all right. Believe me when I tell you that you will pray for death before I'm finished with you if she should suffer any type of indignity caused by your prejudices against my people."

"Just make sure people see you leave. I'd have no business left if they thought I was rentin' to an Injun."

Hawk spent the night in the woods at the back of the inn within sight and sound of Molly's window. He was relieved when the residents of the inn settled down for the night, making it easier for him to hear any noise from the only room that held his interest.

He thought of his reception at various hotels in the larger cities back east. There had been natural curiosity but he was welcomed as freely as the next man. His Indian heritage had been a thing of interest to most people rather than a thing of repugnance.

The further they traveled into the wilderness, the more lacking the hospitality. It was easy for him to decide to avoid as many towns as possible. Travel would be difficult enough for Molly in her delicate condition, she didn't need proof that her decision to marry him had been a mistake.

Hawk sat on the ground and leaned back against a tree. He, far better than Molly, knew that the marriage was a mistake that shouldn't happen. He knew he could take her to Shawnee Town and leave her with Linsey. Someday she would understand and thank him for taking the wiser course.

But he wanted her as he had never wanted anything in his life. He needed her gentleness and humor, her tenderness and faith. He wanted to be the reason she smiled, the reason she laughed. He ached to walk with her hand-in-hand into the forest and never return to civilization. He wanted to show her the ways of his people. He needed to show her the gentle side of himself that few people even knew existed.

He wanted to fold her into his arms and never let her go. Now he understood why Bear protected Linsey with a fierceness that was astounding. Hawk felt the same way about Molly.

He had never applied the word *love* to any emotions he'd felt for any of the women he'd dallied with in his past. He'd felt liking, friendship, even lust, but the gentler emotion of love had always been lacking.

Until Molly. She had wiggled her way into his heart simply by being herself. Liking had grown to fondness; fondness had become love.

Hawk stared at the darkened window and urged himself, for her sake, to get up and leave.

Love kept him firmly seated beneath the giant elm.

Sunlight streamed into the open window as Molly snuggled beneath the blanket. The inn was small and she had been forced to share with another lady and her maid. The lady, a Mrs. Fitzmyar, shared the bed with Molly while the maid slept on a pallet in front of the door. They had left at daybreak but Molly had easily drifted back to sleep, oblivious to the noises made around the bustling inn.

She watched the dust motes drift through the sunlight and wondered where Hawk had spent the night. He had explained that the inn was full but that he wouldn't have trouble finding some place for himself. A firm rap on the door interrupted her thoughts and brought her fully awake.

"Mrs. Royse," the innkeeper shouted through the door. "I'm 'spose to give you a message that Mr. Hawk will be downstairs in an hour to escort you into town."

"Thank you, sir," Molly called back. "I'll be ready when he arrives."

Reluctance to leave the bed vied with impatience to start the day that would see her as Hawk's wife before it was finished. She climbed from the bed and poured fresh water into the bowl on the washstand. A bath would have been delightful but she made do with a thorough scrubbing with the last of her bar of soap.

Refusing to wear trousers for her wedding, Molly

shook the wrinkles from a dress she had packed for the occasion. Sitting down on the rickety stool at the dressing table, she stared at her reflection in a poorly silvered mirror. As she pulled the brush through her tangled hair, her eyes came to rest on the gold band on her left hand.

Molly stopped and stared at the ring. She remembered the pleasure she had felt when Adam had placed it there. She thought of the hours she had spent sitting on the hard seat of the wagon, watching it catch the sunlight.

Lowering her arms, Molly turned the ring around and around on her slender finger. The innocent young bride had grown up cruelly fast when her husband had died in her arms. In her place was a woman who was stronger and more self-assured. A woman who knew that life had to be lived for the moment—tomorrow might never come.

Molly had learned to grab at happiness before it could slip through her fingers. Marriage to Hawk, with all of its inherent problems, was the right thing for her to do.

She loved him. Nothing could change that. And somehow they would find a way past the problems as they rose.

Slowly, reverently, Molly slid the simple gold band from her finger. She clutched it in her hand before laying it on the dressing table. She stared at it as her fingers mechanically braided her long hair and wrapped the braids around her head. It stayed within her sight as she slid the dress over her head.

A multitude of buttons closed the front of the

simple gown but she soon found that they would not close. She stared with disbelief at the inch of space left between the buttons and buttonholes at her waist and breasts. She had worn the dress only a couple of weeks earlier and it had been snug but it had fit. Now the dress was simply too small.

Reluctantly, Molly pulled out the clean shirt and trousers from her bag. She wadded the dress up and shoved it into the bottom of the bag along with her dirty clothes. She muttered about the impropriety of wearing trousers in general and to a wedding in particular as she hurriedly dressed.

A harsh voice at the door informed her of Hawk's arrival. She tried to smooth some of the wrinkles from the shirt as she gathered together her belongings. Hoping that the Reverend Childers would find it in his nature to overlook her dishevelled appearance, Molly picked up her bag and walked to the door.

On the dressing table, the golden band caught the morning light and sparkled with a rich luster. A symbol of what had been momentarily forgotten in the excitement of what would be.

"Look at me," Molly said to Hawk as she walked down the stairs. "I've never heard of a bride getting married in trousers and a wrinkled shirt!"

Hawk barely noticed her clothing. He was entranced with her sparkling eyes and rosy cheeks.

"You are beautiful," he replied quietly.

"Beautiful?" Molly chuckled and shook her head.

"You must have spent the night standing on your head if you can look at me and say I'm beautiful." She handed her bag to him. "Look at this shirt, it hangs nearly to my knees and there isn't room for even one more wrinkle. And my hair is badly in need of a good scrubbing. And trousers—"

"I see the glow of motherhood," Hawk interrupted her, his deep voice soft so that it didn't carry beyond her hearing. "I want to reach out and catch the joy that surrounds you. I long to place my head against your belly and hear the life within you."

Molly's breath caught at the unspoken hunger blazing in his dark eyes. A blush climbed up her cheeks when she silently acknowledged that she was eagerly anticipating their wedding night. She couldn't lie to herself by denying her fascination with the masculine perfection of Hawk's body.

"If you haven't changed your mind, let's go get married, Molly."

"I haven't changed my mind," she answered firmly.

"Ahxk wài la teè wai thùk a tai," he said softly, his dark eyes alive with emotion as he traced the angles and slopes of her face.

"Which means?"

His gaze moved from the gentle curve of her cheek to sear into her own. "To love is to burn." His voice was suddenly harsh from the repressed emotion.

"Do you burn, Hawk?" A shiver of excitement raced down her spine.

She didn't think he was going to answer as he

reached for her elbow and escorted her out of the inn. Their horses were tied to the hitching post and she waited patiently as he secured her bag to the packhorse. He turned, placed his hands at her waist and lifted her to the saddle. Holding her in place, sitting on the saddle rather than straddling it, Hawk's grip tightened until it was just short of painful.

"I burn, *aín jel eè,* I burn."

Chapter Fifteen

Self-conscious in her highly unorthodox clothing, Molly smiled shyly when Hawk introduced her to John Childers and his parents. Mrs. Childers's censorious expression belied her cordial greeting, but Molly didn't know if it was caused by her trousers or by the man at her side or maybe both. Hawk was doing his best at the role of an intimidating Indian, and Molly longed to kick him.

John and his father, the Reverend Childers, made up for any lack of friendliness on Mrs. Childers's part. John in particular seemed delighted to meet Molly.

"Are you sure you want to marry this blackguard, Miss Royse?" John asked with a grin. When Hawk had introduced her, he had neglected to give her status as a widow and Molly didn't feel inclined to correct the misimpression.

"Is there something I should know about him?" she asked, liking his irrepressible humor and friendliness.

"Miss Royse, I have been an intimate of Mr. Hawk's for an extended length of time. Please believe me when I say that it would take years for me to give you the details of his escapades." He lowered his voice to a conspiratorial whisper, his eyes twinkling. "And those are only the ones acceptable to a lady's ears. I'm afraid I'm too much of a gentleman to give you details of his more raunchy exploits."

"Call me Molly, please," she invited as she waved her hand dramatically beneath her nose. "I fear that I must take my chances with him, since I don't have years to spend listening to your discourse on his character."

"John, please remember that you are no longer twelve years old," Reverend Childers said firmly, but the same twinkle in his son's eyes was evident in his own as he turned to his wife. "Katherine, please take Miss Royse upstairs and help her to prepare for the ceremony. Mr. Hawk has expressed his desire to continue on his journey as quickly as possible."

Molly regretfully followed Mrs. Childers up the steep stairs. She remembered the warm reception she had received from Mrs. Cobb the day before and couldn't help but compare it to the coldness of her current hostess.

"You may use this room to change." Mrs. Childers opened the door to what was obviously a guest room. Sparsely furnished, the room had an air of disuse. "I'll have one of the girls bring you a pitcher of water."

"I will appreciate the water, Mrs. Childers, but I'm afraid I'll be wearing my trousers for the wedding." Disgusted by her attitude, Molly deliberately pulled her shirt snugly against her stomach. "Nothing else fits and I just don't know what I'll do when these trousers become too tight."

She lowered her voice to a conspiratorial whisper. "Hawk has so many . . . ah, needs, that he leaves me little time for domestic necessities such as sewing an adequate wardrobe."

If possible, Mrs. Childers's nose rose even further in the air. "I was going to discuss this marriage with you and possibly try to dissuade you from your chosen course but I see that it is entirely too late. So be it, you will suffer the consequences of your misguided decision for the rest of your life, young woman. Marriage to a heathen will be hell on earth; may God have pity on your soul for your sins."

Disbelief at the woman's attitude mingled with satisfaction, successfully keeping Molly tongue-tied until long after the door had closed behind Mrs. Childers.

"Meddling old biddy!" Molly fumed as she attempted to straighten her hair. "Always looking for the worst in someone and ready to believe any gossip that comes along. How someone like her can have such a delightful husband and son I'll never know!"

She was still muttering definitely unladylike comments several minutes later when she descended the stairs and found the three men in the parlor. Mrs. Childers was nowhere to be seen nor had the promised pitcher of water appeared.

"Please forgive my wife's absence, Molly," Reverend Childers began.

"There is no reason to apologize for your wife, Reverend." Molly kept a firm hold on her temper but it sparkled in her eyes. "She was eloquent in stating her position on my marriage to Hawk."

The older man took Molly's hands into his own. "Katherine's seemingly irrational behavior is based on a devastating experience from her past. As I have just explained to Hawk, who is generous enough to forgive her, Katherine was just a small child when she witnessed the annihilation of her family at the brutal hands of the Iroquois. She is normally a generous and loving woman but she can't overcome her ingrained fear and hatred of Indians."

"I am sorry for her past, sir," Molly stated firmly, "but to condemn an entire race of people because of the actions of a few of its members in not a Christian attitude."

Hawk walked up to Molly and, placing his hands on her stiff shoulders, turned her face to him. "If you marry me it will be this way the rest of your life, Molly."

"If you tell me that one more time, Nathan Morning Hawk," she snarled between gritted teeth, "then so help me God, I'm still going to marry you but I'll make your life miserable for the rest of mine. I'll whine and cry and do anything I can think of to make you remember that statement!"

A smile played at the corners of his mouth. "Is that a threat, *aín jel eè?*"

"No, Hawk, that is a promise!"

"Whoa! I think you've met your match, Hawk ole buddy," John interrupted with a chuckle.

"You should see her when she really gets worked

up," Hawk replied, his gaze never leaving Molly.

"Something worth seeing, huh?"

"Stunning!"

"If you two are finished testing fate, and the lady's justifiable anger at your teasing, I suggest we get on with the ceremony," Reverend Childers commented. "I fear that if you continue to push your luck, Miss Royse may decide to show you an example of her temper."

"Wise suggestion, Reverend." Molly knew the two men were simply teasing her but her frayed temper couldn't tolerate too many more of their comments.

Wanting to soothe her, Hawk pulled Molly into his embrace, his hand lightly rubbing her back. He buried his face in the sweet softness of her hair and closed his eyes. Somehow, someway, he would protect her from the abuse their marriage was destined to attract. He never wanted to face the day when he'd see regret in her eyes.

Molly rested her cheek against his shoulder and let the steady beat of his heart calm her frayed poise. Here was strength to conquer any adversary, intelligence to overcome any obstacle. His gentleness and compassion would be her sanctuary. She found security in his arms and maybe, if she was very, very lucky, someday she would find love there, too.

"Anytime you're ready." Reverend Childers cleared his throat, uncomfortable with the display of affection in his parlor.

"Looks like he's ready to me," John said softly.

Hawk opened his eyes and speared his friend with

a look that could kill—had John been less knowledgeable of Hawk's personality.

With John as their witness, Molly and Hawk became husband and wife. Her voice was clear and firm when she promised to love, honor and obey, but she noticed his eyebrow raise when she repeated the last word.

Molly's breath caught audibly when he slipped the ring onto her finger. It was as different from the gold band she had removed earlier as night is from day. The wide band was a blue-black braid, tightly woven from strands of Hawk's hair.

"I didn't remember until late last night that I didn't have a ring for you. I will replace it with something more appropriate later."

"No you won't," Molly's eyes expressed her delight in the unusual ring. "There isn't a ring anywhere in the world more appropriate."

Hawk lifted her hand and kissed the finger that wore his band. "It won't last forever as a band of gold will."

"Then you'll just have to make me another one." Molly looked at his thick, black hair. "I trust you aren't planning on going bald?"

"Gray, maybe."

"After years together, I think a ring with gray in it will be appropriate."

"I have a feeling, Mary Helen Hawk, that you will be directly responsible for more than a few of those future gray hairs."

"If we may continue?" Reverend Childers interrupted.

"Of course."

"With the giving of this ring and the pledging of these vows, so you have committed to living as husband and wife. By the power vested in me by God and the sovereign state of Tennessee, I hearby pronounce you man and wife." Reverend Childers's eyes twinkled merrily. "You may kiss your bride, Mr. Hawk."

"Neè wàh, my wife," Hawk murmured as he raised her head with a hand beneath her chin. His lips were soft and warm as they closed over Molly's. The kiss was over nearly before it started but not before Molly's breath became erratic and a tremble settled in her legs.

Hawk's black eyes were unreadable when he lifted his head and gazed into hers. He had felt her trembling and she wanted to reassure him that it wasn't from fear, but her suddenly dry throat prevented the passage of words.

"This is an occasion that deserves celebration!" John's smile was sincere as he clasped Hawk's hand and patted his friend on the back.

"Celebration will have to wait. We've still got most of the day available to us. We can travel many miles in those hours." Hawk watched Molly to see her reaction.

Smiling shyly, she agreed with him. She was anxious to put miles between them and the animosity of their hostess.

"But surely you can spend one night with us?" John protested, his gregarious nature needing little reason for a party.

Molly watched as the Reverend Childers fought a silent battle, caught between the friendship of his

257

son and the hostility of his wife. She wanted to reassure him that nothing on earth would prevent them from leaving, that she would do anything to save Hawk from facing Mrs. Childers again. She didn't want her wedding day further marred by the ugliness of hate.

"I think it would better serve everyone involved if we were to leave immediately," Hawk replied firmly. "Your mother's feelings are justified and I dislike making anyone feel ill-at-ease in their own home."

She saw relief pass Reverend Childers's face as he offered to show Hawk to the stables around back of the house. After assuring his host that he was capable of finding the barn, Hawk left the room.

Molly sipped impatiently at the glass of wine John had insisted she have as she waited for Hawk to bring their horses around to the front of the house. Reverend Childers nervously cleared his throat several times, attempting to say something.

"Just say whatever it is that's bothering you, sir," she finally encouraged.

"Perhaps it is better left unsaid," he replied. "After all, the ceremony is completed, you are now his wife."

"Yes, Reverend, I am his wife," she agreed quietly.

"Yes . . . well, . . . what I mean is, I feel that since you don't have a father to advise you, it behooves me to offer my home to you should it ever become necessary for you to . . . ah . . ."

"Reverend, Nathan Morning Hawk is a Shawnee warrior," she stated firmly. "He is also one of the most scrupulously honorable men I have ever known. My husband was killed several months ago and

Hawk stayed with me to help complete the construction of my home and to help me settle in the area. Not once in all the months we lived and worked side-by-side have I been concerned for my safety; either physically or morally.

"In fact, his very presence reassured me that I was safe, safe from white men who have no honor or morals, the very same men who are accepted by our society merely because they are white."

She placed her glass on a side table and turned toward him. "Hawk is not the father of my baby, but he insisted on our marriage so that my child would know a father. I know it is his intention to see me settled in Shawnee Town with his white family. I expect he plans to see that we lack for nothing."

Her voice lowered with promise. "It's my intention to see that Hawk honors his marriage vows. He will be my husband and I will follow wherever he goes. And I'll fight anyone who tries to separate us."

"Forgive me, my dear, for the interference of an old man."

"There is nothing to forgive, Reverend. Your concern was honorable, if somewhat misguided."

Rev. Childers took her hand in his. "It is my wish that my son may someday find a woman who will love him as you love Hawk." His smile was sincere with warmth. "Go with God, my child. Ask for His guidance when troubles seem to overwhelm you. Remember that He is always there."

Her hand was still in his when Hawk entered the room. Ebony eyes narrowed in speculation.

"Are you ready to leave?" he asked.

"Yes." There was no hesitation in her voice or her

eyes when she looked at him. "Let's head for home, Hawk."

In a matter of minutes they were once more in the saddle heading in a northwesterly direction. Jonesborough was quickly left behind and they were again surrounded by massive trees and abundant undergrowth.

"So, where are we headed?" Molly asked, when the silence between them had grown as thick as the leaves on the trees.

Since the trail allowed them room, Hawk reined in his horse slightly so that they were riding side by side.

"Ever heard of a man named Daniel Boone?"

"Good heavens," she exclaimed with exasperation. "Who hasn't? But I do find it hard to believe some of the things I've heard!"

Hawk smiled. "You can believe most of it."

"Do you know him?"

"Never had the privilege, but Bear and Kaleb can tell you some stories that'll make your hair curl. Last I heard of him he was still alive but had moved west. He has to be pretty old by now so he might even have died."

"I've always wanted curly hair."

He ignored her. "Boone is said to have *discovered* a trail through the western Virginia mountains."

"You sound skeptical. Did he discover it or not?"

"The path he found is now called the Wilderness Road but it's been used for centuries by the Indians. They called it the Warrior's Path, for obvious reasons."

"Battles?" Molly guessed accurately.

260

Hawk nodded and continued to explain. "Northern tribes traveled south for trading or raiding, southern tribes traveled north for the same purpose. In 1750 a Virginian named Dr. Thomas Walker did some surveying for the Loyal Land Company of England and documented the path. He named the area through the mountains, the Cumberland Gap.

"Then about twenty-five years later Boone came along with six or seven others and they marked and cleared the path from the Tennessee border to Boonesborough, which is about two hundred miles north into Kentucky."

"Which just happened to be named after Mr. Boone, of course," Molly added.

"Are you going to listen to the story or tell it?" Hawk asked with mock annoyance.

"I'm sorry," she replied. "Please continue, I'm all ears . . . except for my eyes . . . and nose . . . and—"

"Does wine always affect you this way?"

Molly giggled. "It's either that glass of wine or getting married. I just feel like I want to throw my arms up in the air and dance with the wind."

Hawk smiled indulgently. "Please don't let me stop you."

"No, I'll behave, please continue your story."

"Not much more to tell. They say that upwards of three hundred thousand settlers have used the Wilderness Road to move west."

"That's a lot of people looking for a better life," she replied seriously.

"Most of them found it. It's beautiful land, Molly." Hawk thought of the area he had always known as home. "It's rich land, with gently rolling hills. There's plenty of water and game."

"Then I'll be happy there, too."

Hawk's dark gaze studied the young woman who had become his wife. "You'll be happy there, Molly. But it's still a long trip before we're home."

"But we're headed in the right direction . . . I assume . . ."

Hawk smiled at her light-hearted mood. "I haven't gotten you lost yet, have I?"

"Couldn't prove that by me, Oh great Shawnee warrior! I've been lost since we left the cabin."

"Guess you'll just have to trust me then."

Suddenly her mood changed. "I do, Hawk. Not only with my life but with the life of my child."

Hawk grabbed the reins of her horse and pulled it to a halt beside his own.

"Our child Molly. From this point on that baby is as much mine as it is yours."

Her heart melting with joy, she nodded in agreement. "Our child, Hawk."

Molly looked for something around the campsite to throw or slam. She regretted the loss of the huge highboy dresser in her bedroom in Charleston. The drawers gave such a satisfyingly resounding bang when she'd slam them shut to relieve anger. Right now she'd willingly travel the several hundred miles back to Charleston just to have the opportunity to slam a drawer.

Finding nothing in their few possessions that worked sufficiently, she attempted to stamp her feet as she moved from one spot to another. Even that failed because of the heavy ground cover of newly fallen autumn leaves.

As if unaware of her anger, Hawk saddled the horses in preparation of their departure. All that remained to be done was to clean up from their breakfast . . . and to discover the exact reason for Molly's bad mood.

"We'll enter the gap by midafternoon," Hawk said quietly as he began to load the packhorse.

"Well goody for us!" Molly muttered just loud enough for him to hear.

Resting an arm across the broad back of the animal, Hawk turned and looked at his wife of three days.

"You want to tell me what's wrong or do I get to spend the morning trying to guess? I think I should warn you that my patience with temper tantrums is extremely limited."

"Poor you, having to put up with me," Molly mocked. "Why don"t you just tell me which direction to take and then you can ride off by yourself and you won't have to worry about my temper!"

Hawk's audible sigh filled the sudden silence. "I'm not going anywhere, with or without you, until you tell me what's wrong."

"Nothing's wrong!" Molly turned and grabbed her bedding. Rolling it tightly, she tied it with the hide thongs and threw it toward him.

Hawk nimbly caught the bedroll and secured it to the horse. He quickly gathered up the remaining items and tied them into place. As was his custom, he walked to where Molly waited beside her horse for his help in mounting.

Putting his hands at the side of her waist, Hawk held her in place. His dark eyes sparkled with determination and she knew he would hold her there until he found out what he wanted to know, even if it took all day.

"All right, Mrs. Hawk, what's wrong?"

"Mrs. Hawk? Really?" she scoffed. "I certainly don't feel like Mrs. Hawk."

His eyes narrowed with suspicion. "Explain!"

"Why should I explain anything to you?" Molly attempted to pull free from his grasp but he only held her tighter.

"Molly?"

"I should think it would be very clear to you."

"Well think again."

The intimidating look she had grown to know so well months earlier turned his countenance to granite, but it no longer filled her with terror.

"Well if you don't know I'm sure not going to tell you!"

"Molly!"

Suddenly, tears clouded her honey eyes and she leaned her forehead against his chest.

"Just put it down to my condition," she mumbled, trying to wipe the tears from her cheeks.

"Not good enough, Molly." Hawk gathered her closely against him and rubbed his chin against the top of her head. "Tell me what's troubling you."

Embarrassed by her uncharacteristic outburst, Molly hoped Hawk would tire of waiting for her answer and suggest that they get on their way. After long minutes when he continued silently to hold her, she knew she had no choice but to explain.

"Am I really your wife?" she finally asked.

"That's a dumb question, Molly."

"Is it?" She pulled as far away from him as he would allow and stared into his dark eyes. "We've been married for three days. If I'm really your wife then why do I sleep alone each night?"

Color darkened her cheeks, but Molly refused to lower her gaze from his. Hawk suddenly released her and stepped back.

"You can't answer that, can you, Hawk?" she asked quietly. "Or is it won't? Perhaps you won't answer."

"Are you ready to leave now?"

Without waiting for a reply, Hawk grabbed her waist and gently lifted her onto the horse. He handed the reins to her before mounting his own animal.

"Why, Hawk?" Molly insisted quietly before he could ride away. "Why can't I be your wife?"

"You are my wife!"

"No, I'm not. A wife shares her husband's bed."

A nerve jumped erratically at his jaw. "We won't discuss this now, Molly."

"We will discuss this now! Why, Hawk? Just tell me why!"

He looked at her, his gaze filled with longing, anger and determination. "If the marriage is not consummated then it can be terminated with little problem."

An equal determination filled Molly's gaze. She pulled her horse away from him.

"And how will you prove that it wasn't consummated, Nathan Morning Hawk? This marriage will not be terminated until one of us is dead." She moved the horse further away. "And if you continue to use the excuse that you're an Indian and I'm white then your death may be a lot sooner than God originally planned because I'll be tempted to do it myself!"

Chapter Sixteen

The well-traveled Wilderness Trail wound through valleys of breathtaking beauty, with mountain slopes towering into the clouds. Enormous trees, dressed in their best autumn colors, provided shade from the sun in the late afternoon and protection from the cold breeze of early morning.

In places the trees were so thick Molly began to feel oppressed by their abundance. Just when she thought she'd give anything for the sight of the sun, the trail curved and the trees thinned out to reveal a meadow or mountain clearing.

But even breathtaking beauty can become commonplace, and after three days of mountains, valleys and awe-inspiring vistas, Molly began to long for wide-open spaces. And solitude.

Rather than being isolated, as Molly had assumed she and Hawk would be on the trail, they were rarely alone. Looking back at the wagon that currently followed their path, she shook her head with disgust. Another night of a shared evening meal, life histories around a campfire and Hawk sleeping three feet away from her.

Most of the travelers accepted Hawk without question, but in the faces of a few she had read suspicion whenever they looked at his ruggedly sculptured face, and speculation when they looked at her rounding belly. They were always eager, however, to eat from the game he regularly provided each night.

"Tired?" Hawk's quietly asked question interrupted her less-than-pleasant thoughts.

"Of mountains and trees and people," she replied.

At his gentle smile, Molly suddenly felt guilty for her sharpness. "I'm sorry, blame it on my condition." She smiled hesitantly. "I guess I've been a poor traveling companion."

"On the contrary, *Aín jel eè*, I can't think of anyone I'd rather be with right now."

He pulled his horse to the side of the trail and motioned for her to do the same. Hawk signaled for the wagon to go on without them and they waited patiently for it to pass before he turned and started backtracking.

"I hate to be the one to point this out to a mighty warrior, but we've just come this way," Molly said with her usual impish grin.

Satisfied with the return of her good humor, but aware of the deep fatigue betrayed by the grayness beneath her eyes, Hawk continued back down the trail.

Within a short time he turned off the main path onto one that Molly had overlooked earlier. The new path, so overgrown it was barely visible, soon began a steady climb up the side of the mountain.

The horses did all of the work, but Molly had to readjust her position frequently to allow for the angle of ascent, and she soon noticed a nagging pain in her back.

"Is this going to be a short side trip?" she mumbled grimly after what seemed like hours of climbing.

"Just a little further, *Neè wàh,*" Hawk promised.

"*Neè wàh?* What's that mean? And that thing you called me just before we started this new trail. What was that?"

"*Aín jel eè* is angel," Hawk replied, his deep velvety voice a soothing sound in the quiet.

"Angel," Molly smiled softly. "I was acting like a spoiled brat being denied a sugar candy and you called me angel."

"You were acting like a woman who is carrying a precious gift within her body and desperately needs to rest."

"Not desperately enough to excuse rudeness."

"I have traveled with you for hundreds of miles, from the shores of Charleston," he reminded her needlessly. "I know that you don't usually complain about anything, always accepting things with a smile. I think we can allow for the babe you carry within your body and overlook an occasional bad mood."

"Complaining never did get me anything but I really am tired, Hawk."

"It has been a long trip, *neè wàh,* with many more long days ahead of us, but it should get a little easier once we clear the mountains."

"*Neè wàh?*"

Hawk's dark eyes deepened with intensity. "My wife."

A tingling awareness rippled through her body. "How do I say 'my husband'?" she asked in a husky whisper.

"*Wài see yah.*"

"*Wài see yah,*" she repeated softly. "My husband."

Molly began to feel light-headed as her gaze remained caught by the enigmatic expression on his usually unreadable features.

As if he had come to some decision known only to himself, Hawk suddenly turned his horse and brought it up alongside hers. When only inches separated the two animals, Hawk reached over to cup the back of her head.

"*Neè wàh,* my wife," he said quietly as he lowered his head to hers.

His lips were soft and firm, the kiss as gentle and tender as a new spring day. His hold on the back of her head was so light that Molly knew she could pull away with little or no effort. It never entered her mind to resist.

He raised his head until his face was the only thing filling her vision. "I will protect you for the rest of my life, *neè wàh.* At times you may not understand or accept a decision I've made concerning you or the child. You might grow to hate me, but your tears and recriminations will not change my mind. Words spoken in anger will not turn me from my chosen way. If you trust me then you must trust my decisions."

Releasing her, Hawk again turned his horse and

270

headed it up the trail. Reeling from the unexpected gentleness of his kiss, Molly automatically began to follow him.

Her thoughts were a mass of confusion as she tried to understand his puzzling actions. Any other wife could safely assume that her husband was reassuring her but Molly knew better. There had been something in his eyes that forced her to believe that he had made a promise—one she wouldn't be happy with. It was a long time later before the discomfort that had been overcome by the caress again tormented her exhausted body.

"How much longer, *wài see yah,* before I can get off the back of this horse and feel the ground beneath my feet?"

Molly arched her back to stretch her aching muscles, unaware of the way her shirt tightened across her breasts. Hawk's gaze was captured by the action as the buttons threatened to pull loose from the holes. His attempt to ignore the way her breasts had enlarged with her pregnancy was thwarted as he watched her unintentional display.

"Just a little further," Hawk finally replied, tearing his eyes away from her. "There is something I want you to see, and, if you're a good girl, there may even be a special surprise waiting for you."

"I'm always a good girl. So what's the surprise."

Hawk turned his horse back toward the trail. "It won't be a surprise if I tell you."

"But if you tell me then I'll know exactly how good I want to be." Reluctantly, Molly fell in behind him. "I mean, if it's something extra special then you'll be amazed at how good I can be."

"And if it's only a little special?" Hawk asked with a chuckle.

"Then I only have to be a little bit good. Why waste all that effort to be extra special good if the surprise is only a little bit good?"

Hawk's rich laugh floated on the breeze and Molly was surprised at her own reaction to it. She longed to ask him to turn around and face her so that she could see his humor reflected on his face.

"You'll just have to wait, *màh chee mun ết o.*"

"What's that mean?"

"There isn't a direct translation. It roughly means little devil."

"Oh, so now I'm a devil!" Molly smiled at his broad back. "How can I be an angel one minute and a devil the next?"

"I admit that would be a problem for most people, but you seem to have an unique ability denied to most of us."

"And which do you prefer, *wài see yah?*" For some reason this silly, uncharacteristic chatter was making her forget the fatigue that had seemed so overwhelming just minutes earlier.

"I prefer them all, sweet Molly." Hawk's voice had lost its teasing sound and she wished even more that she could see his face. "I want you in all of your moods, be they happy or sad, tired or teasing."

"If you want me, then why haven't you made me yours?" she asked solemnly.

No reply came from her suddenly quiet companion. Only the clip-clopping of the horses' hooves broke the stillness. As the silence continued, the aches and pains—the small discomforts—again

272

descended to plague her as she followed him up the mountain trail.

"Hawk, I'm giving serious thought to being bad." Molly tried to keep her voice light as she lost the battle with exhaustion. "And it'll be all your fault if I don't get my surprise."

Hawk stopped his horse and motioned for her to join him. "Listen closely. What do you hear?"

Molly tried to detect a strange sound, but everything sounded the same as it had during most of the afternoon.

"I give up, what do I hear?"

"Woman, we're going to have to work on your trail sense."

"Later, after I've had my surprise. Now what am I supposed to hear?"

"You tell me."

Molly strained to identify the sounds around her. "I hear the wind in the trees and the birds singing."

"Very good, but what else?"

"The horses breathing, my stomach growling with hunger and," Molly stopped, a surprised look crossing her face. "A roar?"

As she listened, she realized that vaguely audible in the distance was a distinct sound reminiscent of never-ending thunder, but the sky overhead was a clear, crystalline blue with no evidence of forth-coming rain.

"It should still be warm enough for you to have a long leisurely bath," Hawk commented.

"A bath? A real sit-down-scrub-up-water-everywhere bath?" Molly's eyes sparkled with delight.

"As long as you don't object to bathing in a river with a waterfall."

"Right now I wouldn't object to bathing in a bucket beneath a pump as long as it's big enough to get my whole body into!"

"I think this'll be big enough." Hawk grinned at her, the smile crinkling the corners of his eyes and showing his strong, white teeth.

"Let's get to it." Her smile matched his. "My bath is waiting and I've been *soooo* good!"

The sound of the waterfall grew steadily louder as they approached the river. Molly sighed with delighted pleasure as the trail brought them to within sight of the cascades.

It was not a particularly large waterfall, but its beauty was in the surrounding trees and the huge slab of rock both above and below the falls that allowed easy access to the river.

"Is it named?"

"It's had many names. My people used this land for centuries and it was once known as Shawnee River Falls. The white map-makers have called it Falls of the Cumberland after the Duke of Cumberland in England. I have heard reference to the fact that the crookedness of the river greatly resembled the Duke's own character.

"The locals, however, have the most romantic name for it. They call it the Moonbow Falls."

"Moonbow? Don't you mean rainbow?"

"Just wait," he replied mysteriously. "You'll have to see it for yourself."

"I'll wait for just about anything if I can take a

bath first," Molly responded. "Even supper!"

Hawk set up camp on a grassy meadow a comfortable distance from the river while Molly hunted through her bags for clean clothes and a drying cloth. Unlike some waterfalls where the roar of the water is so loud that ordinary conversation must be spoken in a raised voice, the Moonbow Falls provided a comforting sound in the background that allowed for normal speaking voices.

When she was ready, Molly walked toward the river, wondering where she could find the best place for her bath. Alert, as always, for any sign of danger, Hawk followed her.

Putting a hand on her shoulder, he stopped her when she reached the rocky slab. He pointed slightly upriver, above the falls.

"There're some rocks there that will provide privacy but there are few trees, so you'll have plenty of sun for warmth."

Molly walked to his chosen place and set her clothing on a narrow ledge of one of the boulders.

Hawk carefully studied the area to reassure himself that she would be reasonably safe. Boulders jutting into the river slowed it to a gentle flow, enough to allow the water to wash away the natural debris but not enough for him to worry that she would be swept over the falls.

"Don't wade out too far or you might be caught in the current," he cautioned, needlessly.

"I won't," she replied impatiently. "Now go away so that I can bathe."

"The water will be pretty chilly," he warned.

"I realize that! Go away, please!"

"I'll be within sound of your voice so scream if you need me."

"I appreciate that, but now that I know what my surprise is I don't need to be good any longer and if you don't go away so that I can enjoy it, Nathan Morning Hawk, I have a feeling that I'll become very, very bad!"

"That might prove to be very interesting," Hawk teased.

"Hawk!"

With a grin, he turned away. "This isn't your surprise *màh chee mun ét o.*"

"It isn't?" Molly stopped unlacing her leather shoes. "Then what's my surprise?"

"You'll see," he replied mysteriously as he headed back to camp.

Her natural curiosity was temporarily waylaid by the overwhelming desire to wash away the days' accumulation of trail dust. She nearly tore the clothing from her body in her excitement to get into the river.

The clear, blue water was chilly but Molly decided even a warm bath in a tub wouldn't have felt as good, as she lowered her aching body into the river. With the water swirling just beneath her breasts, she repeatedly soaped her hair, dipping briefly beneath the surface to remove the lather.

When her hair squeaked between her fingers, she began to wash her body. She sighed with pleasure as she attempted to rub some of the soreness from her arms and shoulders. Hanging onto the reins as the horse had climbed the side of the mountain had required constant vigilance and the use of muscles unaccustomed to such exercise.

Her soapy hands lowered to her breasts and she was pleased that they no longer ached as they had earlier in her pregnancy. Their new fullness seemed strange to her and she tried to ignore the budding of their peaks in response to her innocent touch.

She softly caressed her rounded stomach, her thoughts turning to the child cradled within. For several days, the first time on the day she became Hawk's wife, she had felt a gentle flutter that already seemed to be growing stronger in its intensity and frequency. She had longed to share the knowledge with Hawk and had waited for the right time to do so, but that time had never come. Perhaps tonight she would find the right time to tell him and soon he, too, would be able to feel the movements within her body.

Her movements slow and dreamy, in spite of the cool water, Molly finished her bath. Wading from the river, she stood at the edge drying with the bath sheet and relishing the warmth of the late afternoon sun. Already the air was hinting at the chill that would come as the sun lowered in the sky, but for now it was warm enough for her to linger in her task.

Wrapping the bath sheet around her body, Molly sat on a convenient rock and scrubbed at her dirty clothes. Wringing the moisture out, she spread them to dry, pleased that she would have something fresh to wear later in the week. Men's pants and shirts were unbelievably comfortable but she missed the feel of a skirt around her ankles. She knew it would be many weeks before she would be able to wear her dresses, and by then they would be a poor fit across her swollen stomach, but she would be relieved to see the last of trousers and shirts.

Her leisurely movements became more rapid when she began to detect the delectable odors drifting on the breeze. After pulling on her trousers and buttoning up her shirt, Molly grabbed her shoes and the bath sheet and walked toward camp. She wrung water out of her long hair as she walked, enjoying the feel of the grass beneath her bare feet.

Unaware of the fetching picture she presented with her pink cheeks and bare feet, Molly smiled sweetly when she approached Hawk.

Squatting beside the fire to check on the cooking food, Hawk was all too aware of the enticing femininity of her presence. He breathed deeply, enjoying the flowery scent of the soap lingering on her skin and hair. He watched as she sat on a quilt he had spread out for her and as she attempted to untangle her hair.

She was serene, tranquil and so female that the male in him threatened to overtake his iron-fisted control.

"I have never had anything feel so good!" Molly sighed as she pulled a brush through her hair.

You have never felt me touching you, Hawk thought to himself, fighting the urge to speak aloud.

"That water felt like satin."

My touch would be a feather stroking your skin.

"If it hadn't been a little chilly I'd still be in there."

There would be nothing but heat when I touched you.

"And that water tasted nearly as good as it felt."

Nothing could compare with the taste of you,

278

Hawk thought feverishly, his desire running rampant through his body. *I would taste and touch and sample until neither of us knew where you began and I ended.*

Molly stopped and stared at the profile he presented to her. "You're awfully quiet. Is something wrong?"

"Watch supper while I take a quick bath," he replied abruptly, turning so that she saw only his back when he stood. The evidence of his desire was blatantly apparent and he wanted to conceal it from her. He remembered all too well the conversations of his friends who had warned him that white women accepted lovemaking as a necessary evil, not as something to be enjoyed.

"Hawk? Is something wrong?" she asked again.

"No, I just want a quick bath before it turns too cool." He walked away from her, pleased that his voice had sounded nearly normal.

Molly watched his retreating back, puzzled by the abruptness of his voice. He had been unfailingly pleasant all day and now, suddenly, for no reason he had turned harsh and irritable.

She finished brushing the tangles from her hair and left it loose to dry. The simple meal was ready and the sun was lowering in the sky by the time Hawk returned from the river. His mood was still rather sharp but he was no longer harsh nor did he snarl at her.

"Isn't it amazing how good it feels to get the trail dust off?" Molly asked as she ate her supper.

Hawk looked with disgust at his strong, capable hands holding his plate and fork and wondered why he had thought that the cold water would be enough to control his raging lust.

The sound of her voice on the sweet evening air, the scent of her filling his nostrils, her long hair ruffled by the gentle breeze, her swollen breasts filling her shirt, her bare feet tucked femininely beneath her . . .

Molly drifted into silence when Hawk didn't respond to her simple statement.

Hawk cursed himself for a fool and tried to force his meal down his throat.

She wondered what she had done wrong.

He wondered if he was strong enough to fight himself and win.

She knew she would gladly apologize if only she knew what she had done.

He knew he'd never make it another night with her sleeping so closely by his side. He'd have to make her his.

And he was tormented by the knowledge that she would be horrified if she knew the true extent of his desire for her.

Molly sighed and stared into the fire. She had been raised to believe that a lady never questioned a gentleman when it was obvious that his temper had been aroused. Damn it, she wasn't a lady, she was his wife and she wanted to know what she'd done to make him so angry!

Her soft sigh drifted around him, seeming to settle in the one spot that needed no further invitation. He eyed her with such hunger and passion that she felt it and she lifted her gaze from the fire.

Molly shivered at the intensity of his burning

gaze. His anger was a throbbing, living thing between them. It would be a long night, she decided.

Hawk stood abruptly and left camp. If he didn't put some space between them he knew he wouldn't be capable of controlling this craving to find peace within her body.

Chapter Seventeen

Molly heard Hawk return to camp long after she had cleaned up the supper dishes and settled down for the night. She had watched the dancing flames of the fire as they ate away at the wood she had put on it, feeling no fear as it burned down and the darkness enclosed her, knowing instinctively that he was within the sound of her voice.

Longing to ask him to hold her as he had done for so many nights, Molly closed her eyes, forcing herself to relax. That fatigue from the journey and from her pregnancy were such that she soon drifted into sleep.

Hawk added another log to the fire and watched as the hungry flame took hold. A cold breeze nuzzled its way down the open neck of his shirt causing him to search through his gear to unearth his coat. Shrugging his way into the deerhide garment, he walked quietly over to Molly.

Pulling the quilt up around her ears to protect her from the chill, Hawk studied her sleeping features. It was not the first time he'd watched her as she slept, but he took pleasure in repeating the experience.

In sleep her face was almost plain, losing its familiar animation and sparkle. With her hand tucked under her cheek and her lips pursed in a pout, she had the appearance of a small child.

He thought of the child she carried. He sincerely hoped it was a male, knowing that he didn't stand a chance if the babe was a girl who resembled her mother. He would spoil her unmercifully—her slightest hurt, real or imagined, bringing him to his knees.

He could deal easier with a boy, teaching the child to hunt and track, to face life squarely.

His thoughts sobered as he considered Molly raising the child by herself. Perhaps it would be easier for her to raise a daughter than a son. A boy needed a man, a father, that he could emulate. Of course Bear and Kaleb could provide a measure of that need, but that wasn't the same as having a father.

Hawk fully intended to take Molly to Bear and Linsey, to be sure that she was settled in, and then he would leave. He planned to return at least once a year to be sure she needed nothing, but he knew that she would be safe and well provided for by his foster parents.

But would the child suffer for the lack of attention from the only man he would know as father? Would Molly grow to despise him for not being a husband? Would she ever understand that it was the only way he could protect her from the bitterness and fear his Indian heritage inspired in total strangers? Or would she think that selfishness motivated his actions?

Hawk thought of years far into the future when her warm honey eyes would look at him with loathing. Would she grow old and embittered by the way of life he would force upon her? Would the child be enough to help her overcome the loneliness of long winter nights, the big cold bed meant to be shared with the warmth of a husband?

He remembered the secret smiles, the yearning looks exchanged by Bear and Linsey. Would Molly long for a mate to share the quiet moments, to understand her thoughts with only a look? Would she cry for someone to hold her when she was sick? To laugh with her? To share the good times, and bad, that were part of everyday life?

Would she grow to hate him for not being there when she needed the tenderness a woman expects from her husband?

Could he endure her hate?

As if sensing his thoughts in her sleep, Molly moved restlessly beneath the quilt. Hawk tucked several loose strands of hair behind her ear and tenderly stroked the velvety cheek. Unconsciously, he began to chant the wordless melody and watched as it soothed her back into a deeper sleep.

He wondered what she would think of the pounding rhythm of the drums his people used—or the eerie, haunting sound of the wooden flute as it drifted on the night wind. Would she find them repulsive, so strange to her that they sounded threatening?

Or would the seductive beat, so reminiscent of fevered blood pounding through an erotically alive body, reach deeply inside her to the hidden sensuality he suspected lingered there. Would it mesmerize her to the point that she would let her body sway to the captivating rhythm?

He had heard the fiddle and banjo of her people. He had listened to the melodies of the pianoforte and the violins. There was nothing in her past that even remotely resembled the instruments used in the ceremonies of his people.

Only after the full moon had risen late into the night did he stop his song. He rose from beside his sleeping wife and walked downriver from the falls. When he was sure that the time was right, Hawk returned to the camp and knelt beside her.

"Molly?" he called softly. "Wake up, *aín jel eè.*"

"Humm? Whatsit?"

Hawk smiled at her murmured response. "It's time for your surprise."

"Later . . . sleep . . ."

"Later will be too late, you have to see it now."

When it began to appear that she would sleep through his surprise, Hawk picked her up, careful to keep the quilt around her so that she wouldn't become chilled.

Aware of being carried, but too comfortable to be concerned, Molly snuggled her head into Hawk's shoulder. With the supreme confidence of someone who trusts, she didn't worry about his destination or his reason. She simply enjoyed the feeling of being in his arms.

Hawk stopped on the rocky slab just below the falls. Careful not to dislodge the precious burden in his arms, he sat down with her cradled on his lap.

"Open your eyes, Molly."

"They are," she muttered.

"You're going to miss it and if you don't see it you'll never believe it's real."

"Has anyone ever told you that you're a pest?" she asked as she peeked from beneath lowered lids.

"Look." Hawk turned slightly so that Molly was facing the waterfall. He waited for her response, smiling when she jerked away from him.

"It's a rainbow! At night!" she said in surprise.

"Actually, it's a moonbow," Hawk informed her. "It only happens on clear nights when the moon is full."

The fully formed rainbow hung mysteriously above the falls, its ends disappearing into the mists.

"It's beautiful," she whispered reverently.

"My people have long considered this waterfall to be a holy place, a place to worship Manitou and to thank Mother Earth for the greatness of her blessings."

Molly leaned back against Hawk and he carefully tucked the blanket around her shoulders. They sat in quiet contentment and watched the moonbow until it disappeared as the moon moved below the surrounding hills.

Turning her head slightly, Molly smiled at him. "Thank you, that was something to remember. If I told people about this, nobody would believe me."

"The pleasure was all mine." Lost in the softness glowing in her eyes, Hawk lowered his mouth to hers.

Surprised by the sudden contact of his lips on hers, Molly sighed with pleasure. The kiss was as soft as the mist rising above the falls, a gentle touch slowly igniting the fires burning just beneath the surface.

Feeling her response, Hawk deepened the kiss. Molly willingly opened her mouth to his invading tongue, struggling to free a hand from the cocooning folds of the quilt.

Misunderstanding her struggle as a sign of her disgust with his kiss, Hawk raised his mouth from hers. With an effortless movement that disguised the strength necessary to accomplish it, he stood with her in his arms.

"Time for bed, little one," he said in a husky whisper.

"Hawk?" Her voice was rich with bewilderment.

"I apologize for the kiss, Molly," Hawk replied as he carried her back to camp.

"I don't want an apology!"

"Nonetheless, you deserve one." He lowered her back onto the bed. "I realize that a lady demands certain consideration from her husband and I was negligent in my treatment of you."

Molly freed a hand from the quilt and grabbed Hawk's shirt as he attempted to rise.

"What are you talking about? What *considerations?*"

Sitting down beside her, Hawk freed his shirt from her grasp and raised her hand to his lips. He placed soft reverent kisses on her palm before tucking it back beneath the quilt.

"Hawk, don't you want to kiss me?"

"Of course I do, Molly." He moved restlessly, as if uncomfortable with the discussion. "I have tried very hard not to press you for the rights of a husband. I am fully aware that you are a lady and I know that certain parts of a marriage are distasteful to you."

"What?" Molly interrupted in amazement. "How did you come to that conclusion?"

Hawk looked past her, into the darkness. "I have always known that ladies look upon the marriage bed as a necessity they must bear. It is not my intention to force myself on you any more often than I must, but Molly, please understand that I need . . . ah, I want . . . ah, hell," he muttered to a halt.

Not knowing whether to laugh, cry or rip her clothes off and show her husband that she was far from being a lady, Molly slowly shook her head. His formidable expression did not deter her curiosity.

"Hawk, where did this information come from?"

"Friends during my university days were careful to explain many things that seemed strange to me."

"Did the ladies find you . . . interesting?"

"The first few months that I was there I believed they did," he replied. "Then, when my friends explained several things about ladies to me I realized that I was misreading their intentions."

"Hawk, have you ever wondered if it were possible that your friends were jealous?"

"Jealous?" His head snapped up and his eyes narrowed.

"You are incredibly handsome. Your copper skin invites a feminine hand to reach out and stroke it, while your brooding black eyes dare her to try. You were probably attracting the attention of the ladies while they were all but ignored. It must have been difficult, if not downright impossible, for them to watch while a backwoods *Indian* caught the fancy of all the young ladies but they were left stranded."

Hawk's eyes gleamed. "They wouldn't do that to me. They were, and still are, my friends."

Molly tried, unsuccessfully, to bite back a smile. "I'm sure that they are your friends. However, their lecture on the likes and dislikes of ladies was completely wrong."

"Are you saying that you want me as a lover?" he asked bluntly, hoping she'd agree, praying she wouldn't turn him away.

"I'm saying, Nathan Morning Hawk, that if your friends were correct in their assumption about ladies, then I'm no lady!"

For the first time in a long time, Hawk was unsure of himself. "Molly, I will be gentle with you."

"I don't want gentleness!" Molly sat up and pushed the blanket away. "So help me, Hawk, if you don't make love to me, I'll tie you to a tree and get my own pleasure from your body."

Hawk's smile was a flash of white in the darkness as he removed his coat and began to unlace his shirt. "Perhaps another time. That could be an experience I don't think I want to miss, but this time we'll do it my way," he commented, his voice husky with the desire that was never far from the surface when he was around his wife.

Molly watched with fascination as he pulled his shirt over his head, revealing the width of his shoulders and the rippling strength of his chest. The firelight danced across the smooth dark skin and her hand drew into a fist as she fought an overwhelming desire to touch him. Her breathing became labored as her eyes followed his hands to the laces on his pants.

"Are you sure this is what you want?" he asked, knowing that he could still stop himself—maybe.

Molly looked into his eyes, her own reflecting her need. "Make me your wife."

Knee-high moccasins were quickly unlaced and Hawk stood.

"Do you find me incredibly handsome?" he asked, repeating her own words.

"Yes," she replied, sitting up, unaware of the quilt as it slid off of her shoulders.

"Do you want to touch my copper skin?" His voice was velvet, stoking the fires of her growing need.

"Yes." Molly rose to her knees, unconscious of her hands reaching toward his waist.

Slowly, as time stood still, Hawk pulled the laces free from his pants. The fabric parted to reveal smooth copper skin and, as they slid lower on his hips, a narrow line of coal black hair that disappeared beneath the fabric.

With fingers that trembled, Molly touched the firm ridges of his stomach. She heard his hiss of breath as she softly brushed over him.

"Touch me, *neè wàh*," he whispered, his eyes glowing with desire. "I have longed to feel your hands against my skin."

Leaning forward, Molly placed soft, enticing kisses against the warmth of his stomach. Her hands moved voluntarily up to his smooth chest, across wide shoulders and down muscular arms.

When her hands glided to his, Hawk entwined his fingers through hers. She rested her cheek against his stomach, while the soft breeze playfully wrapped her long hair around his legs, capturing him in a web of silk.

"Look at us, Molly." His husky voice betrayed the serious intensity of his eyes.

She raised her head to look willingly at him. "I see my husband," she whispered, placing another longing kiss on his stomach.

"You see an Indian." He put her hand against his smooth chest. "Look at your pale flesh against mine."

"A beautiful Indian . . . a gentle, caring man . . ." She rubbed her cheek against his stomach. "My husband."

Tugging her hands from his, she wrapped her fingers around the waist of his pants. "It's too late to try to force me away, Hawk. I love you. And I *will* be your wife!"

The battle, the war, was lost. He had no weapon to fight against her words of love when they so perfectly matched his own desires. The future would resolve itself, for now there was Molly . . . and love.

Slowly, deliciously, Molly released the fabric and watched as it slid down heavily muscled thighs. Hawk kicked free of the pants and knelt beside her, pulling her against him.

"You have too many clothes on, woman," he murmured as he placed numerous kisses on her face. "But I fear you'll freeze if I remove your nightdress."

Molly's rippling laugh sent slivers of desire down his spine. "Right now there is no way I could freeze, but if I was in danger I trust you could find a way to warm me?"

Hawk's reply was a growl of desire as he found the hem of her gown and pulled it over her head. He pulled her against him while eager hands skimmed over warm flesh as searching lips constantly found new and different places to taste.

Hawk marveled at her full breasts, as he traced the delicate blue veins just beneath her skin with his tongue.

Molly relished the freedom to touch, savoring each as a treasure to be admired at length—later, when desire wasn't the overpowering force driving her to explore quickly.

Her hands twined in the blue-black hair that had so enticed her as his mouth found the puckered peak of her breast. The gentle tug and pull of his lips made her grasp for a firm hold. With her head thrown back and her back arched to give her better access, her long honey-colored hair tied a lover's knot around their fevered bodies.

Hawk sampled her with his mouth as his hands trailed to new territory. Down her slender back to the firmness of her rounded bottom to the trembling strength of her thighs, he found nothing but delight in her body. A fevered pitch was building in both of them when he found the swelling of her stomach.

Molly was suddenly shy as he drew back so that he could see the mound of her belly. He tasted the tight flesh while his hands explored. She wanted to hide her face as he held the weight of her in his hands but then he spoke, wiping away embarrassment.

His words were Shawnee but they were so

eloquent when combined with his worshipping touch that Molly needed no translation. Her breath caught as he traced the taut skin that cradled her child.

"He will be my son." Both hands caressed her belly with reverence. "I can feel as he grows in your body, nestled in the safety of your womb, but already love for him grows in my heart."

Emotion too deep for simple words to express held them captive and for long minutes their gaze locked, and they were aware only of this moment in time. The cold air danced over their exposed skin and a shiver rippled through her. Hawk grabbed the quilt, draping it over her shoulders but allowing none to come between their bodies. With her hands occupied holding the blanket in place she could only kneel before him as he explored her.

Tender touches and gentle kisses led to fevered caresses and deep moans of desire. When her legs could no longer support her, Hawk lowered her to the bed, throwing the quilt over both of them.

When Molly doubted that she could stand another kiss, another touch, Hawk taught her that she could. Mindless with need, enthralled by a hunger she had never felt before, she parted her thighs, silently begging him to end the torment.

"I've wanted for so long," he whispered, his breath warm against the aroused flesh of her breasts.

"Wanted?"

"Wanted to touch you." His hands journeyed leisurely down her body, stopping to linger in places of special interest.

"Wanted to taste you." His mouth followed the

trail of his hands, tasting, suckling, nipping.

He rose and moved carefully between her thighs. "Wanted to be one with you."

"Love me, Hawk."

Driven by the rhythm of the drums pounding through him, Hawk accepted the invitation. With utmost caution to protect the babe sheltered in her body, he sensuously invaded the damp warmth of her femininity. Copper flesh merged with silky satin as two became one. Each lingering thrust was a pledge of love, a promise of tomorrow.

Together they traveled far beyond the enchantment of the moonbow, the bewitchment of lovers united in a world of two.

Molly woke when she felt cold air invade the cocoon of warmth provided by the quilt. Pulling the blanket snugly around her nose, she watched as Hawk stoked the fire.

The morning sun was only beginning to chase away the night, but it provided enough light for her to appreciate the perfection of his body. Well-honed muscles rippled beneath firm, smooth skin with each graceful movement. Raven black hair hung to impossibly wide shoulders that arrowed down to narrow hips and rock-hard thighs.

His movements were relaxed, almost leisurely, as muscles responded upon demand. The cold air nipped at her exposed nose and a light layer of frost glittered on the bare ground, but he showed no obvious discomfort.

Molly was so enchanted by her silent observation

of him that she was disappointed when he returned to the bed and climbed beneath the quilt.

"You're cold!" she complained as he snuggled his chilled flesh against her warm body.

"Woman, another minute of staring at me and I would have been burning up!" he growled against the soft skin of her shoulder.

"I wasn't staring at you!" she defended herself as her cheeks grew rosy with embarrassment.

"If that wasn't staring what would you call it?" Hawk propped his head up so that he could look at her.

"Your back was to me so how do you know I was staring?"

"I could feel your honey-sweet eyes devouring me." He entwined his long legs with hers, his knee resting intimately at the lower slope of her stomach.

Rather than trying to escape from his chilled skin, Molly snuggled closer.

"I was asleep until you came back to bed and tried to freeze me," she lied complacently.

"My people say that if you lie, your tongue will grow as stiff as tree bark and everyone will know that you can't be trusted."

"I'm not sure I know what you mean. Are you implying that I'm not telling the truth?" Her hands lowered to his thigh across her stomach and she began gently to stroke him from knee to groin.

"It would be a shame for such a sweet tongue to grow thick and useless when I can think of better uses for it," he whispered with a groan when her nimble fingers discovered new areas to stroke.

"If you keep that up," he reached for her hand and

held it firmly in place, "then I'm going to have a miserable day trying to stay in the saddle."

"You don't like it?" she whispered, giving him a gentle squeeze.

"I like it far too much," he groaned. "But as much as I'd like to stay here with you until I've touched and tasted every inch of your delectable body, we've got to get on the trail. It's turning cold sooner than I thought it would and I want to be home before the first snow."

Reluctantly, Molly removed her hand from him. "Don't let it be said that I was the cause of delay. Let's get dressed and hit the trail."

Hawk smiled as he found her hand beneath the quilt and returned it to his body. "I think we've got a few extra minutes, if you're interested?"

"I'm interested." Molly turned her mouth to his, sighing as his head lowered.

Surprise combined with shock to prevent Hawk from completing the kiss. He remained immobile, his mouth mere inches from hers and he waited for a repeat of the movement he had felt beneath his thigh.

"Molly?" Knowing what he had felt and yet waiting for her confirmation, Hawk's voice was rich with wonder.

"Our son has decided to start the day early." Her smile had the mysterious glow of all pregnant women.

His gaze intensified fiercely. It was the first time she had referred to the baby as theirs. As if agreeing to her decision, the baby moved again, this time so strongly that there could be no doubt for either of them.

"Welcome to the morning, little warrior," Hawk murmured. Molly felt him gently caress her stomach, his eyes never leaving hers. "Right now, I'm going to love your maman."

Finally, his mouth lowered to hers in a kiss as gentle as spring rain. His hand moved up to cup her breast, his thumb teasing the nipple into pebble hardness. When Molly moaned and arched her back, putting her breast more firmly into his palm, Hawk changed the tempo of his caresses.

As if appreciating the activity, the baby was still. He was the only one who was.

Chapter Eighteen

"You're tired, Molly." Hawk held her in his arms and gently rubbed her back. "Go to sleep, *aín jel eè.*"

"I'm sorry we had to stop so early this evening, I know you wanted to get to the river." She snuggled into his warmth and tried to forget that every bone in her body ached.

After more than a month on the trail, Molly was so tired she had to force herself to rise every morning and sheer willpower kept her in the saddle all day. But willpower was beginning to waver and she wondered how much longer she could continue at the pace Hawk set.

She tried not to complain, but by the middle of the each day Hawk could see her exhaustion in the cumbersome movements of her body. He began to insist that she have a nap at midday when they stopped to eat and rest the horses, and he began to stop far before sundown each evening. Still, the signs of exhaustion never left her face, and her natural grace was replaced by ponderously halting movements.

Molly's protruding stomach rested against him, and Hawk felt the firm kick of the baby. He moved his hands to her belly to soothingly massage, hoping the child could feel it and would allow his mother to get some much-needed rest.

By Hawk's reckoning, it was nearly December. Until a week ago the weather had been nearly perfect. Warm dry days were followed by cool, clear nights. There had been only a couple of days of rain, but each morning the layer of frost on the ground seemed heavier than it had been on the previous morning.

The snow had held off but now the temperatures were well below freezing at night and only slightly above during the day. He could almost smell snow in the air and he would bet that in a matter of days they would see the first snow of winter.

He was deeply concerned about the effect on Molly if they had to travel through blizzard conditions. Hawk was caught between his concern for her traveling faster to avoid possible complications if it began to snow, and his knowledge that she was already pushing herself to the meager limits of her strength each day.

Hawk had hoped to be on the Ohio River nearly a week earlier, but had slowed his pace when he saw how much Molly was suffering. He wanted to be at the river by this time tomorrow but knew he'd make the trip in two days instead of one if she couldn't handle the miles.

Once they were on the river instead of on horseback, he knew the trip would be easier for her. Hopefully, within a week they would be at Shawnee Town. For the first time in far too many years, he'd be home.

It seemed to Molly that her toes and fingers were always cold, even with the extra socks and bulky gloves she wore. She relished the heat from Hawk's body, snuggling against him beneath the blankets and quilt. She was tired and she desperately wanted to sleep, but she knew that sleep would be denied her until the baby quit moving so fiercely.

"Tell me more about Linsey," she asked. Of all the people Hawk considered family, Molly was most concerned about meeting the woman he considered to be his mother.

As he thought of his adoptive mother, Hawk settled Molly against him, continuing his gentle stroking of her stomach. Until he had met Molly, Linsey had been the most important woman in his life. He more than loved her, he admired her and deeply respected her.

"Do you remember me telling you about her temper and how she swears in Gaelic when she's angry, even though she doesn't know what she's saying? One day she was furious and the Gaelic was flying. She didn't know that we had a visitor—a missionary, a Scot come to the wilderness to minister to the flock. When she turned around, words still tumbling from her lips, there he stood."

Hawk grinned at the memory. "The poor man was beet red and I'm sure he felt he'd arrived too late to save her tarnished soul. In privacy he told Bear exactly what Linsey had been saying for all those years." He chuckled, squeezing Molly to him. "It was months before we heard Gaelic again in the house."

Memories of his childhood with his fiery mother drifted through his thoughts. "She's suffered tragedy and adversity but has never lost the femininity and gentleness of her nature.

"I was nine when she lost her fifth son at birth. While she was still recovering from the birth, Matthew, her third son, drowned."

"Oh my God," Molly moaned in sympathy. "How could she stand to lose two children?"

Hawk closed his eyes and remembered the tragedy so many years ago. "I watched her prepare Matthew for burial. I've never seen such a lost look on someone's face. But she's a strong woman, Molly. She shed tears for her children then put her life back together. She had other children who needed their mother. She didn't have time for self-pity."

"When did you meet her?"

"The day I was born. An outbreak of measles had nearly destroyed our village. Linsey, Bear and Kaleb had worked to try to save anyone they could but there was little they could do.

"My older sister and my mother both caught the disease. Spring Flower died quickly but my mother hung on, maybe because I had yet to be born or maybe because she wasn't ready to relinquish life.

"Linsey, Bear and my father all fought to save her, but after several days of soaring fevers she could

302

fight no longer. She died, but I had yet to be born."

Molly sat up and turned to look at her husband. "Hawk, if she died, how could you be born?"

"Patience," he chided gently, pulling her back into his arms. "It's a long story and you're supposed to be trying to go to sleep."

"I couldn't go to sleep now if my life depended upon it. Explain how you were born please."

Hawk settled her in place and continued his tale. "There was an old woman, called the grandmother by my people, who tended my mother at the last. Linsey has told me many times that while she, Bear and my father stood in horror and watched the contortions of my mother's belly, the grandmother took matters in her own hands. She slit open the womb and pulled me free."

"If she hadn't been there and known what to do . . ." Molly couldn't finish the statement but pulled Hawk's hand to her mouth and softly kissed his palm.

"I'm not sure the grandmother knew exactly what to do, maybe she knew there was little to lose and much to gain. With so many people dying I'm sure a birth gave hope to everyone. After my father welcomed me, I was put in Linsey's hands. She named me and cared for me when it was impossible for my father to do so.

"After the epidemic was over, he took the remainder of the tribe west. Because I was so young, I was left with Linsey and Bear. I was nearly five years old before my father was able to return for me. From that time on I spent my life living with my people for a few months and then with Bear and Linsey for a few months. The Cub always went back and forth with me, not only because we were inseparable but I think Linsey used it as an assurance that Limping Wolf would return me to her when he brought the Cub home."

"Thank God for the grandmother," Molly whispered fervently.

Hawk smiled in the darkness and kissed the top of her head. "Linsey had her hands full. I was only four months old when the Cub was born. Little Kaleb was born the next year and Matthew two years later. Will, John, James and Mark all came along in the next few years."

"Eight boys! The lady had her hands full!"

"There were only four of us after John and Matthew died. It was a couple of years before Jamie and Mark arrived on the scene and then they were too little to get into trouble with us. They were just starting to look for trouble when the Cub and I left for the university."

Hawk's voice drifted away. "They're nearly men now and it's been so long since I've been home, I won't even know them."

"Were you bad and did you cause her all kinds of problems?" Molly delighted in the thought of Hawk as a child.

"None of us was exactly bad," he replied hesitantly. "But we weren't exactly good either. Occasionally Bear would put the fear of God—or usually the fear of Bear—in us and we'd be remarkably good for a few days.

"Linsey will love you," he added, perhaps trying to change the subject.

"You don't know that! She may take one look at me and wonder where she went wrong in raising you!"

Hawk smiled, hugging her tightly. "She'll take one look at you and your expanding belly and be thrilled that she's going to be a grandmother."

Molly frowned, concerned about Linsey's true reaction. "Hawk, do you think she'll accept my child as her grandchild once she sees he wasn't fathered by you?"

"*Aín jel eè,* Linsey took a newborn Shawnee child as her own. Many times she has fought as fiercely for me as for her natural sons. Trust me, she will accept you and the child and dare anyone to comment about his conception."

"I hope you're right." Molly understood Hawk's boundless love for Linsey and was concerned that he might be forced into choosing either herself or Linsey.

Knowing that time, and Linsey, would prove him right, Hawk didn't bother to continue the discussion. He rubbed the tight skin of her stomach and began the familiar chant that would relax Molly and help her to find the sleep she so desperately needed.

Because of the cold nighttime temperatures, Molly had abandoned her long flannel nightdress and she now slept in a warm buckskin shirt that belonged to Hawk. Softer than velvet, the long sleeves hung below her fingers, and the hem came to midthigh.

Feeling her begin to relax, Hawk continued the chant. His hand slipped beneath her shirt and he rubbed her soft tight flesh. His fingers drifted through her feminine curls and he closed his eyes, picturing his dark hand against her creamy skin.

Fearing that he would hurt her or the babe by making love to her in her exhausted condition, Hawk had refrained from intimate touches. The simple act of stroking her began to have a marked effect on him. He shifted his body away from her so that she wouldn't become aware of it.

In spite of his warming passions, Hawk found himself soothed by the intimate touches and he allowed himself to drift into the light sleep that kept him on the point of alertness in case of unexpected danger.

After weeks of wilderness, Molly was not impressed by the waterfront settlement on the Ohio River. Unpainted slatboard houses, weathered log cabins, and tents formed the dusty main street, and only street. The whining screech of a saw mill, the rattling of wagons, raucous laughter and an occasional report from a rifle seemed invasively loud to ears accustomed to bird song, the wind through the trees and rustling from small creatures never seen.

"We can spend the night here if you'd like," Hawk offered.

Molly didn't even have to consider his offer. "No," she replied firmly. "It's only midday, we've still got

306

plenty of daylight left." She held firmly to the reins, wanting desperately to reach for his hand for security as inquisitive, lecherous looks were turned her way.

Hawk was aware of the speculation of the hunters who milled around. He was relieved at Molly's decision, hoping to get her out of the town before the trouble that he could feel brewing erupted into a free-for-all.

"I'm going to get a room at the inn for you. You can take a long hot bath and nap on a bed while I see about trading the horses for a boat."

"I'd rather stay with you." The thought of a bath and a bed were inviting, but knowing that she'd be without Hawk's protection was daunting.

Hawk understood her unspoken fears and felt anger begin to brew beneath his unruffled surface appearance. The looks she was receiving were the very thing he'd warned her about. The men were still uncertain of their relationship but he had little doubt that as soon as they detected her condition they would become obnoxious in their comments and actions. He hoped he could prevent it from happening by installing her in a room and out of sight.

At the battered building sporting a sign that labeled it as an inn, Hawk dismounted and helped Molly from her horse. The exterior of the structure left much to be desired, as did the dirty appearance of the man who stood in the open doorway blocking their entrance but it was the only inn available.

"We don't take Injuns," he said hoarsely, spitting a stream of tobacco juice into the dust at Hawk's feet.

"I want a room for the lady." Hawk positioned himself slightly in front of Molly, his rifle cradled prominently in his arms.

"Don't take no Injun trash, either."

Molly placed her hand on Hawk's arm when she detected the stiffening of his body.

"Let's go, Hawk. It's not worth a fight."

Ignoring her, Hawk kept his burning gaze turned toward the proprietor. "We can do this the easy way or the hard way," he said softly, his voice a threat. "Either way, the lady will have a room and hot water for a bath."

Seeing Hawk's intentions clearly stamped on his stoic countenance, the man stepped back into the inn. "I'll give her a room long 'nough fer her to take her bath, but you and she'll be outta here afore nightfall."

"That'll do." Hawk escorted Molly into the building and followed the man to a room at the back. The interior of the building was as shabby as the exterior. Filth was everywhere, while spider webs hung from the rafters, and he suspected that the dark stains on the dirt floor were from more than spitting and spilled drinks. He began to doubt the wisdom of leaving Molly in such a place when he saw the bedroom.

The room was hardly large enough for the rope bed and a battered dresser, and he wrinkled his nose at the smell. With a disgusted snarl he wiped the bedclothes from the mattress and kicked them out the door.

While he waited for the innkeeper to return with the water, Hawk examined the only window in the room and found that the shutter was broken, the latch long gone. He nearly decided to keep Molly with him rather than to allow her to stay here unprotected. One look at her weary face and he knew he had no choice.

"Don't got no tub," the innkeeper stated when he returned with two buckets of water, one cold and one barely warm. He tripped over the smelly blankets on the floor and sneered at Molly. "Ain't good enough for you?"

"Those aren't good enough for a pig," she replied softly. "But from the appearance of this room I'd say that's what usually sleeps here."

"Uppity bitch, ain't ya? Take me 'bout ten minutes to knock that outta you."

"You touch her and you're dead," Hawk snarled as his fingers closed around the man's throat.

"Ain't gonna touch no Injun leavings," the man whimpered while his hands shook so badly water sloshed out of the buckets he still held.

"If you're smart enough to remember that you might still be alive when we leave."

"Are you threatenin' me, Injun?"

"No threat," Hawk stated quietly, abruptly releasing his hostage. "That's a promise."

The man set the buckets down on the floor and backed out of the room. Hawk slammed the door in his face, his temper boiling just beneath the surface.

When Hawk turned he found Molly in his arms. She rested reassuringly against his chest and smiled when the babe kicked firmly, sending his own message of support.

"Will you bring in my bags before you leave?" Molly asked quietly. "I'd like to change into something clean."

Hawk placed a soft kiss on the top of her head and hugged her tightly. He left the room and quickly returned with Molly's bags. While she searched out her sole remaining clean shirt and pants, Hawk shoved the dresser in front of the window.

"This won't keep a determined man outside for long," he told her. "But it should cause enough noise to waken you. I'm going to leave the gun here. If you have reason to use it, don't waste time aiming, point it at the top of the dresser and fire."

Worried about Hawk facing the unfriendly townspeople without the protection the long rifle offered, Molly protested. "Take it with you, I won't need it. No one has a reason for wanting to bother me."

"For the most part, I'll be ignored if I'm on the street by myself."

"I've caused you problems," Molly interrupted quietly as guilt made her realize the real danger Hawk faced with her at his side.

"No, *aín jel eè.*" He smiled softly and cupped her cheek in his hands. "The problems are caused by people who have no reason to think they are better than anyone else but act that way anyway.

"Now, the door is flimsy, but when I get out I want

310

you to use this piece of rope to secure it."

Hawk handed her the rope and showed her how to tie the door closed. "I'll knock when I return, but it'll probably take a couple of hours before we're ready to leave. I want to get some supplies after I trade the horses for a boat or a canoe. You bathe and then try to rest. We'll be gone long before dark."

"Be careful, Hawk." Molly wrapped her arms around his waist and hugged him.

"I will, *neè wàh,*" he gently caressed her stomach. "I have to much to return to, I won't take careless chances."

He kissed her and walked out of the room. Waiting until she had tied the door as he had shown her, Hawk pushed against it, satisfied that anyone trying to enter through it could have to struggle to get it opened. He prayed that if it were necessary, Molly would use the gun first and regret it later.

Molly stripped off her shirt and pants and used the warm water to clean some of the grime from her skin. It was barely warm but after cold river water it felt heavenly. After donning her remaining clean shirt and pants, she used the water to wash her clothing, then found there was nowhere in the room that she wanted to lay the damp clothes. Wadding them up, she put them back into the empty bucket. She decided to wait until they were on the boat to spread them out to dry.

It took only a quick look at the bed to see the fleas jumping around and she shuddered at the thought of what else might be on the dirty ticking. Deciding that the hard dirt floor was preferable to the dubious

311

comfort of the bed, Molly spread her bedding on the floor and lay down. Within minutes, even as worry for Hawk plagued her thoughts, she drifted into a light, troubled sleep.

"Molly, wake up, *aín jel eè.*"

At the sound of his voice from the other side of the door, Molly jumped up and hurried to the door. Her fingers were clumsy in her haste to untie the rope and it seemed to take forever before the knots were free.

Then she was in his arms, tears of relief flowing freely down her cheeks.

"What is this?" Hawk caught one of the crystalline drops.

"I know it's silly, but I was so scared." She sniffed, wiping away the tears. "I seem to cry all the time. I guess that goes with the condition."

"Did someone bother you?" His voice promised immediate retribution for anyone foolish enough to trouble her.

"No! No, I wasn't bothered. I was safe enough here."

Hawk looked at the flimsy door and the doubtful protection of the dresser in front of the window and he was glad she didn't know how easily someone could have entered the room.

"It's time to leave, sweetheart. Let's gather up your things and head for the river. The current is running strongly and we should be miles away from here before dark."

Anxious to be on the way, Molly rushed to leave. In a matter of minutes the bedding was tied in a firm

312

roll and her wet clothing gathered in a bundle. With Hawk's hand firmly at her back, she walked from the inn, delighted to be leaving, as she took every footstep.

For the most part, they were ignored as they walked toward the river. A few fools risked taunting the Indian, never realizing that they owed their lives to the woman who walked confidently in front of the Shawnee warrior. Had it not been for his fear of causing her further anguish, Hawk would have slit the throat of each man without a moment of regret.

They stopped at the river where a young boy whom Hawk had paid to guard the boat, waited patiently. He tossed the boy a coin and watched the child run off to spend his unexpected booty. He turned the canoe over, stashed their gear in the middle and pushed two-thirds of its length into the water.

Hawk had hoped to find a flatboat large enough to allow Molly to stretch out and sleep, but the only thing available was a canoe. It was well crafted and watertight, but even though the canoe would be faster, it was far less comfortable than a large craft.

"A canoe!" Molly exclaimed with delight. "I used to watch them float up and down the river in Charleston and always wanted to ride in one."

"Here's your chance, sweetheart." Hawk took her hand and helped her into the bow. He instructed her to sit on the plank seat and fold her knees under her. He pushed the craft the rest of the way into the river and jumped into the stern. Picking up a paddle,

Hawk guided the boat into the current.

Molly felt as if they were flying, so fast did the little canoe move. The water line was only a few scant inches beneath the sides but only occasional drops splattered onto her.

"How do you say canoe in Shawnee?"

"O lah ka see," Hawk replied, feeling relief slip past on the current as they put the settlement behind them. "Paddle is *cho mah lee* and water is *nup ee.*"

Having quickly discovered that the slightest movement caused the small boat to rock from side to side, Molly carefully turned so that she was looking at her husband.

He controlled the craft with the expertise of long practice. He knelt and his arms moved rhythmically, pausing between strokes then dipping the paddle into the water and strongly digging in to get as much distance as possible out of each stroke.

He had discarded his heavy coat before they had set off. Molly soon saw a film of perspiration cover his copper skin. His shoulder-length black hair hung freely and shone blue in the bright sun. A red band was tied around his forehead, and it served double duty by keeping hair out of his eyes and by catching sweat as it beaded down his face.

Never had he looked more the Shawnee warrior.

"How do you say I love you?" she asked softly, her eyes overflowing with emotion for him.

"Ahxk wài la teé wai." His voice was richly husky and his black eyes glowed with tenderness.

She could believe he meant the words for her.

The paddle dipped, lifted, then dipped again. The

water sparkled and rippled, carrying them at long last toward a home filled with welcome and love for the weary travelers.

"*Ahxk wài la teé wai,*" she repeated, her eyes never leaving his. "*Ahxk wài la teé wai,* Nathan Morning Hawk."

Chapter Nineteen

Molly sat in the front of the canoe and tried her best to appear relaxed. The gentle flutter of the baby kept her company as if he were doing his best to bolster her courage.

She watched the leafless trees as the boat glided silently past mile after mile of riverbank. The light snow that had been falling when they'd wakened before dawn had stopped and now the sun shone feebly through the thick clouds that hung threateningly just out of reach.

Before the day was over they would reach their destination. And Molly wished they could travel past Shawnee Town and settle alone in the wilderness.

After four days on the river, three of them spent reassuring Molly that she would be accepted by his white family, Hawk decided to let time prove him right. He could see the false courage in her shaky smile and firmly squared shoulders, and he longed to take her into his arms and hold her. If he doubted for even a moment that she would be greeted with anything less than warmth he would never have wanted her to endure the meeting. But Linsey would make Molly welcome with a smile and her knew that Bear would greet her with one of his rib-shattering hugs.

A sigh of relief drifted past Hawk's lips, as familiar landmarks came into view. Home. After years spent at the university and then drifting from place to place, he was home.

Hawk pulled the canoe up on shore and jumped out, landing in ankle-deep water. Reluctantly, Molly handed him the things piled neatly in the middle of the craft, then held her hand out for him to steady her as she climbed to her feet. Her knees were shaky from the hours spent in the folded position . . . and from fear.

"Hawk . . ." Molly hesitated, not knowing what she wanted to say.

"Come, we're home." Hawk wrapped his arm around her for a brief hug then shouldered the packs and, taking her hand in his, started up the trail.

Having no choice but to follow, Molly clutched his hand and watched the trail ahead of them. Far too soon, they came upon the house and she gasped with surprise.

The white two-story house seemed to be all full-length windows and tall, graceful Grecian columns. From each end of the house, chimneys poured white smoke into the air. Three giant weeping willow trees, their spindly branches bare of leaves, seemed to stand guard at the front entrance. Molly knew that in the summer the trees would provide a cool haven from the heat of the sun.

As they approached, a man walked from around the side of the house. He stopped abruptly when he saw them. Even from a distance Molly could see the smile that split his face and she heard as he yelled to the occupants of the house.

People seemed to spill into the yard. As she and Hawk walked closer Molly saw that, except for a woman wrapped warmly in a hastily donned cape, these dark-haired men were of massive proportions.

"Thought you might have gotten lost and couldn't find your way home," one of the men said with a grin as he reached for Hawk's hand.

"Kaleb!" Unabashedly, Hawk wrapped his arms around the man who was about his own age but several inches taller. "God, they surely don't still call you Little Kaleb. Did you forget to stop growing?"

"He has a way to go yet before he's big enough for this family to keep."

"Will! Jamie?! Mark, you were just a little kid when I left!" Hawk hugged the men he claimed as brothers, each seeming to be larger than the other.

One by one each man greeted Hawk while Molly stood back and watched. She saw their honest joy in Hawk's return. Unaware of the polite, but nonetheless speculative glances being thrown her way, she turned her gaze to the tiny woman who seemed as if she couldn't possibly be the mother of these massive men.

She saw tears that flowed freely down an unlined face of rare beauty. The love the woman felt for Hawk glowed in eyes the color of summer grass. The hood to her cape fell back as she moved to greet Hawk and Molly saw the autumn-red hair tied demurely in a bun at the nape of her neck.

This could only be Linsey.

After the boisterous greetings from his brothers, Hawk turned to the woman and took her into his arms.

"Nathan, my son, oh how I've missed you," Linsey said as she reached for him.

"*Nee ke yah,* my mother." Hawk bent, wrapped his arms around her waist and twirled her with abandon. "If it was half as much as I've missed you then you've been miserable."

"I've been miserable," she replied with a smile. "but now all of my sons are home and I'm filled with joy. Luc will be so happy to see you."

"Where is Bear?" Hawk asked, returning Linsey to her feet.

"He, Kaleb and Daniel are helping a neighbor finish his harvest. We were all there most of the day but since it was finished early this afternoon everyone has drifted back home but them."

"Daniel is here?" Hawk's grin widened and Molly saw the special place Daniel held in his heart. Daniel, the Cub, who had grown up with Hawk, was more of a real brother to him than his Shawnee brother.

"He's been home since spring."

"Aren't you forgetting someone?" Will asked, looking pointedly at Molly.

Four pairs of dark masculine eyes turned in her direction and Molly wished for a hole to crawl into to escape their friendly curiosity. Had she looked,

Molly would have seen the sympathetic understanding in the sole pair of feminine eyes.

Her turn had come, and Molly wrapped her coat tightly around her, holding it firmly to keep her hands from shaking. She watched Hawk walk toward her, unaware that all her fears glittered in her worried gaze.

With a gentle hand under her chin, Hawk tipped her head up. His head lowered until his mouth covered hers in a kiss of gentle reassurance. Wrapping his arm around her shoulders, he turned and walked with her up to his family.

"I would like to introduce you to Mary Helen . . . my wife." His smile grew wider at the various expressions of surprise from his family.

Understanding how overwhelming her large sons could be to strangers, Linsey moved over to Molly. If the men hadn't been there towering over her, Molly would have felt huge and gawky in front of the petite Linsey, but no one could feel huge when surrounded by four human mountains.

"Mary Helen," Linsey said quietly, reaching for Molly's hand. "What a lovely name for a lovely young woman. Welcome to our family. We take some getting used to but you'll find that my sons have been raised as gentlemen . . . even if they do tend to forget it at times."

"Thank you," Molly said softly, turning from Linsey as Hawk began to introduce the men.

It was easy to identify them as brothers—not only were they all similar in size but they shared the same dark hair and eyes. At a closer distance Molly could see that Jamie and Mark were far younger than she had assumed. Their size disguised their ages—both were obviously still in their teens, with Mark not more than fourteen.

They were studiously polite as they were introduced, each warmly welcoming her to the family. Kaleb was the only one to hug her, his eyes widening when he felt the obvious bulge of her stomach. He kept the knowledge to himself, seeming to relish knowing her secret.

"Mama! Mama, me need help!"

A tiny girl with bright red hair and glistening green eyes approached from behind the house. Her skirt was gathered in her arms and she seemed completely unconcerned about the cold air chilling her bare bottom.

"Who is this?" Hawk asked, his eyes glowing with surprised delight.

"Dara Bevin LeClerc, where are your drawers?" Linsey asked, fighting to keep a stern expression on her face.

"They wet!"

"How did they get wet?"

Dara knew exactly how to change the subject. She approached the strangers in the midst of her brothers and stared up at first Molly and then Hawk.

"Who're you?" she asked.

Hawk knelt in front of the tiny girl and carefully pulled her dress down. Dara helped him to smooth it in place, completely unconcerned by this stranger. After all, she had been surrounded by men all of her short life, and one more didn't make any difference to her.

322

"I am Hawk, your brother," he answered quietly.

Searching green eyes stared at him. Seeming satisfied, she reached for him and snuggled into his arms. Hawk stood, carefully balancing this unexpected surprise in his embrace.

"I think you forgot to mention this little bundle, Maman." He turned to Linsey, a smile crossing his stern features.

"This little hellion was a complete surprise to all of us three years ago." Linsey motioned for everyone to enter the house. She held Molly's arm as she led the way inside.

"Not only did I think I was through with having babies, but to have a girl after so many sons, we almost didn't know what to do with her. Luc still hasn't completely recovered from the shock. Dara has her daddy firmly wrapped around her tiny little fingers . . . and her brothers are not far behind. I'm glad there will be another woman in the house to help me prevent her from becoming totally spoiled.

"I decided not to write either to you or to Daniel about her. She was to be a surprise."

Linsey looked at her daughter snuggled in Hawk's arms. "I didn't expect your first meeting with her to be a display of her bare backside." She reached for Dara and balanced her on her hip. "You still haven't explained to me what happened to your drawers, young lady."

Linsey turned and smiled at Molly. "I'll take this imp upstairs and get her properly dressed and then we'll get Hawk's room ready. I'm sure you'd like to bathe and change clothes."

Molly didn't know how to tell her hostess that

these, and others exactly like them, were the only clothes she had. She watched the gentle sway of Linsey's skirts as she climbed the stairs.

"Come sit down, *aín jel eè.*" Hawk took Molly's hand and led her into the drawing room.

The room was huge—Molly came to realize that everything around her was huge. Stretching from front to back of the house, it was filled with comfortable chairs, several tables and a fireplace that was large enough to walk into. The men were spread out around the room, waiting impatiently for Hawk to join them.

Hawk helped Molly remove her coat, and four pairs of masculine eyes immediately found her rounded stomach. Kaleb grinned as he watched the looks of surprise cross his brothers' faces.

"I'm going to be an uncle!" Mark cheered gleefully. He stood and grabbed Molly and hugged her tightly. "Wait until the Bear hears about this! Can you imagine him a grandpa!"

The others chuckled with enjoyment as Molly blushed a vivid red with embarrassment. In polite society, men didn't acknowledge a woman's expectant condition. Obviously, in this family, some rules of behavior were ignored! She knew that if she wanted to be a member of this family she would have to learn to accept their good-natured teasing. But she suspected that she was in for some rough times before she became accustomed to their easygoing manner.

And after such a short acquaintance, Molly knew she wanted to be a member of this family more than she had ever wanted anything in her life.

Conversation flew, questions were asked and answered, as the brothers caught up on each other's lives. The closing of the front door brought a sudden, expectant silence to the room. Hawk stood up from Molly's side, his eyes glued to the door.

A man, larger than any in the room, with hair as red as the setting sun, walked in. A smile crossed his handsome features as his voice boomed into the stillness.

"Did you take the long way home and get lost?"

Molly knew this was Daniel, the Cub, the Mountain with Voice of Thunder. She was intimidated by his stunning size and she found herself trying to sink into the chair. Black eyes, so like those of his brothers, quickly found her but before he could do more than smile gently, another voice broke into the noise.

"Welp, it's 'bout time you come home, boy." The old man grabbed Hawk and hugged him tightly, tears unashamedly rimming his eyes. "Missed ya, boy, missed you somethin' bad."

Her mind a whirl with so many impressions, Molly stared in shock at the old man. His face puddled in massive wrinkles above his shaggy eyebrows. A badly scarred bald spot at the top of his head attested to the scalping he had survived nearly thirty years earlier.

"It's been too long, Kaleb."

"What? You think yore too old to call me grandpa liken you always done?"

"I'm not too old if you're not," Hawk replied with a chuckle. He had missed this old man almost as much as he'd missed Linsey and Bear.

325

The only missing member of the family filled the doorway. Molly's eyes were drawn to the man who had been a father to Hawk. While he was smaller than Daniel, he was larger than his other sons. Thick black hair, with only the slightest touch of silver at the temples, hung to his wide shoulders. Sharp black eyes narrowed in on Hawk, but his stern features didn't change.

Linsey returned from upstairs and walked up beside her husband. When he turned his head and wrapped his arm around his tiny wife, Molly couldn't prevent her gasp of surprise as she saw the horrible scars that disfigured the left side of his face.

As if separating good from bad, the right side of his face was incredibly handsome while deep scars from hairline to jaw on the left side destroyed the beauty that should have been there.

Every eye in the room turned to Molly but her eyes were glued to the man in the doorway.

"They are only scars, little one," he said softly, repeating the words he had used to reassure Linsey so many years ago.

Finding herself drawn to the gentle understanding of his voice, Molly stood and walked across the room. Face to face with him, she found herself speechless, wanting to apologize for her rudeness and yet knowing it wasn't necessary.

"I'm Molly," she introduced herself, feeling foolish.

Bear took her extended hand and brought it to his lips. "I am Luc LeClerc." He studied her closely, and a smile crossed his dark features.

"Did you arrive with my long-missing son?"

Releasing her hand, he turned to Hawk.

"A wife usually travels with her husband," Hawk said.

"Son." Luc gathered Hawk close. No further words were exchanged as the two strong men held tightly to each other, their mutual love needing the physical contact.

Finally they parted and Bear bent to pick up his tiny daughter. He kissed her soft cheek then nuzzled his daylong growth of beard into her soft flesh. Her childish giggle filled the room as he carefully set her on her feet.

"Go find a brother to spoil you." He gently pushed her toward the men, any of whom would willingly fill the request.

"Don't be gone so long ever again," he said, turning to Hawk. "Your mother worries when her sons aren't within her sight."

Finally, to the satisfaction of the waiting men in the room, his gaze came to linger on Molly.

"*Mon dieu,* she's breeding," he whispered, his voice conveying his pleased shock. "I'm going to be married to a grandmother!"

Laughter erupted, confusion reigned and Molly found herself the center of concerned masculine attention. Dara selected Hawk's lap as her place of choice while Linsey disappeared up the stairs.

The loud masculine voices put Dara to sleep while they bewildered Molly. Her head began to ache as she tried, with little success, to follow the many conversations that flowed around her. Her sigh of relief was audible in the noisy room when Linsey returned and motioned for her to come upstairs.

"I know you want to rest." She took Molly's hand in hers and signaling Hawk to follow with their bags, led her up the curving staircase. "My family takes some getting used to, their voices ring through the house and will startle a deaf person. But when even one of them is gone, his is the voice that I miss, the one I long to hear."

Leading Molly to a door at the end of the hall, Linsey ushered her inside. "This is Hawk's room when he is home. Now it will be yours."

The room was masculinely comfortable, with several chairs that seemed to invite a weary body to sit and linger, a desk and dresser and a massive bed. But what drew Molly's attention were the windows. The corner room was at the back of the house and the two exterior walls consisted of row after row of floor-to-ceiling windows. The view looked out on a thick forest and the dull glitter of the river was just over the tops of the trees.

"I have always thought that Hawk chose this room because it was as close to being outside as possible. When he was a child he used to open the windows and sleep on the balcony. Many times, when the weather turned bad late at night, Luc would come in and carry him back to bed."

"On a clear day the view must be breathtaking," Molly said, entranced.

"When it rains it seems like a magic place, with the thunder booming in the distance and the lightning bringing fire to the sky." Hawk walked up behind Molly and wrapped his arms around her. He pulled her gently back against him and she rested in the strength of his embrace. "In the winter the snow touched here first, so I could always claim to be the first to know it was snowing."

Unseen by the two at the windows, Linsey silently slipped from the room. She didn't want her presence to intrude on their moment of tender quiet. Besides, she wanted a few minutes alone with the men of the family. She had seen how easily Molly became flustered by their boisterous teasing, and she intended to see that they took care until she had a chance to know them better.

"In the spring, I used to sit on the balcony, with a blanket wrapped around my shoulders, and watch for the first sight of my father," Hawk continued, his deep voice soothing Molly. "And in the summer I never slept anywhere but on the porch. It seemed to me that I was closer to my people when I had the stars overhead instead of a roof."

Hawk softly kissed the side of her neck then turned her in his arms. Her willing lips met his, softly, gently, in a restrained kiss of heart-melting tenderness.

"Linsey has a bath prepared for you," Hawk stated as he lifted his head. "I'll help you wash your hair, if you wish."

"I wish," Molly replied.

Sitting on one of the chairs, Molly didn't protest when Hawk knelt and removed her shoes. He pulled her to her feet and reached for the lacings on her pants. Exhaustion overrode any embarrassment she might have felt as the trousers slid down her legs and she stepped out of them.

Hawk pulled her against him and Molly rested her head on his strong chest as he removed the pins from

329

her hair. The long, honey-colored mass cascaded down her back, the color almost matching exactly the buckskin shirt she still wore.

He took her hand and led her behind a screen in a corner of the room that Molly hadn't even bothered to look at yet. A huge tub, large enough for the masculine bodies that usually used it, filled with steaming hot water, waited invitingly. Molly looked at it longingly, wanting to sink her aching body into its depths.

"Hair first," Hawk said, a smile lighting his eyes.

Molly sat on a low bench and hung her head over an empty bucket as Hawk poured warm water through her hair. Hawk worked the soap gently into the wet tresses and she would have purred with pleasure if she had had enough energy. Finally, he repeatedly poured clean water over her hair to remove the soap. Twisting the strands into a long rope, Hawk again pulled her to her feet.

He quickly dispensed with the laces of her shirt and pulled it over her head. Gathering her into his arms, Hawk lowered her into the tub.

When Molly sat down, the warm water came to just beneath her chin. She leaned against the rounded back, her eyes closed in bliss.

"Slide up, Molly," Hawk's voice drifted into the dream world she had slipped into.

"Hum?"

Hawk reached into the tub and slid her forward. Careful to support her head, in fear that in her relaxed state she would slip beneath the surface, he stepped into the tub behind her. He eased her between his open thighs, her head resting on his chest, the long rope of her hair thrown over his shoulder to hang nearly to the floor.

He held her gently and his hands moved slowly over her body. He carefully soaped her breasts, lingering to feel their growing weight and to tease the nipples that had reacted to the heat of the water by softening and flattening. He only moved on to other areas when he felt them begin to pucker in response to his soft tugs and pulls.

He felt her ribs and realized that she had lost weight on their trip, pounds that her thin frame couldn't afford to lose. The mound of her belly enticed him, as always. The baby was quiet, as if he too enjoyed the warm water cradling his mother's body.

Hawk spent a long time massaging her belly before his hands ventured further, into the feminine warmth waiting for his exploration.

Molly moaned softly and opened her thighs for his questing fingers. Feeling his growing desire pressed into the small of her back, she found his free hand and guided it back to her breast.

"I thought you were asleep," Hawk whispered, his breath warm against the tender skin of her back.

"If this is a dream, please don't wake me, yet," she murmured.

"It's only the beginning, *neè wàh,* but the water grows cool so we must move our play to someplace warmer." Hawk stood and pulled her to her feet. Picking her up, he stepped from the tub and let her body slide down the length of his. Supporting most of her weight, he managed to dry her body and most of his own.

Once more picking her up, Hawk carried her across the room to the massive bed. He carefully placed her in the center, following her down.

"Open your eyes, Mary Helen," he requested quietly.

When she complied, Hawk carefully joined his heat to hers. His eyes burned with more than the passion that he carefully kept in control.

"I love you, wife," he whispered softly.

Chapter Twenty

Molly woke to an empty bed and voices in the distance that she suspected were trying to be quiet. Feeling remarkably refreshed from her short nap, she listened to the voices, trying to identify Hawk's.

Her stomach growled noisily as she stretched beneath the warm quilt and she wondered if Linsey had delayed serving dinner while Molly was taking her nap.

A muffled shout drifted through the closed window, followed by the giggle of a little girl. A warming fire burned merrily in the fireplace but suddenly Molly was lonely, wanting to be a part of the activity outside.

She threw back the quilt and spied her bags sitting on a chair across the room. Digging through them, she pulled out a clean shirt and pants that smelled of the wood smoke that had helped dry them. Hoping Linsey would understand her lack of clothing, Molly searched for her shoes.

Her stomach rumbled again and she gave up her

search for the missing shoes. Surely if Linsey could overlook her unconventional mode of dress she could also overlook bare feet.

She hurried from the room, hoping she could find the kitchen without much trouble. As she started carefully down the stairs, a voice from below startled her.

"Let me help!" Mark stumbled in his haste to reach her and solicitously took her arm. "Can't be too careful," he muttered as he needlessly helped her down the steps.

"Thank you." Molly hid a grin of amusement at his attentive assistance.

"You are most welcome," he replied seriously when they reached the main floor.

Molly could have sworn that he heaved a sigh of relief as he released her arm. She looked around the foyer, wondering which room hid her husband and which hid the kitchen.

"Hawk's outside, Ma went to check on a neighbor who's been sick for several days and everyone else is somewhere. Now that you're up, I can go too."

Molly frowned as it began to dawn on her that her nap had been considerably longer than she'd originally thought.

"You didn't have to wait for me to come down here if there was someplace else you wanted to be."

"It was my turn," he explained with a casual shrug.

"Your turn?"

"Sure, Ma waited as long as she could but she finally left and Pa wanted to show Hawk some of the changes that have been made around here in the last couple of years. They took Dara with them because she couldn't be quiet if you gagged her. So we took turns waiting for you. I was last 'cause I'm the youngest. I was just wondering if I'd need to get Daniel for another turn when I heard your door open."

"I appreciate your concern for me, but it really wasn't necessary."

"Sure it was." He grinned when he heard her stomach growl. "Sounds like my new nephew is hungry."

Molly blushed and put a hand to her stomach. "I guess I missed dinner."

"And breakfast and lunch," he confirmed with a nod. "Follow me, I know where Mom hides the good stuff. Guess she won't mind if we invade her kitchen."

Appalled that she had slept so long, Molly followed her irrepressible brother-in-law. They walked through a formal receiving room that appeared to be seldom used, into a dining room that could comfortably seat thirty, and finally into the kitchen. It was huge, like most of the rooms she had seen.

Unlike the kitchens in houses she was familiar with—where the kitchen was in a separate building—this kitchen was part of the house. She counted twelve chairs pushed up to the oak table, but several others stood around the room. Delicious mouth-watering aromas drifted from a pot bubbling gently over the fire, but Mark continued through the room to a door at the back.

It opened up to reveal a fully stocked pantry and

she watched as he grabbed things from the shelves. When his arms were loaded to his satisfaction he nodded toward the table.

"Guess I'll have a little bite to keep you company. No one wants to eat alone."

The impromptu meal was a delight, as Molly was kept entertained by her youngest brother-in-law. She stopped eating long before her plate was empty and she had difficulty convincing him that she was full. If she had eaten everything he placed before her she would probably have been unable to move.

She was pleased to watch him clean up the table, returning things to the pantry and placing the dirty plates in the sink to be washed.

"Well, what do you want to do now?" he asked.

"I appreciate your care," she replied. "But I'll just wait in the parlor for Hawk to return."

"Why do that? I'll take you to him."

Molly held up her bare feet and wiggled her toes. "Couldn't find my shoes," she explained with a grin.

"Don't worry!" Before she could ask his intentions Mark ran from the room. He returned minutes later, her shoes in one hand and her coat in the other. "Under a chair," he explained, handing them to her.

Molly slid her feet into the shoes but knew from experience that lacing them was impossible with her belly in the way. Seeing her dilemma, Mark knelt at her feet and quickly laced them up. He helped her to stand, wrapped her coat around her and led her to the back door.

Feeling slightly breathless, Molly had no choice but to follow him. She stepped out the door and was quickly surrounded by overly helpful males. Seeming to come out of nowhere, they all offered their services.

Kaleb asked if she was warm enough and pulled her coat tightly around her neck before she could reply. Will offered to find a chair for her, while Jamie held out his arm for her. Mark hovered at her side, dogging each footstep.

Perplexed and overwhelmed by their attention, Molly searched desperately for Hawk.

"Back off before you smother her," a booming voice demanded from behind her. "Her condition is delicate, not fatal—unless one of you steps on her. And I sure wouldn't want to be the man that did that. What is left of you when Hawk's finished skinning you alive will have to explain to Mother exactly what happened."

Molly turned and watched Daniel approach. His years of living with the Shawnee showed in quiet, graceful movements. He walked softly, his moccasined feet barely crinkling the dried grass beneath them.

Knowing that Daniel was now in control, the others quickly departed for their own pursuits and Molly was left alone with the one brother-in-law that most intimidated her.

"They meant well," she stuttered. "They were just trying to be helpful."

"You would defend them from me?" he asked in an amazingly soft voice.

"I wouldn't want you to think they were doing something wrong."

A softness crossed his handsome face and he held his hand out to her. Her own hand looked lost when she hesitantly placed it in his and she watched with bewilderment as his eyes seemed to glare fiercely into hers.

"You are a fitting wife for my brother," he said after long minutes of studying her. "You have a strength that is rare in most women. Your son will grow strong and brave with the guidance of Hawk. You and he will be accepted as Hawk's, though he will look more like me than like the man he will call father."

"Look like you?" Molly asked with bewilderment.

Daniel grinned and released her hand. "His hair will be as red as mine."

"No one will know that until he's born! How can you say such a thing?"

"He has the sight."

Startled Molly turned and discovered that Hawk had walked up behind her without her knowing of his presence.

"The sight?" she asked.

"The ability to know something, sometimes long before it happens," Hawk explained, wrapping his arm reassuringly around her shoulders.

"A gift, though sometimes it is more of a curse, from my mother." His voice filled with pain. "I suspect that Dara may have it too, but only time will confirm that.

"I'll be gone from here before the child is born," he continued. "Make his first breath of life yours when he arrives in your hands. He will grow to be a fine man."

Shaking her head in confusion, Molly looked at Hawk. "You told him that the baby isn't yours?"

338

"There was no need," Daniel interrupted before Hawk could reply. "I have known from the moment I first saw you. But he will be Hawk's first-born son, the first of several."

At her surprised expression, Daniel's booming laugh filled the air. He turned and walked away, leaving Hawk to explain and to reassure his wife in any manner he chose.

Hawk chose to pull her close and lightly kiss her soft mouth. "Did you sleep well?"

"I think I'm still asleep." She leaned against him, taking comfort from the strong beat of his heart. "Mark greeted me on the stairs, said it was his turn to watch over me. He fed me enough food for an army and he found my missing shoes. Your other brothers hovered over me like I was in imminent danger of giving birth, and then Daniel comes along with his knowledge of things that have yet to happen."

"It's going to snow," Hawk said, changing the subject.

Molly pulled away from him and stared into his black eyes. "How do you know that?" she questioned suspiciously.

"Daniel told me," he replied with a chuckle. "The sky is filled with snow clouds and I can smell it. And, if that isn't enough to convince you, Kaleb came by early this morning with a little surprise of his own to introduce us to and left because his bad leg started throbbing. Said it only did that when there was going to be snow, and he was too old to be riding around in snow when he had a perfectly good home waiting for him."

"What was his surprise?"

Hawk grinned, remembering his shock of delight when Kaleb had pulled his wagon into the yard. Numerous children of mixed ages and sizes tumbled from the back, but Hawk's eyes had been glued to the big, rawboned woman sitting at Kaleb's side.

Kaleb had proudly introduced her as Ethel Mae, his wife. Ethel Mae took no nonsense from her children or her husband, but her clear blue eyes melted with love each time she looked at him.

There hadn't been time for Hawk to learn how this marriage had come to be, but he intended to hear an explanation, an amusing one, he knew—as soon as he could.

"You'll meet her and her brood when the weather clears," Hawk continued. "But first we'll have to wait out the snowstorm."

Having never seen snow, Molly was more interested in it than in Kaleb's new wife, and she was impatient for the first real storm. "Well, if I'm sleeping when it happens, wake me up."

"I will."

"Probably not, you'll think I need my rest more than I need to see snow."

She turned and watched Luc walk toward them, with his tiny daughter riding on his wide shoulders. "You were well provided for?"

"She's complaining that everyone was trying to suffocate her in their care," Hawk answered with a chuckle.

"Linsey complained of the same thing when she was carrying this one," Luc bounced Dara on his shoulder. "You must understand, daughter, we men have a deep respect for an expectant mother. There is nothing like it in our life and so it remains a mystery that leaves us weak with fear."

Molly shook her head at the thought of him or any of his sons being afraid of anything. They looked like they could conquer any foe single-handedly without breaking into a sweat.

"Tell us about Kaleb's wife and family," Hawk requested.

"Two summers ago, Ethel Mae and her family were traveling downriver on a rather dilapidated flatboat. Everything they owned was piled sky high in the middle. When it capsized they thought everyone was safe but they quickly discovered that one of the youngest children was missing. Her husband returned to the water and dived repeatedly trying to find him. After one dive, he didn't return to the surface.

"Ethel Mae and the children walked the rest of the way to the settlement, searching the river banks for either body. Neither one was found."

Hawk hugged Molly when a moan of sorrow escaped her lips. "Kaleb was in town when they trudged in. You know how Kaleb is about kids. I don't think he even saw Ethel Mae at first. All he knew was that these kids had lost everything. He loaded everybody on his wagon and took them back to his place.

"A few months later, everyone for miles around was invited to attend their wedding." Luc chuckled. "It hasn't been all bliss for Kaleb, that woman is fierce enough to scare the war paint off a Shawnee warrior, but I've never seen him so content. And those kids love that old man as much as you and your brothers always have."

"How many families are around here now?" Hawk asked as they walked back to the house.

"Fourteen at last count. And a trading post was constructed last summer just east of here. The settlement can no longer use the name of Shawnee Town since the government began surveying for its mail distribution center about fifty miles west of here. They're calling it Shawneetown and are using it as a mail route for the territory.

"Guess they were concerned that there might be some argument over rights at the Great Salt Springs on the Saline River so they moved in. I haven't been down there in a couple of years but Daniel says there's a federal land office, some taverns and about thirty or so log cabins right on the river."

Luc shook his head, disgust obvious in the movement. "The Indians have used that salt spring for centuries but now the white men claim it as their personal possession.

"Many times I traveled with the people of your village to gather salt. It was always a time of hard work and hard play. Now they have a salt works built there and you have to *buy* salt."

Luc stopped walking and lowered Dara from his shoulders. He watched as his young daughter ran off to chase the chickens pecking at the grass. "A man used to be able to come and go as he pleased, to raise his family as he saw fit. Now the government is moving in, watching every move a man makes.

"I'd walk away from everything here without a second thought except that I know that Linsey needs

342

the security of her own home. She'd go with me but I just couldn't ask that of her."

"All changes are not bad," Molly said quietly.

"I know, little one." Luc reached out and laid a gentle hand on the swelling of her stomach. "You are like my Linsey, you would follow your man wherever he leads, keeping your discontent to yourself. You, and she, are happier with having other people within your area. But I am a man of the wilderness, I begin to feel trapped when I know that each curve in the trail shelters the home of yet another settler."

They both felt the kick of the baby and Molly laid her hand on top of his. "Will you go or stay?"

"I'll stay, there is nothing without my Autumn Fire and her happiness is mine."

"Is anyone using your old cabin?" Hawk asked as they entered the house.

"Daniel has been down there this morning getting it ready for you," Luc replied with a chuckle. "He said you'd be wanting a place of your own."

"Is there nothing he doesn't know about before anyone else?" Molly shook her head with disbelief.

"He didn't need the sight for this decision." Luc added a couple of logs to the fire and looked for his pipe. "It was his knowledge of your husband. He knows his brother well."

Molly removed her coat and sat in one of the oversized chairs. The room was crispy warm and inviting.

"Daniel does not have an easy life," Luc continued, sitting in a chair near Molly's. "He sees things that will happen, but because the images are hazy, he can't do anything to prevent them from happening."

"How awful!"

"Sometime in the last few days he's seen something that's bothering him more than anything has in a long time. I expect him to be leaving here shortly."

"Has he said that?"

"It's not necessary for him to tell me, little one," Luc said softly, his voice filled with pain for his son. "I know him too well. I can see the agony he's suffering. He's been here for several months and it's never easy for him to be around people for long. There are more events to happen, there is more pain for him to feel, and anger because he can't stop it.

"I think he's stayed so long only for the sake of his mother—and because he knew that Hawk was returning home. He and Hawk have a special relationship, far stronger than brother for brother. Hawk is about the only one who can absorb some of Daniel's pain. Hawk and sometimes Dara.

"Daniel and Dara have been nearly inseparable since he came home. I fear greatly that my little daughter also has the sight." His voice had lowered to a whisper filled with anguish for his children. "God spare her the agony her brother has lived with."

As naturally as if she'd done it all her life, Molly stood and walked over to her father-in-law. She knelt at his feet and took his work-worn hands in her own. No words could relieve his troubles, but the touch of hand on hand showed that she understood and cared.

Returning from the kitchen with a cup of hot tea for Molly, Hawk stood in the doorway and stared at his wife kneeling at his father's feet. Emotion ran rampant through him as he witnessed the silent exchange between them. With a gentle touch, Luc smoothed the hair away from her face, then leaned forward and softly kissed her brow.

"Welcome to our family, Mary Helen," he said quietly.

Molly blinked back the tears that threatened to spill down her cheeks. There could be no doubt of the intensity of his greeting. She was now as much his daughter as Dara. She suspected that he would make an ominous enemy and an even more formidable friend.

Seeing Hawk in the doorway, Luc helped Molly to her feet. Their conversation became lighter, discussions about crops, the weather, and mutual friends. Leaning into the corner of the chair with her head against the padded back, Molly soon drifted to sleep, the quiet sounds of their voices fading away.

"It's 'nowing, Papa, it's 'nowing!" Dara rushed into the room, chubby cheeks pink with cold. "Come on, Papa, it's 'nowing!"

Molly sat up and wiped the sleep from her eyes. Snow! She felt almost as excited as the little girl. Having been born and raised in Charleston, she had seen little of the fluffy white stuff familiar to northern residents. She climbed awkwardly to her feet and looked around the room for her coat.

"It's going to snow for days, pumpkin." Luc pulled his daughter onto his lap.

"Gonna build a 'nowman and a cave and fight

345

Marky with snowballs and Mama says we'll have some 'nowpudding and . . ."

"Whoa! You keep that up and you'll be too tired to play in the snow." Luc stood, lightly holding Dara on his arm. "Now, where did I put that coat?"

"In the closet, Papa, hurry!"

Hawk helped Molly into her coat, grabbed Dara out of Luc's arms and carried her to the door. Careful to give Molly extra support, they walked into the drifting snow.

Large palm-size flakes floated lazily to the ground. Already the bare branches of the trees sported a light covering of white.

"'now," Dara whispered in awe.

"Snow," Molly agreed, equally in awe. She tipped her head up and caught a snowflake on her tongue while others clung to her eyelashes and hair.

"Down, Hawk," Dara demanded, wiggling free of his grasp. She ran into the yard, catching the flakes as they fell.

Jamie and Mark sneaked up on Dara and pelted her with hastily constructed snowballs. Dara screamed with delight but her tiny hands couldn't make the balls stick together. Taking pity on her, Hawk joined her side of the war, making the balls and handing them to her to throw.

Wanting to share the fun, Molly joined them. Abruptly, the fight came to a halt. Hawk looked at his wife, her pregnant belly pushing out the front of her coat and shook his head.

"No, *neè wàh,* this game is not for you."

"Can't I have any fun?" she asked, disappointment thick in her voice.

Hawk handed one of the snowballs to her and pointed toward his brothers. Jamie and Mark stood patiently, waiting for her to pitch it, refraining from teasing her when it fell short.

"That was your fun," Hawk said as he grabbed her arm. "Back to the porch."

"Some fun," she mumbled. "One puny snowball!"

"Later, if you're good, we'll hitch up the team and go for a ride. But for this winter you're going to have to leave the games to the others." When she started to protest, Hawk placed his hand gently on her stomach. "They do not carry my son in their body, *aín jel eè.*"

Molly sat on a rocker on the porch and watched them play until the cold drove her inside. As she dispiritedly closed the front door behind her, a smile began to grow. Almost sneaking, she tiptoed through the house to the back door.

The snow fell as heavily in the back yard as in the front and there was no one to tell her she couldn't play. Molly grunted as she bent to scoop up some snow. She carefully formed the snowball, taking extra care to make it perfectly round. She aimed for the branch of a nearby bush and clapped her hands when it splattered dead on target.

"Very good, but does Hawk know you're out here?"

Molly groaned as she turned and faced Daniel. He grinned knowingly, a eyebrow arched in question.

"Are you going to tell him?"

"Yes."

"Tattletale," she mumbled, taking his outstretched hand and walking back toward the house.

Maybe this being a member of a large family wasn't going to be as great as she had first thought. With this many brothers a person couldn't get away with anything! There was always someone around when you least wanted them.

Molly was muttering under her breath as she preceded Daniel into the house. Hawk stood in the entry way, his arms folded across his chest as he watched her guilty expression. She removed her coat and threw it on a convenient chair.

"Out back, throwing snowballs," Daniel replied to Hawk's unasked question.

"I wanted to play, too," she defended herself.

Hawk's expression didn't change, his dark eyes glaring accusingly at her. "Well, I've never seen snow before either and I didn't want to be stuck inside while everyone else was having fun!"

Unaware of her lower lip pouting, Molly fought back the tears that rimmed her eyes. Hawk walked over to his wife and picked her up as easily as he picked up Dara. Ignoring the amused faces of his gathered brothers, he turned and climbed the stairs. Molly leaned her head against his broad shoulder and closed her eyes.

This wasn't playing in the snow, but if she had a choice, she'd take this any day.

Hawk carried Molly into their room and over to the windows. Setting her on her feet, he pulled the heavy curtains back until nothing stood between them and the snow falling heavily outside except the pieces of glass.

After throwing some wood onto the fire, he pulled a chair in front of the window, grabbed Molly's hand

and sat down, pulling her forcibly onto his lap.

"This is where you'll see most of this winter, Molly. It's too dangerous for you to be outside. Snow is slippery and there's usually a layer of ice underneath the fluffy top layer. One wrong step and you're on your backside in a snow drift."

He turned her head to face his and he saw the defiance and disappointment in her eyes. Hawk nuzzled his nose against hers then softly kissed her lips.

"You'll see the snow, sweetheart, but only if someone else is with you. You are too precious to me. I don't want you to take chances.

"Don't you know yet," he asked softly, his voice filled with emotion, "You and our son are my whole world?"

Molly's heart soared, and the baby kicked fiercely as if he, too, had heard Hawk's voice.

Hawk's head lowered to hers. His tongue tasted the soft silhouette of her waiting lips. Teasing turned to invitation, expectation became demand as fires of passion grew to surpass the fury of the storm building outside.

The tip-tapping of the snow on the window panes was soon forgotten as Hawk showed his wife another, more pleasant, way to spend a cold snowy day.

Chapter Twenty-One

The branches of majestic evergreens swept to the ground from the weight of their blanket of snow. Bushes sported snow flowers and layers of ice, as winter wrapped the world in a wonderland of white. Familiar landmarks became strange. Even an old barn badly in need of a coat of paint turned into a charming structure with rainbow icicles hanging from its drooping roof.

Molly had been surprised to discover how noisy snow was as it crunched underfoot or tapped against the windows. And after two months of nearly continuous snow, she was still delighted by its strange appearance. Her sizeable stomach made it difficult for her to maneuver on its slippery surface and Hawk forbade her from leaving the cabin without him.

They had moved into the old cabin that had been Linsey and Luc's first home. The tiny two-room structure with its polished plank floors and glass-paned windows quickly became home for Molly. Furniture and other household necessities had been scrounged from the attics of the larger house and carted the short distance to the cabin.

In the last couple of weeks, as if sensing that Molly's time was drawing near, Linsey had been a constant visitor. The two women had become more than friends as they openly shared their past with each other.

Molly had been surprised to discover that Luc had delivered all of Linsey's children. The first two births had taken place before a midwife was in the region but Linsey had insisted on his help with the others.

Her voice had softened with sorrow when she spoke of the stillbirth of John. Her pain had been increased by the agony she had witnessed on her husband's face when he held the small lifeless body in his large hands. She smiled as she told of Dara's birth and the fact that Luc had expected yet another son and so he hadn't checked on the baby's sex. She chuckled when she described the way he rushed to confirm it for himself when she had brought it to his attention.

Molly stood at the door and watched as Linsey headed home on the well-traveled trail between the cabin and the house. The path was used frequently during the day, since the brothers were not at all bashful about stopping in to visit Hawk or to check on her when they knew he'd be gone.

They made no pretense that their visits were anything other than what they were. They would question her about the state of her health, carry in armloads of wood or buckets of snow to be melted for water. When they were satisfied, they left, but Molly was never alone for long. Soon another brother, or Kaleb or even Luc would stop in for a visit.

She enjoyed the visits, getting better acquainted with each man, but her days were lonely when Hawk wasn't around. He had spent several days hunting with Daniel before restlessness forced Daniel to leave. If he had told Hawk of his latest vision, Hawk had not shared it with Molly. She shivered at the horror of knowing something tragic was about to happen and being unable to prevent it. Her heart went out to the gentle man who kept his grief buried deep inside his massive body.

Molly rubbed her aching back as a twinge of pain traced from the middle of her back to her stomach. The light twinges, more of a nuisance than real pain, had started earlier in the day.

She had been plagued with similar aches and pains for several weeks, but rather than abating, these grew stronger in intensity as the day progressed. She knew that within a day or two, before daylight tomorrow if she were lucky, she would hold her child in her arms.

And, as the Bear had delivered his sons, so would Hawk deliver this child.

Molly grew restless and grabbed the broom to sweep the already spotless floor. That chore was finished all too quickly and she looked for something else to do. She wiped off shelves, rearranged clothing and food supplies, remade the bed and looked through Hawk's clothing to see if any of it needed repairs. Finally, when everything had been straightened, cleaned, swept or polished, Molly picked up the dress she had begun sewing.

With Linsey's help, Molly's wardrobe had grown to several dresses, skirts and blouses and underthings, most of which wouldn't fit until after the birth.

Plying the needle in and out of the fabric, Molly bit back a moan as a strong pain gripped her middle. When it released her from its clutches, she carefully folded the dress and climbed from her chair. With hands that shook from both excitement and fear of the unknown, she removed her shirt and skirt and slid into a warm, flannel nightgown. Another pain worked its way through her body, forcing her to grab for the support of the bedpost.

Between pains, Molly readied the necessary items for the birth. She had questioned Linsey repeatedly on the procedure and had gotten Linsey's promise that she wouldn't interfere unless there was an unexpected problem.

Molly was sitting at the table, a warm shawl around her shoulders and a soothing cup of tea in her hands when Hawk returned.

"The sawmill will be in production by spring," he said as he closed the door and placed his long rifle beside it. "I'm starved, what's for dinner?"

"Humm . . ." Molly bit her lip as she waited for the pain to subside. "Nothing . . . I guess I forgot."

"Molly?" Hawk stopped in the process of re-

354

moving his coat and looked at his wife. "Are you all right."

"I'm fine, I just got busy and forgot to cook anything for your dinner."

"Busy with what?" he asked suspiciously, carelessly dropping his coat onto a chair.

"Things . . ." She wasn't as successful at hiding the new pain, her moan alerting Hawk to her condition.

"Is it the babe?" He knelt beside her, taking her cold hand in his.

Molly nodded, unable to speak. Hawk remained beside her until he felt her relax then he gathered her into his arms and carried her to the bed.

"When did this start?" he asked, when he saw that the bedding had been folded back and a heavy padding of fabric was waiting to receive her. He placed her on the bed and noticed the other things she had placed within convenient reach.

"A few hours ago," she muttered, unbuttoning the top of her gown.

"How many hours ago?" Hawk demanded, his arms folded across his chest as he stared down at her.

"Don't you think it's getting hot in here?"

"Don't try to change the subject. How long ago did your pains start?"

Molly successfully changed the subject as another contraction laced knife-sharp through her body. Sweat beaded her forehead as she fought back against a moan.

"I'm getting Maman." Hawk ran from the room and grabbed his coat.

355

"No, Hawk!" she called. "She won't come."

"Won't come?" Hawk stood at the doorway, frantically pulling his coat on. "Woman, what do you mean she won't come? She's my mother and you're my wife, of course she'll come."

"No, she won't!" The last word was nearly screamed as the peak of the contraction stabbed through her.

Hawk turned and ran from the cabin. The house was a pleasant ten-minute walk from the cabin, he ran the distance in less than three minutes. Linsey was in the kitchen preparing the evening meal when he burst into the room.

"Maman, you must come, Molly is having the baby." He grabbed her cloak from a hook by the door.

"I thought she was having some discomfort when I was there this afternoon. When did her pains start?" Linsey asked as she dried her hands on her apron.

"You left her when she was in pain?" he asked in astonishment. "I don't know when they started but there's no time to ask questions now. Come!" He threw the cloak around her shoulders and tried to usher her out the door.

"No, Hawk." Linsey pulled herself free from his grasp and removed her cloak.

"No? No?" he asked in confusion.

Linsey stood firmly, "Molly wants you to deliver the baby. I'll only come if you need me."

"I need you! I can't help her."

"Yes, you can, son," a deep voice said quietly from

the doorway. Luc walked over to his wife and wrapped his arm around her shoulders. "Go home to your wife, by now she is probably frantic with both pain and worry. We'll send someone over periodically to check on her progress, but she needs you."

"I've never asked anything from you before. You would deny me this one request?" Hawk asked with disbelief.

"It's her decision, Hawk." Linsey explained gently.

A frantic, terrifying emotion ran rampant through Hawk. He looked at the two people who had never betrayed him before and he suddenly knew how thin the line was between love and hate. He squared his shoulders and raised his head proudly, generations of Shawnee warriors were reflected in his face.

"From this day forward I will never again ask for anything from you. I will take Molly and the baby from the cabin as soon as they are able to travel."

His eyes narrowed as he stared at them and his voice was harsh when he spoke. "I am no longer your son."

Turning away, he didn't hear Linsey's gasp of anguish or see the fire of retribution that burned in Luc's eyes. His thoughts were centered on the woman who waited for him, though his heart nearly broke at the betrayal of the two people he had always loved beyond all else.

"He didn't mean it," Luc said soothingly as he gathered Linsey into his arms.

"I know," she mumbled, her face buried in his

chest. "But it hurts so much to deny him something he so desperately needs."

"Do you regret having me deliver our children?" he asked softly.

"No. I wouldn't have changed that for anything in the world."

"Then don't deny him this chance. Molly is wise enough to know if she needs help. She'll ask for you."

"It's going to be a long night!" Linsey sighed.

"It always is when you're waiting for a new life to begin."

Hawk raced back to the cabin and found Molly standing beside the bed, trying to remove her damp gown.

"What are you doing now?" He rushed over to her but wasn't sure what to do once he got there.

"This gown is wet and hot and I want to get it off." She turned to him, a pleading look on her face. "Will you help?"

Shaking his head with exasperation, Hawk grabbed the gown and jerked it over her head. She grabbed for the support of his arm when another contraction began.

Wanting to put her on the bed and afraid to move her, Hawk held her and watched with amazement as her stomach hardened to granite with the pain. When it eased he nearly threw her on the bed, pulling a blanket over her naked body as he went in search for something cooler for her to wear.

"Linsey won't come," he stated bluntly, digging haphazardly through Molly's things.

358

"I know." She grabbed for his hand and held it tightly. "Hawk, I asked her not to come. Please understand that she isn't refusing you she's simply following my request. I don't need anyone but you."

"Ah, *neè wàh!*" He sat on the edge of the bed. "I don't know how to bring your child safely into the world."

"It's my understanding that there's really little for us to do. He'll come when he's ready but I want your hands there to hold him."

He held his hand out to her. "Look at me, my hands shake like those of an old man. I'll drop him on his head and you'll never forgive me."

Molly smiled as she reached for him. "No you won't, *wài see yah,* your grasp will be steady and firm."

"If I admit that I am afraid, will that change your mind?"

"That'll just make two of us," she gasped as another contraction began to build. "I was hoping for more from a warrior."

"*This* was never mentioned in the many lessons from either of my fathers!"

He was amazed at her strength as she clutched his hand, her fingers biting into his palm. The nightgown was forgotten as he began the soothing chant, his volume building as the pain crested.

Throughout the long night, the touch of his hand and the wordless chant soothed her through the agony. He wiped the sweat from her brow, marveling when she smiled reassuringly at him. He couldn't begin to conceive of the torture she was

359

enduring but his respect for her became boundless as he watched her suffer in silence.

He stayed at her side, leaving her only when one of his brothers came to the door to inquire about her progress. His greetings to them were harsh and they quickly went on their way to report that Molly was doing fine but that Hawk was about to buckle under the stress.

Just as dawn was breaking, the final stage of labor was reached. Hawk was too busy tending to his wife to notice when Luc appeared in the doorway. He stood quietly, observing the closeness between the two involved in the birth, then slipped silently out of the cabin. He sat on the top step of the porch, knowing the birth was imminent, and he relived the thrill and terror he'd felt each time Linsey gave birth to one of his children.

"Is everything all right?" Linsey asked softly as she sat down beside him.

"I thought I told you to stay home?" Luc wrapped an arm around her shoulders and pulled her tightly against him.

"And miss all the excitement?" She chuckled as she snuggled up to him.

"Can it really be that long ago when we watched Hawk's birth or when I caught Daniel in my hands?" he asked quietly. "They are men now—fine men— but *mon ange* I miss those little boys."

"You'll soon have another little boy to tag along behind you, Grandpa," Linsey teased. "And you'll come in complaining that you can't get anything done because he's always in the way—just as you did

360

about Hawk and Daniel and each of the others in turn."

"Have I told you yet that I love you, woman?" he asked, pulling her onto his lap.

"There's no better time than the present," she replied, her lips ready for the kiss she saw in his eyes.

"Oh, Hawk, this hurts!" Molly muttered between clenched teeth.

"I know, *aín jel eé,* just a little longer." He tried to encourage her. "It can't be much longer now!"

Molly panted and gulped shallow breaths of air, her body a whirlpool of pain. Wave upon wave, the contractions built without break, until she began to wonder if pain would be her lasting impression of the birth of her child.

The blanket had long ago been discarded and her distorted body lay bare in the warm room. Sweat beaded Hawk's face, running into his eyes until he found the familiar red band and tied it around his head. He'd removed his shirt and his copper skin gleamed in the early morning light.

He knelt on the bed between her spread thighs, his eyes widening in wonder.

"I see his head, Molly!" he exclaimed in amazement. "Daniel is wrong, his hair is as black as mine."

Molly bit back the scream that tried to force its way through her clenched teeth. She grabbed the back of her thighs just beneath her knees to give him better access to the birth area. She was unaware of her fingers digging into her own skin.

The scream she'd tired so hard to suppress was torn free as the pain crescendoed and she expelled the tiny body into Hawk's waiting hands.

His hands were firm and sure as he laid the child on Molly's stomach. He followed the instructions she had given him during the long night of labor—and he cleared the mucus from the tiny throat and nose.

Holding the child close to his own body, the cord of life still connected to Molly, Hawk blew gently in the tiny nose. The baby gasped, arched his back and bellowed to the world that he had arrived. His first breath of life came from the man he would know as his father.

"Neè wàh, our son."

Hawk held the baby up for Molly's inspection. A more careful inspection would be done at leisure later, for now, Hawk returned the infant to her belly and carefully tied and cut the cord.

As Hawk ministered to her, Molly stroked her angry son's tiny head. She smiled at his furious cry, pleased that he was breathing so well. Using a warm, wet towel, Hawk cleaned his new son and wrapped him in a small blanket. He placed the baby in Molly's arms and watched as she encouraged him to suckle at her swollen breast.

The cabin was filled with new silence as the baby closed his lips around her tender nipple.

"Thank you," Molly said softly to Hawk, her eyes filled with love for her new son and for the man who had safely delivered him into the world.

Hawk knelt beside the bed and stroked the soft cheek of his son. He made no effort to hide the tears that spilled down his cheeks.

"It is I who owe you thanks, Molly. I would have run from this and missed the beginning of his life. You gave me no choice but to stay and I will forever be grateful for your wisdom."

She smiled gently and his head lowerd to hers. The kiss they shared was filled with the emotion of life, a promise of tomorrow and all the days of their lives yet to come.

Hawk could have knelt by the bed all morning and watched the baby nurse, but there were things to be done. He listened as Molly spoke softly to the baby as he tenderly washed the traces of birth from her body.

The room grew cool and he pulled the blanket up to her breasts before adding more wood to the fire.

"Daniel was right, you know," Molly stated as she watched Hawk pull on a shirt. "His hair is red."

Hawk turned and stared at the tiny head resting against her breast. The soft, fluffy hair had dried and now it showed definite traces of red. Hawk grinned and gathered up the soiled linen.

"I'll dispose of this and go to the house." He stopped, emotion playing across his face. "I owe Maman and Bear an apology. When she wouldn't come with me I'm afraid I said some things that they didn't deserve."

"They'll understand," Molly said quietly. "You were scared and worried about me."

"I hope you're right, Molly. I can't think of what my life will be like if you're wrong."

Hawk walked through the cabin, grabbing his coat as he passed the chair. He opened the door to

363

find Linsey and Luc sitting comfortably on the top step. They smiled at his look of amazement.

"We were always here in case you needed us," Linsey said softly, standing and opening her arms to the man who had always been her oldest son.

"I'm sorry," he started, only to be interrupted.

"Then come, be the second person to kiss the new grandma," Linsey invited. "I've waited about as long as I intend to wait to see my new grandson."

Hawk hugged Linsey, his gaze turning to Luc who stood with his arms folded across his chest. He released her and watched as she hurried into the cabin, closing the door behind her.

"Every man should experience the birth of his child," Luc said quietly. "It makes him remember the pain a mother feels all of her life when her children disappoint her."

"I disappointed Maman, for that I will never forgive myself," Hawk replied.

"No, you didn't disappoint her, son." Luc placed his hand on Hawk's shoulder. "She knew that it was your fear for your wife that was speaking."

"I would rather face a grizzly than go through that again!"

"You have accepted the boy as yours, as I accepted you?"

"From the moment he slipped from his mother's body, he became mine." Fierce pride crossed Hawk's face. "No man will take him from me!"

"Ah, but someday, Son," Luc said with a chuckle, "a cute little girl will smile at him and he'll be gone!"

"Maybe I'll just tell him about childbirth and

grizzly bears!" He looked at Luc. "Does it get any easier?"

Luc shook his head slowly. "Each one is as scary as the last one. Every time Linsey gave birth I swore that would be the last time. The only problem was that I couldn't stay away from her once the fear faded!"

Masculine laughter drifted on the morning air as the promise for the future slept undisturbed in his mother's arms.

Chapter Twenty-Two

Leaves budded pale green on the branches of the trees. New grass peeked from beneath dead underbrush and bird song cheerfully filled the air. The days were blessedly warm but the nights were still cool enough to welcome a blazing fire.

Molly sat on the porch, with her two-month-old son sleeping in her arms, his lips puckered around her nipple. She smoothed the fiery red hair back from his brow and caressed his satin-soft cheek. She still marveled that she had produced this perfect child, although the memory of the pain had faded.

She closed her eyes as she thought of his father. She realized now that what she had felt for Adam had been a combination of girlish infatuation and gratitude for the escape he had offered her. Her feelings for him didn't begin to compare to the soul-shattering love she had for Hawk. He was her other half, the person necessary to make her life complete. She knew that if Adam had lived, she would have been contented to live out her life as his wife, never

367

knowing the love she had missed.

But without Hawk at her side, she would only be existing.

Molly had waited to decide on a name for her son until after his birth, hoping that holding him would help her select the right one for him. Hawk had taken the decision out of her hands by announcing the day of his birth that he was to be called Adam after the man who had fathered him.

Molly still remembered the love she had felt at his decision. Nothing could have told her how much he loved her than his choice of that name for his son— or how secure he felt in her love for him.

Hawk walked out of the cabin and looked down at the sleeping babe. He had discovered that he enjoyed fatherhood, holding the baby whenever possible and taking care of even the most repulsive chore—which he knew he'd never like!

He no longer planned to leave Molly and his son, knowing that the separation would destroy him. They were his life, his reasons for living.

A noise from the woods drew his attention. He stared hard as a shadow, darker than those surrounding it, faded into the trees. He reached for the rifle just inside the door and checked to see that it was loaded.

Molly opened her eyes and bit back a scream as an image from a nightmare stepped into the sunlight. Pitch black hair was pulled into a topknot on his head with several feathers protruding from both sides. His face was painted red to just beneath his eyes, while black stripes crossed both cheeks.

Hawk aimed carefully and fired. The bullet

landed just to the left of the Indian brave.

"A little to the right," Molly suggested quietly, trying to soothe her son, who woke at the blast of sound.

Hawk reloaded and aimed again, this time his bullet going to the right side of the man.

"At this rate he'll grow old before you hit him," she stated as she stood, straightening her bodice to cover her breast. "Would you like me to try?"

A tomahawk whistled through the air, landing on the planks between Hawk's feet.

"He aims better than you." Molly turned and walked toward the vision of terror. "Welcome to our home, Quiet Otter," she said softly. "Your brother is badly out of practice with his rifle."

The Indian looked down at her. "You are a witch woman—to know who I am?" he questioned.

"He wouldn't have missed if you had been a threat to me or his son," she answered.

Hawk walked up to his brother. Arm clasped arm as the two men greeted each other in the language of their people. Turning, Hawk took the baby out of Molly's arms. Wanting to linger, but knowing this was a time for the two brothers, she turned and walked back to the house.

Unwrapping the baby, Hawk presented him to Quiet Otter. "My son."

Quiet Otter examined the infant's bright red hair and tender white skin. His dark gaze met with Hawk's and he nodded as he accepted the child into his own hands.

"My nephew," he stated firmly.

The baby squirmed and tried to focus fuzzy blue

eyes on the man who held him. His hands waved in the air, and more by luck than intention, his thumb found its way into his mouth. Trusting in the hands that held him to keep him safe from harm, he yawned around his thumb, sighed and closed his eyes.

The fierce warriors, father and uncle, smiled at the child. Adults would run in terror at sight of the ferocious Indian, but this small boy found security in his arms. It was the beginning of a relationship that would last through the years until Quiet Otter's long life was finished.

Molly returned to the yard, a cup of coffee and some freshly baked bread in her hands. She saw her son in the warrior's hands and smiled at him.

"I'll take the baby, if you'd like something to eat."

Quiet Otter shifted the child to the cradle of his arm and reached for the bread. The white man's soft white bread was something he remembered from his visits with Linsey and Bear. Butter and honey oozed from the slice as he greedily ate the offering. He took the cup of coffee from her and breathed deeply of its rich aroma.

"Some things the white man knows better than the Indian," he stated as he drank the brew. "My nephew will know both worlds, as does his father."

Molly's face softened as she realized that Quiet Otter had accepted her child. She stared at this newly met brother-in-law. Of similar size to Hawk, she suspected that beneath his war paint was a face every bit as attractive as her husband's.

"His name?" Quiet Otter asked.

"Adam," Molly replied.

Quiet Otter shook his head as a look of disgust crossed his face. He shifted the baby so that his head lay in his strong hand while the rest of his small body was supported between Quiet Otter's arm and hip.

Reaching up to his face, Quiet Otter smeared red paint on his fingers. He gently traced lines across the baby's chubby cheeks and over his forehead. Spots of black paint were added to the lines until Quiet Otter was satisfied with the results.

"His name is Little Hunter," Quiet Otter stated firmly. He removed one of the feathers from his hair and tucked it into the baby's swaddling. "As his uncle it is my right to name him and so it shall be."

He looked at Molly, waiting for her nod of assent. She couldn't help wondering what he would do if she disagreed. Deciding not to find out the answer to that question, she nodded agreement.

"Good!" Quiet Otter shuffled that baby back into the cradle of his arm with such expertise that Molly suspected he had several children of his own.

"We will greet Autumn Fire and Bear and then will talk."

The Shawnee warrior, dressed in feathers and war paint, turned with the tiny child in his arms and walked away.

"Why am I not surprised that he speaks such fluent English."

"When we were boys he insisted that Daniel and I teach him. He seemed to know even then that someday he would need the language."

"I guess if we want our son back we'd better follow him," Molly stated with a sigh as she watched Quiet Otter disappear from sight.

"We can still call the baby Adam," Hawk commented.

She smiled softly, "His name was chosen by his uncle and it will remain Little Hunter, but I think I'll shorten it to Hunter."

"You don't mind?" Hawk wanted to please her in every way. He had selected the name Adam because he knew she'd be happy with the choice.

"I am very proud that your brother has accepted my red-haired, blue-eyed son as his nephew. Hunter is a good, strong name for a boy to have."

Hawk took Molly's hand in his, raised it to his lips and kissed her palm. They leisurely followed the path Quiet Otter had taken. It had been years since Hawk had seen Quiet Otter and he worried that something was seriously wrong for his brother to have traveled the many miles from Missouri, but Hawk knew it would be a while before he learned the reason.

"Chattering Squirrel . . . oops, Quiet Otter," Linsey greeted the warrior, a smile of delight dimpling her cheeks. She hugged the intimidating man, easily overlooking his severe visage, as memories of a toddler running to her arms filled her thoughts. "It's been far too long."

"Autumn Fire, your greeting warms my heart," Quiet Otter said. He turned to Luc and greeted him more formally but a smile lingered in his dark eyes.

"Me want some!" Dara demanded when she saw the paint on the baby's face.

Quiet Otter knelt down to the little girl and repeated the steps he had used for the baby, only this time he drew a picture of a bird on one cheek and a leaf on the other.

"I have not met this little one before now but she is her mother's daughter so I know she is yours," he said as he stood.

Molly and Hawk walked up as Linsey finished her humorous explanation of Dara's birth and Luc's shock. Sensing that the men needed to be alone, she took her grandson from his arms and led Molly into the house. Dara followed reluctantly. This new visitor was much more interesting than the baby who only seemed to sleep or cry.

Visiting with Linsey was enjoyable, as always, but Molly grew restless as the afternoon wore on and Hawk still hadn't returned. Finally, she decided to return home. As she carried the baby down the path, a feeling of dread filled her with every step.

Putting the sleeping baby down in his cradle, she grabbed a hoe and began to attack the new weeds in the garden. It was a job that Hawk disapproved of, insisting that she hadn't recovered completely from childbirth, but she needed the physical activity to help suppress the premonition of disaster that weighed so heavily on her mind.

"What do you think you're doing, Molly?"

Hawk's deep voice startled her so much that she dropped the hoe. She bent to pick it up and he took it out of her hands.

"We need to talk." Leading her to the creek behind the house, Hawk sat down and pulled her onto his lap. He was unaware that many years earlier another man had sat down beneath the same tree, pulled the woman he loved beyond reason onto his lap and tried to find the words to convince her that she had to leave his wilderness home.

"My father is dying," he stated bluntly. "He is the leader of my people and without him they will be lost. Quiet Otter will take his place but he's come to ask for my help."

"I'm so sorry, Hawk," Molly leaned her head against his chest, offering the comfort of her presence. "Of course you must help. When do we leave?"

She had gotten right to the heart of the matter and Hawk sighed, knowing she wouldn't be pleased with his decision.

"We don't," he said quietly. "I've spoken with Bear and Linsey. You and the baby will move in with them and I'll go to Missouri with Quiet Otter."

"Wrong!" Molly pulled away from him. "I won't stay here while my husband is hundreds of miles away."

"*Neè wàh*, my brother, my people—they need me. Every day more white settlers are moving into the land of my people. With my education and knowledge of whites I can help my people adjust to the changes that will come."

"I don't argue with that, Hawk. However, I will be there, too, not stuck here waiting for you to remember me and come to see me when time permits."

"I will carry you in my heart, always. But there is untold danger for you in Missouri. Here, you and our child will be safe."

She stood and walked to the creek. She watched the gently bubbling water as it drifted downstream. "How about lonely, Hawk? I'll be safe and provided

374

for but what about lonely?"

It was a question he'd been asking himself ever since he realized he would be leaving her behind. Already loneliness was a mantle around his shoulders and he hadn't even left yet.

The rattling sound of a wagon attracted their attention. Molly turned, her eyes, blazing with anger, met the stoic Shawnee warrior who was her husband.

"You certainly didn't waste any time, did you?"

"We leave in the morning. I want to make sure you're settled before I leave."

"How thoughtful!" she hissed. "Why wait? Leave now. Your son and I can be moved without your help."

She walked up to the house where Luc and his sons were already carrying her possessions to the wagon. Quiet Otter talked softly to the infant in his arms and Molly felt an irrational urge to pull the knife from beneath her skirts and attack him. He was destroying her family, forcing her husband to leave his wife and child and travel far from his home.

He was breaking her heart.

Ignoring the men, Molly took her child and rushed away from the activity. Her pain was too deep for tears. She walked up the path, hoping that Linsey could help ease the agony she knew was just beginning.

The cool evening breeze drifted through the open window as Molly watched the men below. She was aware that Hawk had spent the afternoon preparing for his departure and now he was spending some time with his brothers. It would probably be many years before they would all be gathered together again and she knew he was creating memories to take with him.

Knowing that food would lodge in her throat, Molly had missed dinner. She had nibbled at the food on the tray Linsey had thoughtfully sent to her room, and she had lingered in the warm bath that had followed. Soon Hawk would walk up those stairs and she would spend her last night with him.

They had made love only once since the baby's birth . . . and tonight would be the last time she could hold him, but her anger, her feeling of rejection made her want to lash out at him—not make love with him.

She nursed her son, kissed his downy head and put him in his cradle for the night. Blowing out all of the candles except for the one by the bed, she slipped into her nightdress and climbed into the massive bed.

As Hawk's footsteps echoed down the quiet hall, she determined not to let him see the pain he was causing. If he could leave her without a second thought, then she wasn't going to cling and beg.

Hawk entered the bedroom. With only the feeble light of the single candle, he could see the agony in her eyes and he wondered if his own eyes reflected the same torment. He removed his clothes and climbed into the bed.

Molly welcomed him with open arms. He loved her with soft words and slow, lingering caresses. He tasted her sweet, milky breasts and the hot, moist essence of her femininity. As they merged into one he wondered how he'd ever be able to ride away from her when dawn broke the night.

As his sweet weight imprisoned her, Molly knew that without him she would cease to exist.

Their loving teetered on violence as they sought to hold back the dawn. In the aftermath, no loving words were whispered nor gentle caresses exchanged. With his body still a part of hers, Hawk began the chant that had become so much a part of them both. With his chest against hers she could feel the steady rhythm of it as he whispered it in her ear.

Against her will, tears traced silent paths down her cheeks.

Hawk lowered himself to the bed and pulled her into his arms. Through the lonely night, he held her tightly, finding no peace in the wordless chant.

Molly woke before dawn and found Hawk gone. She raced out of the bedroom, fearing he had already left, and sighed with relief when she heard his voice in the kitchen.

As she turned to trace her steps back to the bedroom, her eyes locked with Linsey's. With the help of a willing accomplice, a decision was made.

Hawk led his horse from the barn to the back of the house. Quiet Otter stood beside his own horse, talking with Bear. With his long hair hanging to his shoulders and his face without war paint, he looked remarkably like his younger brother.

"I have to see my wife and son before we leave,"

Hawk said quietly, handing the reins of his horse to Will.

His steps moved slowly as he approached the house. Now that the time to leave had come he wondered how he could do it. Duty vied with love, tearing his heart in two directions. He looked up as the kitchen door opened and he found his wife walking into the yard.

Dressed in the pants and shirt she had worn on their journey from the Carolinas, she carried a bedroll and pack.

"No!" he stated firmly.

"You don't have a choice." She ignored him as she waited for the horse Mark was walking into the yard.

Hawk grabbed her arm and jerked her around to face him. "What do you mean I don't have a choice? You aren't going."

"I don't remember asking your permission." She pulled herself free and threw the bedroll and pack to Mark. Turning to her husband, she placed a gentle hand on his chest. "I'll go with you or I'll follow along behind, either way, you aren't leaving me here!"

Hawk pulled her into his arms and closed his eyes when her body leaned against his. "No, *aín jel eè,* I can't let you go." He raised his eyes to Bear. "You'll watch over her for me?"

"Of course," Bear replied quietly.

Molly turned and stared at her father-in-law. "You won't keep me here."

"Not against your will," Bear agreed, his dark eyes brightening with a smile.

"So," Molly turned to her husband. "Go ahead and leave. I'll be right behind you. If I get lost I'll ask some friendly trapper which way you went."

Hawk moaned at the thought of her alone on the trail. "Don't do this to me, Molly. I have to go!"

"I know you do, Hawk," she replied quietly. "But you don't have to go without me."

"And our son, madam, what about our son?"

Sorrow drifted over Molly's face. "Linsey has agreed to keep him until he is older and we can come back to get him. He won't be the first baby she's raised who wasn't her own," she reminded him.

"You would leave your son?" Hawk asked increduously.

"Not easily, Hawk." Her eyes showed the torment of her heart. "I will miss him every day, wondering if he's hungry or sick, knowing he'll call another woman Mama and that he won't even know me the next time I see him.

"But Hawk, as long as I know he's safe, I can live without my son. I can't live without you."

Hawk buried his face in her hair and breathed the sweetness he'd come to know as hers. Relief flowed through him as he realized she'd left him no choice. He only prayed to her God and to his that he wouldn't regret the decision.

"Go get our son, Molly."

As if on cue, the kitchen door opened and Linsey walked into the yard carrying the baby in her arms. He wore a gown yellowed with age but soft as velvet. A design of flowers and vines worked in red trailed around the neckline and down to the hem. His tiny feet were covered by moccasins intricately ornamented with beads.

"Many years ago I worked to make a gown for a baby yet to be born," Linsey said softly. "When I realized how plain it was I used some of my own hair to embroider the design on it."

She handed the baby to Hawk. "Your mother saw how poorly it was constructed but she also saw the love I felt for her in every stitch I had sewn for her unborn child. The moccasins show the gift she had. They've always made my poor gown seem so much worse, but you wore it until it was too small. It was her intention to resew the gown as you grew, so that you'd always have it as a talisman but I put it and the moccasins away, hoping that someday you'd have a child who could wear them.

"None but you has worn it, until today. There were some beads that your sister made but they've become lost over the years."

"They're not lost," Hawk said hoarsely. "I've carried them with me since the first time my father came to take me back with him."

"When she knew she was dying, your mother asked me to love her children." Linsey's warm green eyes went drifting past Hawk to Quiet Otter. "I have, like they were my own." She reached up and softly caressed his cheek. "I'll miss you, son." She kissed the baby in his arms then turned to Molly.

"This cradleboard was made to fit your husband, I hope it will hold his son." As she handed Molly the decorated cradleboard, a smile of understanding spread over her face.

Quiet Otter took the baby from Hawk's arms and slipped him into the cradleboard. He carefully adjusted the laces, then strapped it on Molly's back.

"How many children do you have, Quiet Otter?" she asked out of curiosity.

"Nine," he answered proudly.

"How many wives?" she asked.

"Two."

Molly hugged Linsey and Luc. She hugged each of her large brothers-in-law, then turned to her husband. He helped her mount the horse, supporting the cradleboard until she adjusted to its weight.

Molly reached down and grabbed his hand. Her face grew stern, but love for him filled her honey eyes.

"One wife, Hawk," she cautioned adamantly.

"One wife, *aín jel eè,*" he agreed with a smile. "Nine kids?"

"If you deliver them."

Hawk shuddered as he climbed onto his horse. "That is something we'll have to talk about, *nèe wàh.*"

"We have time . . . unless last night . . ."

Author's Note

One of the fun aspects of writing is discovering strange facts, new places and wonderful people.

It has been documented that settlers crossing over the newly opened lands west of the Appalachian mountains sometimes lived in the hollowed out trunk of a dead tree until they could construct their cabins. These trees, usually sycamores, were of massive size and provided adequate, if not comfortable, temporary living space.

The waters of the impressive Cumberland Falls create the magic of the moonbow. It is visible only during a full moon and can be found nowhere else in the western hemisphere. Cumberland Falls is located in the Daniel Boone National Forest, twenty miles southwest of Corbin, Kentucky.

Shawneetown is in southeastern Illinois on the

beautiful Ohio River. I would like to thank Betty Head, Librarian at Shawneetown Public Library and Lucille Lawler, local historian, for their friendliness and help.

Pamela K. Forrest